W9-BRW-707

Praise for the novels of Sharon Sala

"Drama *literally* invades the life of an A-list Hollywood star, and the race is on to catch a killer."
—*RT Book Reviews* on *Life of Lies*

"A wonderful romance, thriller, and delightful book. [I] recommend this book as highly as I can…. Exciting…and will keep you glued to the pages until you reach the end."
—*USATODAY.com's Happy Ever After* blog on *Life of Lies*

"In Sala's latest page-turner, staying alive is the biggest challenge of all. There are appealing characters to root for, and one slimy villain who needs to be stopped."
—*RT Book Reviews* on *Race Against Time*

"[An] emotional thriller, packed with action, love, regrets, and criminal activity that will make your blood boil…. A phenomenal story."
—*Fresh Fiction* on *Race Against Time*

"[T]he Youngblood family is a force to be reckoned with…. [W]atching this family gather around and protect its own is an uplifting tribute to familial love."
—*RT Book Reviews* on *Family Sins*

"[A] soul-wrenching story of love, heartache, and murder that is practically impossible to put down…. If you love emotional tales of love, family, and justice, then look no further…. Sharon Sala has yet another winner on her hands."
—*Fresh Fiction* on *Family Sins*

SHARON SALA

DARK WATER RISING

mira

mira

ISBN-13: 978-0-7783-6917-2

Recycling programs for this product may not exist in your area.

Dark Water Rising

For questions and comments about the quality of this book, please contact us at CustomerService@Harlequin.com.

www.Harlequin.com

Printed in U.S.A.

It is rare when life gives you a chance to undo
a terrible mistake you once made, but when it happens,
it doesn't take long to realize how blessed you are.

This book is about second chances and a forever kind
of love. I know what that's like. I lived it. Even now,
after thirteen years without him, his love holds me steady
on the hard days and fills my soul on the sad days,
because forever never dies.

I dedicate this book to the second-chance lovers
who were brave enough to try it again.

DARK
WATER
RISING

One

Divorced.

Haley Quaid couldn't stop shaking from the sound of the word, and when Sam reached for her as they exited the courtroom, she leaned into his strength just as she had last week when they buried their son.

Robbie had been battling leukemia for more than three years before finally going into remission. When he came out of remission again, the last-gasp treatment failed. Robbie knew what was coming and accepted it before his parents did. He was tired of fighting. He wanted to quit. He begged them to take him home to die, and so they did.

For the next three weeks, the weaker their son became, the stronger and angrier Haley grew. She hated God. She hated herself. And she couldn't look at Sam without seeing Robbie. People used to say when Robbie was born that Sam Quaid had cloned himself, and the older Robbie grew, the more obvious the resemblance became.

Same black hair and blue eyes. Same jut to their chins. Same likes and dislikes in food. Now, with Robbie gone, all that was like a slap in the face to Haley. She already knew that she would never be able to look at Sam again without seeing their son, and that pain seemed impossible to bear. Her rage had carried her through the physical exhaustion of caring and then saying goodbye to her beloved son, but without him, the rage had transformed into a desperate grief—a feeling that was intensified every time she looked at Sam.

She'd filed for divorce in a knee-jerk reaction to bury that grief, to take control of her unraveling life in the only way she could. Her solution was insane, but Haley was already there, so in her mind, leaving Sam would lessen the pain of loss.

Sam was shocked. He'd just lost his son and now his wife wanted a divorce? It made no sense. He kept begging her to reconsider, but she hadn't been able to think past the overwhelming need to make all this go away.

Robbie's death happened between one breath and the next. Haley had turned away to answer the phone when she heard the catch in Sam's breath, heard him call her name. She'd turned around, but it was too late. She hadn't been holding her boy. She hadn't even been touching him, and now he was gone.

How had that happened?

She'd lived through nineteen hours of labor to bring him into this world, and he'd left it without her attendance, leaving her with enough pain to last a lifetime. All she remembered was Sam's arms around her before everything went black.

One day passed into the next as they went about the business of laying him to rest. Getting the court date for their divorce hearing came before the flowers had wilted on the grave. Robbie was gone, and what was left of their marriage had died with him.

And now that was over, too.

The back of her throat was burning as Sam led her out of the courtroom. She needed to cry, but the tears wouldn't come. She'd used them up watching Robbie's casket being lowered into the ground.

Haley was broken, both in heart and spirit, and Sam Quaid could not work miracles. He'd lost his son, and now he'd just lost his wife.

The sun was in their eyes as they walked out of the Dallas County Courthouse and paused on the steps. He heard Haley take a deep breath and then she looked at him—really looked, something she hadn't done in weeks.

Haley saw his tears. She'd done that. Then he shook his head, as if in disbelief, and pulled her into his arms.

He was shaking.

She'd done that, too.

She had to say something, but what? His pain was her fault.

Before she could think what to do, he let her go and thrust something into the palm of her hand.

"If you ever need me, for anything or any reason, call this number. You're the only woman I've ever loved, and that damn piece of paper in your purse changed nothing. I'll always be here for you, Haley."

Her fingers curled around the card as she watched him turn away. His steps were slow, but as the distance lengthened between them, they gained momentum. Then he turned a corner and disappeared.

She looked down at the card.

Samuel Quaid—Private Investigations. The phone number was printed beneath his business name. The only link she would have left.

Reality hit.

He was gone.

What have I done?

Houston, Texas—Three years later

Haley Quaid was getting ready to leave for work when her phone beeped. She glanced down, and when she realized it was the weather app with an update, she frowned. It was not good news.

The storm path of Tropical Storm Gladys was still moving toward Houston and she was anxious about it. It would be the first hurricane she'd experienced since moving here, and if it weren't for that showing at the Lawrence estate this morning, she wouldn't even go into the office. But she made a living selling houses, and the Richards family was interested in a very large, very expensive property in the Energy Corridor in West Houston. They knew about the storm, but were set on the showing today. So as long as there was a potential buyer, she was on the job. She sent a text to the office, letting them know that, at the clients' request, she was going directly to the property to meet with them there, and made a mental note to pick up a half-dozen blueberry muffins to take to the showing. Real food in a kitchen always gave it a homier touch, and she wanted to make this sale.

A quick glance at the darkening sky tightened the knot in her gut, but she had an umbrella and a raincoat in the car, so she grabbed her purse and the tote bag she'd packed last night, and headed out the door.

There was no such thing as a slow traffic day in the city, but Haley was adept at getting through it. After stopping at her neighborhood bakery to get the blueberry muffins, she headed for the west side of Houston, going over the key points of the property as she drove.

About halfway there she passed by a car wreck, an all-too-common event on the massive expressways. As she passed, she saw men from a rescue unit pulling a young boy out of the back seat. He was crying, and she immediately thought of Robbie, and looked away.

"God bless all those who are in need," she said, and clenched her jaw, as if daring the world to hurt her again.

She had exacerbated the heartbreak of losing her son by losing Sam, too, and it was her burden to bear. It had taken six months of counseling to feel human again, and that's when the real pain hit. She'd had to face the fact that it was all her fault Sam was gone, and then figure out how to live with that decision. She didn't have the guts to call him up and say she'd changed her mind. And she had no idea if he'd moved on, or if he was dating someone. Her solution had been to lose herself in her new profession and become a successful Realtor. It was days like this that kept her on the top-ten list with her company.

She glanced at the sky again, eyeing the distant clouds of the tropical storm out over the water. She had plenty of time to do this and get home.

A few minutes later, she exited the freeway and drove until she reached the neighborhood where the property was located. She loved coming into Thornwood. The amazing homes and beautifully manicured grounds were all indicative of the extremely wealthy people who lived here.

When she finally reached the property and pulled up into the driveway, she smiled. It was a stunning, white two-story antebellum with four massive pillars spanning the front facade, and a pathway layered with redbrick pavers that led from the curb, straight across the lawn to the front door.

It dawned on her, as she walked toward the property, that the owners had made no attempt to stormproof this house. Considering its value, she thought it was a careless thing to do.

She pulled the key to the lockbox out of her purse, grabbed her tote bag and the box of muffins, and headed for the front door. All of the utilities were on, including the alarm, which she quickly disarmed as soon as she walked in. She carried everything into the kitchen, took a small glass plate from her tote bag and arranged the muffins on it, adding a small stack of napkins beside it.

Last time she'd shown this house, she'd left a six-pack of water bottles in the refrigerator, and she was pleased to see they were still there. She pulled them out and left them beside the napkins, and then made a quick check of the downstairs, turning on lights as she went.

As soon as she was finished, she headed up the stairs to turn those lights on, as well. Once she was satisfied she had everything ready, she went downstairs, plopped down in a chair near the window so she could watch for the Richards and began checking her messages.

She returned two texts, made three calls, then pulled up the local news app. The first thing she read was a front page story about a van belonging to the US Marshals Service wrecking last night and catching on fire. The two prisoners they'd been transporting to a federal prison had escaped in the ensuing chaos and were still at large, one marshal was dead and another crippled for life.

"Good grief," Haley muttered, then scanned past that story, glanced at the time and kept reading.

Outside, the wind was rising. She knew enough about hurricanes to remember that there were often heavy downpours before the storm made landfall. She went to the window, looking out for a sign of the Richardses' white Lexus, then frowned. Surely they didn't get lost. With GPS on both phones and cars, being lost was becoming a thing of the past. She was about ready to give them a call when her phone signaled a text.

It was Patty Richards. Haley pulled up the message.

So sorry. Family emergency in Phoenix. At the airport getting ready to take off. Call you when we get back.

Haley sighed as she returned the text.

No apology necessary. Safe travels. I'll keep you all in my prayers.

She hit Send, and then got up and began going through the rooms turning off lights. At least now she was certain to make it home before the storm. She boxed up the muffins and put the bottled water and plate back in her tote bag, then took it into the hall and left it on the table at the foot of the stairs while she ran up to the second floor to turn off those lights, as well.

She was thinking about stopping at Whole Foods on her way home, but as she started down the stairs, she missed the first step, and turned her ankle on the next. Pain ripped up her leg as she screamed, and then she was falling, falling. One blow to a shoulder, another to the back of her head that popped her neck, toppling head over heels down more steps, until she went face-first into a balustrade and everything went black.

Roy Wayne Baker and Hershel Arnold were still on the run when dawn broke over Houston, and Dude Santos was not a happy man.

Alejandro, aka Dude, Santos, was the third man in their armored car heist, and after the initial robbery when they all made their getaway, they separated on purpose. They were to meet up later and divide the money. What he didn't know was that Hershel and Roy had decided to go behind his back and kick Dude out of his cut. They'd made sure the money was well hidden, but less than two days later, and before Dude could meet up with them again, they were tracked down and arrested.

Dude was pissed that they'd been caught, but when he found out that the money was not recovered with them, he wasn't ready to quit looking for it.

Months went by as they were held pending trial, and then attending the trial itself. Once they were finally sentenced and had been remanded to Bureau of Prisons in Bryan, Texas, a federal facility, he knew they would be out of jail for the time it took to transport them from Houston to Bryan. He spent a good deal of money and went to a lot of trouble to make that escape happen during the move.

Unaware Roy and Hershel were dodging him, he thought it was just panic when they ran the wrong way from the wrecked van. But once again, it messed up his plan to pick them up at the designated location and get his share of the loot.

Now Dude was still out his share of the money, and Roy and Hershel were on the move without means of communication.

Roy and Hershel were free again, without giving Dude Santos a thought, but they wouldn't be free for long if they didn't find wheels and ditch this prison orange.

They kept to the back alleys, knowing a lot of businesses would be receiving early-morning deliveries, and were looking for a delivery van to steal. They knew there was a bad storm coming, and they wanted to be long gone from Houston before it hit.

They'd spent a night sleeping in an abandoned building and were back on the move before daylight. It was just before 7:00 a.m. when they spotted a produce truck parked in an alley with the motor running.

Roy pointed. "You get the driver. I'll get the truck."

Hershel nodded and raced toward the back entrance of the deli. He took down the driver just as he exited into the alley, knocked him out cold and tossed the body in a nearby dumpster.

Roy was behind the wheel when Hershel jumped into the passenger seat, and off they went, out of the alley, winding their way through the streets, and not relaxing until they got on the beltline and disappeared within the constant flow of traffic.

Hershel was fidgeting. He kept looking in the side-view mirror and running his hand through his hair.

Roy frowned. "Sit still, dammit. You're breaking my concentration."

Hershel glanced at Roy, then back to the side-view mirror. "You don't understand. I can't take being locked up again. I'd rather die. I grew up in the Kentucky hills and I need to go home. I need fresh air and sunshine…and woods so thick you can get lost and never be found."

Roy frowned. "Then why the hell did you ever leave it if it was such a great place to be?"

"Because I didn't know how good I had it until I was gone," Hershel said solemnly.

Roy nodded. There was no sense arguing with truth.

Back at the Lawrence estate, the wind was rising. Within a few minutes, rain arrived in a downburst, running down the windows in rivulets, much like the blood running out of Haley's hairline.

She roused once, disoriented by the fact that she

was lying belly down on the stairs with her feet higher than her head.

"Help me," she mumbled, but when she tried to move, the room began to spin, and she was gone again.

Momma, can I have a drink of water? Will you read me a story? Momma, my hair is falling out. Am I gonna die?

Haley roused enough again to open her eyes, but something was wrong. She wasn't in Robbie's room. She was upside down and she hurt. That didn't make sense, she thought. She was in the wrong place. The room began to spin, and once again, she blacked out.

The next time she came to it was dark and she could hear rain. It took a few seconds before she realized she was lying headfirst down a flight of stairs. And then she remembered the showing that didn't happen, and going upstairs to turn out lights.

Oh my God. I fell. I'm hurt. I have to get up.

But getting up was a whole other thing. Even the motion of lifting her head made her nauseated. When she tried to rise up, everything began to spin, and as she reached out to steady herself, the back of her hand hit the balustrades. Grateful for something to hold on to, the spinning slowly stopped.

She finally managed to get up, but the moment she put weight on her feet, the pain in her ankle reminded her of the reason she fell. There was something sticky on her forehead—probably blood, because her head was throbbing and her vision was blurring.

But instead of going downstairs, she got confused and climbed up. She staggered down the hall without thinking to turn on the lights, found her way into the master bedroom and collapsed upon the bed, and it was none too soon. Her head had barely hit the pillow before she passed out again.

Downstairs, the phone she'd dropped when she fell began to ring, but she didn't hear it. It rang and rang and rang, then went to voicemail.

Rhoda Bates, the secretary from Truman Realty, had been trying to reach Haley for hours. She always called in after a showing, but this time she didn't. At first, Rhoda thought nothing of it. Everyone was hustling around doing last-minute prep for the incoming storm, and then Rhoda forgot until after dinner. She was doing dishes when it dawned on her that Haley had never checked in, so she dried her hands and made a quick call, expecting to get an immediate answer. But when that didn't happen and the call went to voicemail, she left a message.

"Haley. It's me, Rhoda. You didn't call in, and I'm a little concerned. Just let me know you're okay."

After she disconnected, she thought of their boss, Will Truman, and wondered if Haley had talked to him. Now that she was on the trail, she wanted to follow up, so she called him.

"Hey, Rhoda, what's up?" Will asked.

"Haley had a showing this morning, but she never

called in after it was over, and she always checks in. Have you spoken to her?"

Will frowned. "No, I haven't. Did you call her?"

"Yes, but she didn't answer. I left a message on her voicemail."

"That's not like her," he said.

"I know. That's why I became concerned."

"Now I'm worried," Will said. "If you hear anything, please let me know."

"I will. Batten down the hatches," Rhoda said.

"For sure," Will said, and disconnected.

Rhoda laid the phone aside and went back to the dishes. She could hear the wind picking up and sighed. God, but she hated hurricane season. She was wishing she had evacuated. This wasn't the hurricane, it was a precursor. She still had time to get out, and it was still in the back of her mind.

Sam Quaid was eating Chinese takeout and watching the evening news, waiting for the weather report. He and Haley had been divorced a little over three years now, but he still had dreams of her coming back to Dallas. In the dream, he opened the door, saw the smile on her face and then she disappeared.

With this tropical storm heading straight for Houston, he couldn't help but worry about her. He knew the lower level of her apartment building might flood, but her apartment would not. She was on the fourth floor.

When the weather report began to air, the warnings that came with the incoming storm put knots in his gut. He told himself she was fine, but his appetite was gone. He got up, dumped leftovers in the garbage disposal and then sat down to go through his email.

Roy and Hershel's grand plan of getting out of Houston was over before it started, when they began running out of gas.

"What the hell?" Roy muttered, when he saw the gas gauge. "What delivery driver goes out to make rounds without a full tank of gas?"

Hershel was getting nervous. "We can't run out here on the beltway. If we get out and start walking in these orange jumpsuits, this escape is over."

"Right," Roy said, and took the next exit. They were on the west side of Houston now, and driving through neighborhood alleys, looking for a place to hide out until dark, after which they would steal another vehicle and some food and clothes, and keep moving.

The van quit somewhere in the Thornwood area. They left it in the alley and started running, passing wall after wall of privacy fences.

Momma, I'm cold. Can I have the green dinosaur quilt? The one I got for Christmas when I was six?

Please, Momma, I don't want to go back to the doctor today.

Momma, will you fill the hummingbird feeders so I can sit out on the patio and watch the birds?

* * *

Haley roused. "Gotta fill bird feeders," she mumbled, but when she rose up on one elbow, the bed began turning so fast that she collapsed back into the dream where her son still lived.

The next time she woke it was morning, wind was blasting rain so hard against the windows it sounded like hail, and she wasn't back home in Dallas. Robbie didn't need the bird feeders filled, and she knew they'd covered him over in his casket with the green dinosaur quilt.

The hole in her life where her son used to be would never be filled, and her heart hurt from the memories. Then came the realization that she'd been here in this house most of twenty-four hours—and the danger she was in filled her with fear. Tropical Storm Gladys was arriving and in hurricane force. She'd lost her chance to get home. She was trapped.

She started to get up, but the pain in her body stopped her. She hurt in so many places she dreaded moving, and then saw the blood all over her hands and clothes.

"Good Lord. I have all the wounds of a bar fight with none of the fun," she muttered, and eased herself off the bed, then hobbled into the adjoining bathroom.

One look in the mirror, and she knew she was lucky she hadn't broken her neck. From what she could feel of the cut in her hair, it probably needed stitches, but that wasn't going to happen anytime soon, so she began looking around for something to clean up with. The house was staged well enough that she had access to a washcloth and bath towel, so she turned on the water, let it get warm and then began to wipe off the blood as best she could.

Her navy slacks were ripped at the knee and her red-and-navy-striped blouse was ripped under one arm and splattered with blood. There was dried blood in her dark hair and a large purple knot above her left eyebrow. It was going to clash with her brown eyes. Not fashionable at all.

Everyone always said she looked a little bit like Sandra Bullock, only with a heart-shaped face. But she didn't look like her now. She didn't even look like Haley.

The knuckles on both hands were raw and bloody, and the ankle she'd turned was twice it's normal size and badly bruised. She cleaned the cut on her head and wiped blood out of her hair, then dried off.

It wasn't until she went back into the bedroom that she realized how strong the storm sounded now, and she hobbled to the window to look out. Rain was a gray wall of water blowing sideways, and the wind had plastered all kinds of limbs and debris against the rock wall surrounding the grounds.

Standing made her shaky, but when she reached out to steady herself and felt the bedroom wall vibrating beneath her hand, her skin crawled. That wasn't her. That was the wind.

She quickly moved away from the windows and left the room to go look for her shoes and phone.

Halfway down the hall, everything began to spin again. She stopped, grabbed her knees as she bent over and waited until the feeling passed, then kept moving toward the stairs.

She hung on to the newel post to look down, and when she saw the pool of drying blood, guessed it was where she must have laid unconscious. One red loafer was on the second step, the other one about halfway down. Her phone was on the next to the last bottom step, and her tote bag and the box of muffins were on the hall table where she'd left them.

"Easy does it," she said, and slowly made her way down, picking up her belongings as she went.

She sat down on the bottom step with her shoes, and after a bit of struggle got them back on in spite of the swollen ankle. Her phone was at 55 percent battery power as she pulled up the weather app.

Just as she feared, Tropical Storm Gladys had been upgraded to a hurricane. She got up and limped toward the front windows to check on her car. To her horror, there was water flooding the streets and her car was gone. She didn't know whether it had been stolen, or blown away, but it was yet another sign of how trapped she was.

Struck with another wave of helplessness, she leaned against the wall and slid down to the floor with her phone clutched against her chest.

"Think, Haley, think." Then she took a deep breath and called 911.

But the call rang and rang and rang, and instead

of a dispatcher, she got a recording. No police. No ambulance service. No fire trucks available because of the storm.

She thought about checking messages, but her vision kept going in and out of focus. She needed to lie down, so she got herself up and headed back toward the stairs. There was nothing to do but wait out the storm here. She had a half-dozen large blueberry muffins, a six-pack of bottled water and whatever else was in her tote bag. Now all she had to do was get it all upstairs.

It was slow going having to hang on to the railing, and when she passed the dried blood on the stairs, the Realtor in her made a mental note to come back and clean it up. Finally, she made it up to the second floor and back to the bedroom.

She put all of her things on a chair in the sitting area, then dug in the tote bag for a container of wet wipes and headed back to clean up the blood.

By the time she got back to the bedroom again, she was in so much pain she couldn't think. She found a bottle of over-the-counter pain meds in her purse, downed a couple, then plugged her phone into the charger cord before she lay back down. There had to be someone she could call for help. Maybe she'd think of them after the pain pills kicked in, but not now.

Then her phone began ringing, signaling an incoming call. She fumbled to answer, desperate not to lose the connection.

"Hello? Hello?"

"Haley? Oh, thank the Lord! I've been trying to reach you since noon yesterday. Where have you been?"

Hayley eased down onto the pillow, hoping the bed would stop spinning.

"Rhoda?"

"Yes, this is Rhoda. Are you okay? You sound weird."

"Not okay. Fell down stairs at the Lawrence property in Thornwood."

"Oh, honey! I'm so sorry. Were you badly injured?"

"I think concussion. Have cut in my head that's still seeping. Probably needed stitches," Haley said.

"Then why didn't the doctor stitch you up?"

"No doctor… I'm still in the Lawrence house. Unconscious for long time. Still keep passing out. My car is missing. No rescue services."

Rhoda gasped. "Oh, my God! Haley! Houston is flooding everywhere. That house is a two-story. Get up there and stay."

"I'm on the second floor already. Is it flooding everywhere?" Haley asked.

"It's going to, and there's nothing they can do to stop it. The Bayou area is already flooded and backing up through neighborhoods. I evacuated in the middle of a thunderstorm, along with several thousand other people with the same idea. Took hours and hours to get to my sister's house."

The light fixture above Haley's head looked like

it was spinning, but it wasn't a ceiling fan, and there were no blades.

"Oh no! I'm so dizzy. Can't talk. Say prayer."

Rhoda began to cry. "Yes, honey, I'll say prayers for you, and if the rescue services resume, I will call them for you. I promise."

"Address?"

"Yes, yes, I can get the address off our listings. Do you have any food or water?"

"Some. Have to sleep now," Haley mumbled, and disconnected. She rolled over onto her side and passed out.

Horrified, Rhoda called Will Truman to let him know about Haley, then tried 911 services herself. Haley was right. The recorded message gave all the callers the same info.

At this point, there wasn't anything anyone could do but wait.

Two

The phone rang at the Houston Police Department, but no one answered. It made the knot tighten in Mae Arnold's belly. She'd been notified by the US Marshals Service about the van transporting her son, Hershel, being wrecked, and that he and another prisoner were on the run. She was warned that if he showed up at home, to try and convince him that it was in his best interests to turn himself in.

Mae hadn't commented beyond thanking them for letting her know. But now she was scared. Hershel never did call, and she knew if he was on the run, he would be calling her. She'd been expecting him to come home for months to reclaim the box he'd shipped home. They had stored it in the old smokehouse, expecting him to arrive soon afterward, but then they learned he'd been arrested again and soon forgot about the box.

Now the news coming out of Houston was all

about the hurricane, and that's what scared her. Hershel was her only child. She was past judging him. She just needed to know he wasn't dead and floating in floodwaters somewhere in Texas.

Haley slept most of the day, still dreaming of the time they were losing Robbie.

Momma, tomorrow is my birthday.
Momma, will you rub my feet? They're cold.
Momma, I am tired of being sick. I'm not going to get well, am I?

She woke up with tears on her cheeks and an ache in the pit of her stomach. She got up for a bathroom break, ate a few bites of a muffin and drank a bottle of water. She knew to stay hydrated, so she refilled the bottles with water from the tap each time she drank. The six-pack wouldn't last long, and while she still had safe water to drink she wouldn't let the bottles stand empty.

After checking the weather app, she was officially scared. She thought of Hurricane Katrina years back, and of the people who'd been rescued from roofs because their houses had flooded clear to the attics. But this house was two stories, and in a place that didn't normally flood. She should be safe. Only the longer she thought about it, the more uneasy she became. At the least, she needed to check the attic access and see if there was a way to get out onto the roof. It would make her feel better to know what her options were, and she wanted to do it while it was still daylight.

She left the master bedroom, moving slowly on her swollen ankle toward a door at the far end of the hallway. She'd been in the attic once during a showing, and knew there were even more stairs to maneuver, which she was dreading. When she reached the access, she flipped on the light switch, and grabbed hold of the railing to steady her steps going up.

The attic was surprisingly large, with two dormer windows overlooking the grounds behind the house. She couldn't see much for the wind and rain, but saw enough to know if the need arose, she could get out from there.

The attic had actually been finished off like the other rooms in the house, and even had a half bath. Having satisfied herself that she wasn't going to be trapped inside, she made a point to unlock both of the attic windows before she went back down to the second floor.

By the morning of the next day she felt almost normal. Her ankle was still sore, but the swelling was going down. However, the bruising on her face and body was still dark purple, and a long way from fading.

Over the past two days she'd seen the hurricane only through the bedroom windows and from the second story. She was curious to see the front of the property again. Whatever damage was there would be a good way to judge the force of the storm.

She'd plugged in her cell phone to recharge, saving her portable power bank in case the power went off, and left the phone charging as she walked out into the hall. According to her wireless carrier, she should not lose power during the storm. It was part of their sales pitch and something they'd added after Hurricane Katrina happened in New Orleans. And she had been assured that, even if it did fade from time to time, they would be on the job, keeping their customers in service.

As she neared the stairs, she could hear ripping sounds above her head, and guessed the wind was blowing shingles off the roof. But all she needed was for the roof itself to hold.

Then she heard a huge splashing sound and cautiously peeked around the corner, looking down into the floor below. To her horror, the whole downstairs had flooded, and the water had risen enough to cover the bottom two stair steps.

"Oh my God, oh my God," Haley cried, and hobbled back toward the bedroom. A window must have burst while she was sleeping, and the water had come rushing in throughout the night.

As soon as she reached the bedroom, she grabbed her phone and once again called 911, but got the same recording. Desperate to let someone know what was happening, she crawled up into the middle of the bed and began going through her contacts. She was about halfway through the listings when it dawned on her that if 911 couldn't help, no one could.

She took a deep breath and went still, telling herself that if she couldn't change her situation, she could change how she felt about it. Right now, she was safe. She didn't believe that the water would come all the way up to the second story, but the danger could come in what was in the water as it rose, like snakes or gators from the Bayou area displaced by the storm surge. All she had to do was keep her door closed.

She reached for her tote bag and dumped it upside down on the bed to take stock of her supplies. The first thing that fell out was her handgun, a six-shot, Glock 43, with a full clip of the 9mm ammo. She'd had it three years and had yet to use it. Will Truman had encouraged all of his Realtors to get carry permits and take a weapon with them to showings. In this day and age, going into an empty property with strangers was a risky move, but that wasn't the case here. However, if anything slithered or crawled out of the water and up the stairs, she would be ready for it. She popped the loaded clip into the gun, then left it on the bed table while she sorted through the rest of her stuff.

She found a candy bar, an energy bar and a bottle of over-the-counter painkillers, along with a bunch of receipts she kept for taxes and the wallet she used for business cards people gave her. It wasn't until she opened it up and saw the one on top that her heart kicked against her chest.

Sam!

Oh my God!

Could he? Would he?

If there was any chance at all of anyone coming to her rescue, it would be Sam Quaid. Her fingers were trembling when she punched in his number, and didn't know she'd been holding her breath until he answered.

"Hello."

"Sam, this is Haley."

Sam was in his office in downtown Dallas, and the moment he heard her voice, he was on his feet and moving to the rain-drenched windows, as if it would put him that much closer to her.

"I'm so glad you called. Are you okay? I've been concerned."

Then he heard her breathing change, and there was a quaver in her voice.

"No, I'm not okay. I fell down the stairs in a house I was going to show. By the time I came to enough to get up, the hurricane was here. I'm trapped, and the bottom floor of the house is filling up with water."

Sam's voice shifted into a serious tone. "How bad are you hurt?"

Haley was struggling not to cry. "Probably a concussion. Bad sprained ankle. Need stitches on the back of my head, I'm pretty sure. Cuts and bruises."

The thought of her suffering like that alone made him sick.

"How long have you been there?" he asked.

"According to the date on my phone, this is the third day. I have a little food left. The power is still on, but I don't know for how long. No rescue services available." Haley's breath caught. "I'm scared. I don't want to drown."

"You're not going to drown. I won't let that happen," Sam said. "Look, there's always a lull in the hurricane's eye. When that gets to you, would it be possible for you to get out on your roof?"

"Yes. I already checked," Haley said.

"Good job. So listen to me. I'm coming to get you. I will find a way to get as close to Houston as I can now. I know a guy who runs a private airport in the area. He has a chopper, so I'll get him to fly me to your location during that lull. We'll pick you up off the roof."

"That sounds dangerous," Haley said.

"That's beside the point. I need the address so I can program it into the GPS," Sam said.

Haley told him.

"Got it," he said. "Don't be scared, okay? Just trust me."

The deep rasp of his so-familiar voice broke what was left of Haley's self-control. She started to cry, and it wasn't about the hurricane.

"I'm sorry. I'm so sorry, Sam."

It was a gut punch Sam hadn't expected. "Don't cry, Haley. Just one thing at a time, and right now getting you rescued is what matters."

She swiped away tears. "My wireless carrier is supposed to cover this kind of emergency, but this is my first time to test that promise. What if I can't call you anymore?"

"Then just know I'll be there."

"Thank you, Sam. I'll be in the attic waiting, and when I see the chopper, I'll climb out onto the roof."

"You've got this…and have faith, Haley Jo. Stay alive, because I'm coming to get you."

Even after the connection ended, Haley was reluctant to put down the phone. She didn't know how much she'd missed him until she heard his voice again, and for the first time since this nightmare began, she had hope.

Roy and Hershel were in trouble. The garden shed they'd taken shelter in was full of water and it was rising.

"We're gonna die here," Hershel muttered.

"No, hell no! All we have to do is get across the yard and into the big house," Roy said.

Hershel slapped the back of Roy's head in frustration. "Just look out that window and tell me how we're gonna walk through floodwater, and still stand up against that wind."

Roy turned around and punched Hershel on the shoulder. "Don't hit me again. You stand here and drown, then. I'm taking this hammer to bust out a window in that house, then I'm getting inside and up to the second floor to safety. You suit yourself, but if we do nothing, we're gonna drown in here anyway. I'm willing to take a chance and save my ass."

Then he shoved Hershel aside and reached for the doorknob.

"Oh hell. Wait for me," Hershel said. "If we hold on to each other, we might be able to make it."

It was a struggle to open the door against the waist-deep water already inside the shed, but once the latch released, the wind hit the door and slammed it backward, washing both of them down into water from the wave that it created.

Roy fell into Hershel, who was slammed against the wall, shouting and cursing as loud as he could above the wind. "We're dead meat," Hershel cried as he helped Roy up.

"Fuck it," Roy said. "I lost my hammer."

"There's a hatchet," Hershel shouted, pointing to the short-handled tool hanging on a pegboard.

Roy grabbed it firmly, then they locked arms. "You ready?" he asked.

"As I'll ever be," Hershel said, then lowered his head and took the first step across the threshold, dragging Roy with him.

"Oh sh—" Roy screamed, as the wind took away his voice and his breath, and then blew them both off their feet, down into the dark, roiling depths.

Even though the water was less than waist deep, they were struggling to keep their heads above water as they staggered and fell, staggered and fell. But each time they got up, they were a little closer to the house, until somehow they'd reached the back wall.

It was all Roy could do to raise his arm enough to swing the hatchet. It cracked the glass, and the force of the wind did the rest, blowing the glass inward. They used the hatchet to clean out the remaining shards, and then Hershel pushed Roy inside.

Roy hit the water inside headfirst, breaking his fall with outstretched arms, then got up gasping and choking.

Hershel was trying to climb through the opening when Roy turned around and pulled him the rest of the way in.

The broken window let in wind, rain and the hurricane's roar, but being beneath a roof was a huge relief.

"We did it! Hot damn, we did it!" Roy screamed, and then began to laugh. "This will be a good story to tell your mama."

But Hershel wasn't laughing. "Well, hell. We broke into an empty house."

"What do you mean?" Roy asked. "The family probably evacuated."

"No, look at the countertops. No canisters, no toasters, no coffee maker on the counter. This likely means no food, and I'm starving."

Their momentary relief had ended with the new reality of their situation as they both opened cabinets and found them empty.

"I'm not giving up without a search," Roy said. "Come on, we'll go room to room. There still might be something down here. You look in the rest of the cabinets, and I'll check the pantry and the rooms down this hall."

Hershel started banging cabinet doors, and the more frustrated he got, the louder he slammed them.

* * *

Upstairs, Haley thought she heard the sound of breaking glass and assumed it was related to the hurricane. Then the banging started. She slid off the bed and was walking silently toward the landing when she heard men's voices. All of a sudden, the fear of snakes and gators was far less of a threat than being trapped in this empty house with strangers.

She edged her way down the upper hall and peeked around the corner just as a man in an orange jumpsuit moved through the foyer below.

Sweet Mother of God! Prison uniforms!

She slipped backward out of sight and headed toward her bedroom as fast as she could move and locked herself in, her heart pounding. The orange jumpsuits! It had to be the escaped prisoners, and she was trapped with them in a flooding house.

What were the odds of that happening?

She was in a panic, trying to figure out what to do when she spotted the large, oversize black marker on top of the tote bag. Desperation called for desperate measures. She didn't know if this would work, but she had to try.

She took off the top, and very quietly unlocked the door. Once she was satisfied the men were still downstairs, she swung her bedroom door inward, and wrote on the door in big black letters.

Danger—Do Not Enter.

Under Renovation.

Then she eased the door shut and locked it again,

putting everything but her phone and gun back into the tote bag, then sat down on the side of the bed to make another frantic call to Sam.

To her dismay, the call went to voicemail. She left a quick, breathless message and disconnected, then went into the phone's settings, and put all of her notifications on mute.

Just as she did, the light she'd had on in the adjoining bathroom went off. The power in the house was finally gone.

She pinched the bridge of her nose to keep from crying. It had to happen. She was lucky she'd had it this long. Now all she could do was be still and stay silent, and pray they'd bypass this bedroom for any of the others down the hall.

She heard them talking, and when their voices got louder, she knew they were on the upper floor. She palmed the gun, took it off safety, waiting, listening—and then she heard them outside her door.

"What's this all about?" Roy asked, pointing to the warning on the door.

Hershel shrugged. "Seems pretty obvious."

"I wanna see what's in there," Roy said and tried to turn the knob, but it was locked. "It's locked! I'm gonna kick it in."

Hershel grabbed him by the arm. "Right. Wanna fuck up your ankle kicking in a door just to be nosy, help yourself. But if you do, I'm not carrying you anywhere. I'll leave you behind when this storm has passed."

"Fine," Roy said, and pushed past his buddy, and went down the hall to the next room. "This one has a bed."

"I'm not sleeping with you," Hershel muttered. "Find one with two beds or you're in here on your own."

"Whatever," Roy said, and they moved to the next room, arguing all the way.

Haley could hear their voices fading and breathed a quiet sigh of relief. She picked up her phone to check the weather app. The eye was still out over the ocean, but now she had to get to the attic and hide out there, so she wouldn't miss Sam when the time arrived. As soon as it got dark, she was going to make a run for it. She set out a muffin and a bottle of water, and packed the rest of the food in the tote bag.

With her phone in one back pocket and the portable phone charger in the other, she picked up the muffin. She was too scared to be hungry, but she hadn't eaten in quite a while, and had to keep up her strength. So she peeled back the paper and took a bite, chewing and swallowing as if it was a job she needed to finish.

A few moments later, she heard their voices again, coming back up the hall. She froze, hardly daring to breathe. They were fighting about something… something about hiding money, then about their apartment and knowing someone named Dude Santos would kill them if he ever found out they'd betrayed him.

* * *

The hurricane on the Gulf had impacted Dallas weather, as well. Sam drove through rain all the way home from the office, and was still reeling from hearing Haley's voice when he arrived at his house.

The moment he walked through the front door, he headed for his office, and within minutes, was on the phone with Lee Tolson, a man he knew who owned a private airport outside of Houston. Lee also owned a chopper, and after Sam laid out what he needed, Lee was immediately on board, although somewhat doubtful about Sam being able to get there.

"You're taking a big chance driving into this storm," Lee said. "Even if you do make it to the airport, you'll have to shelter in one of the open hangars, if they're still standing."

"I'll make it," Sam said. "I have to."

"I don't know many men who would go to this much trouble for an ex-wife," Lee said.

A muscle jerked at the side of Sam's jaw—a sign of his determination to fulfill that promise he'd made to her.

"I'll just say there were extenuating circumstances to the divorce and leave it at that," he said. "I need to know how much time I have to get there. When is the eye predicted to make landfall?"

"Estimate is sometime within the next twenty-four hours," Lee said.

Sam glanced at the clock. It was still a couple of hours before noon, and the drive to Houston in good weather and bad traffic was usually around five hours. He didn't know how long it would take to navigate it today, but he was confident he'd be there before dark.

"It won't take me that long to get there. You just show up at the airport, and get me where I need to go," Sam said.

"Do you have a location on her?" Lee asked.

Sam gave him the address.

"Got it," Lee said. "Safe travels, and if something happens that you can't make it, let me know."

"Yeah, only that's not going to happen," Sam said. "See you when I see you."

He disconnected and then ran down the hall to get the backpack he used for camping. It was already packed with MREs, the survivalist specials of "meals ready to eat." It also had a sleeping bag and a first aid kit. He added an extra changes of clothes, in case they didn't have time to get out of the Houston area before the eye passed. He was counting on an extra pair of jeans, some underwear and two clean shirts being a safe bet, then remembered Haley already needed a change of clothes, and went back into his closet, got an extra pair of gym shorts, a pair of sweats and another couple of T-shirts. He filled the rest of the backpack with emergency food and extra medical supplies, tossed his rain gear over his arm and carried the backpack into the living room.

As he reached for his phone, he noticed he'd

missed a call from Haley. Frowning, he pulled up her voicemail.

Sam! Two men just broke into the house down-stairs. It's only a matter of time before they come up. I think they're the escaped prisoners that were on the news the day before I fell. I'm going to try and hide from them. I have my gun. I've turned off the sounds on my phone because I don't want them to hear it ringing, but you can text. I'll check messages until my phone goes dead. Wish me luck. I'm going to need it.

"No, no, no!" Sam dropped his phone in his pocket and ran back into his bedroom, grabbing his hand-gun and a handful of loaded clips. Then he opened his safe, took the satellite phone and portable chargers he used for remote locations, and packed it all into his backpack before heading out the door on the run.

His silver Hummer was parked beside the smaller Jeep he drove to work and back, and he dumped his gear into the back seat of the larger vehicle, and took off out of the garage, thankful for the size and weight. It was going to mean the difference between getting to Houston or being blown off the road.

He said a prayer for Haley as he drove through his neighborhood, heading for the feeder road to get him to Highway 75 South, which would connect him to I45 South.

His gas tank was almost full, and the rain on the streets was running toward gutters at breakneck speed. Hurricane Gladys was causing trouble, even this far away.

Once he hit Highway 75, he increased speed as much as he dared, and when he finally got on I45, he accelerated even more. He needed to make good time while he could, because once he drove into the outer edges of the hurricane-force winds, there was no way to predict what he would encounter, or how much it would slow him down. Whatever it took, he had to get there. He didn't want to think about having to bury her, too.

Sam was two hours down the road when he stopped for gas. The wind was stronger here, and it was harder for him to stand up as he refueled, but the size and weight of the Hummer were proving invaluable to bearing the brunt without being blown off the road.

As soon as he pulled back onto the interstate, the southbound traffic went from slim to none. Miles passed without seeing a single vehicle, and then when he did, they were big semis hauling heavy loads, which kept them from being blown off the roads.

He wouldn't let himself think about what Haley was facing, but knowing she was armed gave him hope. She had always been a good shot at the gun range, and he didn't believe she'd hesitate to use the gun to save herself. In his dreams, she always came home to him. He would never have imagined their next meeting turning out like this. He just needed her to stay alive.

He kept playing and replaying that last voice message from her just to hear her voice, and the one thing he got from it was how much she'd changed. He heard fear, but he also heard determination, and a hint of anger.

She'd fought so hard to keep Robbie alive, and in her mind, she'd failed to save him. It had taken him months to figure out that what she deemed as *her* failure had broken her beyond anything his love could have healed.

But he didn't hear that in her voice anymore. Something had changed within her over the past three years, and whatever it was, it was a good thing. She had a weapon, and she sounded perfectly willing to use it. He hit Replay on the message again and let the sound of her voice roll through him.

"Hang in there, baby. Please stay alive. Please be okay."

Three

The sun was shining on the water in the birdbath outside of Mae Arnold's kitchen window. She kept the bird feeder close to it so she could watch the birds as she worked, but today, the sight of them did not soothe her.

She was watching CNN's coverage of what Hurricane Gladys was doing to Houston, and seeing the flooded neighborhoods and the ongoing storm damage was horrifying. Right now, she would rather know her son, Hershel, was spending the rest of his life behind bars than imagine he had become a victim of this storm.

Over the years, he had changed from the gentle little boy he'd once been, to a coldhearted man she didn't know. So she had chosen to think of him as he used to be, and not the man who had killed a guard and put another one in a wheelchair during the latest crime he'd committed.

She'd couldn't bear to follow the trial, and learned of their sentencing secondhand. She didn't like hearing the Arnold name associated with criminal activity and was ashamed that her son had come to this end.

Haley sat quietly on her bed with her swollen ankle propped up, listening to the prisoners fighting. They'd been at it for hours, loudly cursing the fact that there was no food in the house, then running up and down the hall checking on how far the water was rising on the stairs. She'd also heard them talking about getting out of the house as soon as the storm hit a lull, and get somewhere else that would have food. If they knew she had food and water only feet away from their door, she would be in a fight for her life.

As soon as their voices faded again, she moved around the bed to look out the window. There was so much debris in the water surrounding the house that she couldn't help wondering if all of Houston was blowing away.

She thought about Sam, picturing him trying to drive toward Houston through the periphery of the hurricane winds. Would he get here in time to save her? Her life was on the line, and almost anything could send it teetering in the wrong direction.

Please be safe, Sam. Please come get me. I don't want to die.

Trying not to panic, she crawled back up in the middle of the bed, pulled her cell phone out of her pocket and checked to see if Sam had sent her a text.

He had not, but then she told herself it didn't have to mean anything. If anyone could get here, it would be Sam.

She had about 50 percent battery power left and still had bars showing in-service, so she plugged it into the power bank. The time on her phone was already after 6:00 p.m., but the dark skies from the continuing deluge made it seem later. Her shoulders slumped. She ached in every muscle, and she was so tired. If this was a nightmare, she couldn't find the way out to wake up. And her deadline for making her rescue was nearing an end. She had to get out of this room and into the attic tonight, or she'd never be able to get on the roof unseen.

At best guess, Sam was now a little less than two hours away from his destination. His fingers were cramping from the tight grip he had on the steering wheel, but his heart ached more. All of the panic of trying to get to Haley had resurrected the hopelessness he'd felt losing his son.

A man was supposed to protect the ones he loved, and he'd tried. Lord knows how hard he'd tried, but he'd lost them both. And right now, this mad ride into a hurricane felt like his last chance to do something right.

He still loved Haley—probably always would. It had taken her three years to reach out to him, and all he wanted was to keep this promise. The storm-driven winds buffeted the Hummer, but the vehicle's weight was enough to keep it from being flipped. The windshield wipers were mostly useless. He was driving through a gray curtain with about three feet of visibility, when all of a sudden he drove up on the ass end of a jackknifed semi, partially blocking the southbound lanes on which he'd been traveling.

He slammed on the brakes to keep from ramming straight into it, which caused him to hydroplane. The Hummer slid along the length of the tilted trailer without ever coming into contact, ending up right beside the cab.

Sam was shaking; his heart was hammering so hard it almost drowned out the storm. He took a deep breath and put the car in Park until he could get his bearings.

The driver's side door on the semi was missing, and the huge trailer had blown apart in the storm, revealing an empty interior.

Not enough weight.

He hoped the driver had long since been rescued, because he was nowhere in sight. Grateful to still be in one piece, he put the Hummer back in gear, made a U-turn on the interstate and carefully made his way around the cab, hoping there wasn't more debris on the other side.

It appeared to be clear, at least as far as he could see, so he resumed his pace, glancing once at the GPS. Another hour and he'd be at the airport, but this slower pace was making him antsy. What if he got to the airport and everything was in shambles? What if the chopper was damaged and couldn't fly? To calm his fears, he replayed Haley's voicemail once more. She wasn't accepting failure, so neither would he.

He kept pushing south, driving blind into the outer edges of the storm proper, until the GPS directed him off the interstate onto a feeder road. The next time the GPS directed him to turn, it said he was less than a quarter of a mile from the airport. He had to trust the GPS wasn't steering him wrong, because he couldn't see shit. The GPS directed one more turn, this time to the left, and he took it on blind trust that there was a road. Within moments, he drove up on the hangars looming like mountains through the lashing rain.

Relieved that he'd reached his destination, he had a whole new problem—finding a hangar he could shelter in that was still standing. He picked up his phone and sent a text to Lee to let him know he'd made it, and then sent a text to Haley.

I'm at the hangar outside of Houston.

He drove up on one of the hangars that had been flattened, and the small, lightweight planes that had been inside of it were scattered about, all of them flipped, and one crushed beneath a roof. His gut knotted as he kept inching his way through the rain, and he finally drove up on one large hangar still intact. He saw the darker shape of an open doorway—considered it the lifesaver he needed—and drove inside.

The sudden absence of rain was a blessing, and in the glow of his headlights, he saw a space within the plane-filled hangar just big enough for him to park.

"Thank you, Lord," Sam said, and killed the engine.

Even though he was still inside the Hummer with the windows up, the sound inside this place was deafening.

It had been dark outside for hours when Haley decided to make her move. Once she was in the attic, she'd be right where she needed to be when Sam came to get her. She hadn't checked for a message in hours and wanted to look one last time before she turned off the phone.

The time read just after midnight, and she hadn't heard a sound out of either of the men in at least two hours. When she realized she had a new text from Sam, she was so happy she almost cried. And then she read the message. He'd done it! Somehow, he got through.

My Sam. Ever faithful, and I so don't deserve it.

Her belly was in knots as she took off her shoes and dropped them in the tote bag with everything else. After rechecking the clip in her handgun, she made sure the safety was off, and palmed it as she went to her door. The click was minimal when she turned the lock, but it still made Haley flinch. She opened the door slightly then paused, listening.

Nothing.

Anxiety rolled through her as she left the relative safety of her hiding place and stepped out into the hall. Pulling the door shut behind her, she headed toward the attic. Moving as quickly as she could on her bad ankle, she was less than five feet away from her goal when a door opened behind her. Even though it was dark, she knew the outline of her body would be visible. Panicked, she dropped her bag and spun with the gun already in her hand.

Hershel was stunned at first by the sight of someone else in the house, but quickly started yelling.

"Roy! Roy! Someone's in the house!"

Haley fired her weapon without hesitation at the same moment the man bolted toward her. She knew immediately that she'd hit him in the shoulder, when he suddenly spun sideways.

Roy was already out of the room and running when Hershel got hit. "You bitch!" he shouted and lurched toward her as fast as he could run.

Haley fired again.

Roy screamed in pain, but he kept running, and before she could fire again, he took her down in a flying leap, doubled up his fist and knocked her out.

Haley came to with her hands tied to the headboard, and her feet tied together at the ankles with what looked like strips of the curtains that had been on these windows. Her chin ached where he'd hit her, and her swollen ankle was in a bind from where he'd tied her down. But more physical pain was nothing compared to the pain of knowing she wasn't going to make it to that roof.

Suddenly a light flashed across her face. She was so scared she could barely breathe.

"So, bitch! You finally wake up. You've been holding out on us," Roy said, and took a big bite of the muffin in his hand, washing it down with a drink from one of her bottles of water.

Haley shifted her position, trying to ease the pressure of the tie around her sore ankle, and when she did, realized her phone was still in her back pocket, for all the good it would do her. But they didn't have it, either, so there was that.

"What's your name, bitch? Oh wait? I forgot. I already went through your purse, Haley Quaid. Where's your phone, Haley?"

"I fell down the stairs. It's somewhere in the water below."

He frowned but took it as truth, since the fall was obvious by just looking at her face.

"You shot Hershel," he said. He pulled her gun out of the back of his pants and shot at the headboard, just missing her head by inches.

Haley screamed.

Roy laughed, then winced. She'd grazed his side and was pretty sure it had broken a rib because it clearly hurt him to take a deep breath. He waved the gun at her again.

"Hershel is hurt bad," he said. "I can't stop the bleeding. If he dies, so do you, but not yet. You're gonna help me pass some time. You broke one of my ribs, so I won't be fucking you, but I'm damn sure gonna fuck *with* you."

"Sorry I missed," Haley said.

Roy swung the gun back up and shot toward her, hitting the wall above the bed, but this time Haley didn't flinch, and she was counting shots. The Glock was a six shot. She'd used two on them, and he'd just shot two at her. There were only two left.

However, the noise of the gunshots roused Hershel, and it was his groan that shifted Roy's focus.

"Roy, Roy, help me, man."

Roy laid the gun aside and took the flashlight to the other bed. Hershel was bloody as hell, and Roy hadn't been able to staunch the blood flow.

"It hurts, Roy. I hurt so bad. I need to call Mama."

Roy gripped Hershel's shoulder. "We'll worry about your mama after we get out of here. Hang on, buddy. I've got some painkillers. Do you think you can swallow them?"

Hershel shuddered as a wave of pain washed through him, and then nodded.

Roy swung the flashlight at the contents of Haley's tote bag he'd dumped on the floor and fished out the little container of pills. He shook four out into the palm of his hand and then lifted Hershel's head.

"Open wide," Roy said, and dropped them into his mouth, then gave him a drink from the water bottle to wash them down.

Hershel choked trying to swallow.

Roy raised his head a little higher and gave him another sip. This time, both pills and water went down.

"There you go, buddy. They'll kick in soon. Just try to rest."

Hershel reached for his shoulder, then winced when his hand came away red with fresh blood. "I'm gonna die. Tell Mama I'm sorry. Tell her to keep the box."

"I'll call her when I find a phone," Roy said. "Just close your eyes and let those pills do their business."

Haley's eyes narrowed. *So their names are Hershel and Roy. I'm sorry I didn't kill the both of them.* As it was, she was up shit creek. And the moment she thought that, she remembered that was one of Sam's sayings.

Sam.

The pain that went through her was as real as if she'd been shot, too. She wasn't going to see him again after all, and she closed her eyes so Roy wouldn't see her tears.

"Oh hell, we can't have the bitch going to sleep now," Roy said, and swung the back of his hand across her cheek.

Startled by the sudden pain, Haley cried out, and then moaned.

Roy laughed, then grabbed a handful of her hair and yanked her head sideways until she was facing him.

"Do you see my face?" he asked.

She nodded.

"I can't hear you," Roy said, doubled up his fist, and this time hit her in the belly so hard she lost her breath.

"Now did you hear what I said?" Roy said.

Haley was still gasping for air and could only nod.

Roy waved the gun in her face. "Piss me off again and I'll shoot you where you lie. Understand?"

Haley coughed, but the desperately needed oxygen was finally moving into her lungs again.

"Loud and clear," she rasped.

Hershel groaned.

Roy saw blood running from the corner of Hershel's mouth and cursed. The bullet hit more than his shoulder. He never thought to check for an exit wound. What if it was still in him?

"Look what you did, Haley Quaid. Do you see that?"

"I see," Haley said.

"What do you think I should do to you?" Roy asked.

But before Haley could think, something hit the side of the house so hard it sounded like a bomb had gone off.

"Dammit," Roy said, and bolted out of the room with the gun and flashlight to assess damage. It took him a couple of minutes to find the point of impact. One of the windows in the foyer had shattered, and the torrential rain and howling wind were now funneling into the house from the front as well as from the back.

"Shit, shit, shit," Roy muttered, eyeing the water level on the stairs. At his best guess, there was at least five feet of water down there. If he left this house during the storm's lull, he might need a boat, or have to swim it. This was not how he had envisioned their escape.

Frustrated, he went back to the woman and quickly swung the flashlight toward her. She was wide-eyed and watching his every move. He finally had her attention.

Hershel was out of his head, talking crazy, feverish and shaking. This was a damn shame, but at least he wouldn't feel guilty leaving him behind. He picked up the rest of his muffin and wolfed it down in two bites, then chased it with another drink of water.

He was tired and wanted a bed, but Hershel had bled all over that one, and she was tied all snug in the other one. Time to go cruising the rooms again. He came back with a bedspread and pillow, and made a pallet against the door.

"I sleep with one eye open, bitch, so don't even think about trying to escape," Roy said.

"I hear you," Haley said.

Roy swept the flashlight across her face one last time.

"You need to do something about that cut on your cheek. It's bleeding all over," he said and then laughed, pleased with his joke.

"Yes," Haley said, and watched until he moved out of her line of sight, then closed her eyes.

Hurricane Gladys was singing the storm song, blending a bass roar with a soprano whine.

Sam was worried. He hadn't heard from Haley—not even a response to his last text. Either she'd lost battery power in her phone, or she was in trouble. But then Lee hadn't returned his text, either. Maybe the cell towers in this area were all down.

The hangar door he'd driven through was facing away from the direction of wind and rain, but the noise within the hangar was deafening. He reclined his seat enough that he could stretch out, and closed his eyes—just to rest them a bit—and fell asleep, then began to dream.

Haley was naked beneath him, her legs locked around his waist as he rocked within her. Her eyes were closed, her lips slightly parted. She moaned, and then whispered.

"Love me, Sammy, love me, and don't stop. Don't ever stop."

Sam shifted slightly, going deeper, harder, waiting for that catch in her breath. He knew how she ticked. He knew what she needed, and exactly how she liked it.

"Come with me, baby," Sam said.

Haley groaned again, and then all of a sudden the heat between her legs began to spiral, tightening muscles, shortening her breath, setting her on fire as she came in a free fall of lust.

Sam couldn't hold back any longer and let go, chasing the climax as he spilled his seed into her womb.

Haley wrapped her arms around his neck and held him.

"I love you," she whispered. "So much."

* * *

Sam woke himself up, saying, "I love you, too," and then sat up and glanced at the time. He'd been asleep two hours.

Was Haley still okay? Was she hiding, or had her presence been discovered? This was a nightmare. He needed daylight and he needed the hurricane to subside. He needed to see her face—to put his arms around her and know she was still breathing.

Haley jumped at the sound of footsteps coming toward her. Her eyes flew open, her heart racing. And then she remembered what had happened, and saw where she was, and wanted to scream.

But Roy was standing over her, shining the light down in her face. Then, without missing a beat, he swung the flashlight down onto her injured ankle.

Haley swallowed back a sob as she moaned beneath her breath.

Roy tapped the flashlight hard against her forehead.

"Hershel is dying. You're the one who killed him, so I think you need to be awake to watch him take his last breaths."

Haley said nothing, which pissed Roy off. He hit her ankle again with the flashlight and this time, laughed when she began to weep.

"That got your attention," he said. "What do you have to say about that?"

Haley couldn't stop crying, but she let her rage

for him show. "If I'd been a better shot in the dark, he wouldn't be suffering right now, and you'd be stretched out right beside him. That's what I have to say."

Roy cursed her as he swung around. But when pain shot through his rib cage, he grabbed his side, instead. That broken rib was playing hell with him. The more time passed, the more it hurt. If he wasn't so messed up, he'd climb on top of her and show her what real hurt felt like.

Hershel moaned again.

Roy sighed. "Dammit, Hershel. Just let go, then you won't be hurting."

Haley didn't want to think that she was responsible for all that suffering, but she also knew if she had been unarmed, she would have been at the mercy of both men, and from what she could tell, they had none.

Her heart hurt, thinking of Sam waiting for the weather to change, and then imagining what he would think when she wasn't on the roof and didn't answer her phone.

All of a sudden, Roy yanked the pillow out from under her head.

Oh my God, oh my God. He's going to smother me with it!

But he didn't. Instead, he put it over Hershel's face and held it down until the room was silent. Then he tossed it on the floor and moved his flashlight across Hershel's face.

"You're welcome," he said, and then walked out of the bedroom.

Haley was in shock. That was as cold-blooded a move as she'd ever witnessed. Now she was really scared. If he could kill his own friend so callously, there was no way to predict what he would do to her. All she knew was that she would likely die here in this house. Tears kept welling, but she quickly blinked them away and began pulling against the ties around her wrists. The only chance she had to survive this was to get herself loose.

Sam had dozed off. He was dreaming Haley called him, but the call was breaking up and he didn't know what was happening. It was so upsetting that he woke in the middle of it, realized where he was and groaned.

Then he dug into the console until he found one of the energy bars he kept there and got a bottle of water. Within seconds of taking his first bite, he wondered if Haley still had food and water. The thought of eating when she could not almost made him quit, but he finished it anyway. He was going to need all the strength he could muster when they went after her.

He reached for his wallet and pulled out a picture that he'd carried for years. It was Haley and Robbie on a merry-go-round, laughing and waving at the camera as they rode past him. Robbie was five when that picture was taken, and Haley was still the beautiful, happy woman she'd been before the bottom fell out of their world.

"I see you, baby," he said softly. "Robbie doesn't need you anymore, but I do. Please stay safe. I want a second chance to grow old with you."

He looked at it until tears blurred his vision, then he put it back in his wallet, leaned against the headrest and closed his eyes.

Four

Haley had been struggling with the ties around her wrists for what felt like hours. As soon as it began to get lighter, she could see the dead man on the other bed. To the best of her knowledge, Roy hadn't been back since he'd killed him.

Something blew against the house again. Haley jumped when she heard it and instinctively looked up, half expecting to see the roof go flying, but the roof held, and the walls stayed up. The lighter it became outside, the more horrified she was by her situation. She couldn't be more vulnerable. Her sprained ankle was badly swollen below the ties, and both feet were numb.

She was scared. There were still two bullets in the Glock, and Roy had killed his friend with his bare hands. She could hear his footsteps in the hall, and began frantically tugging at her ties, struggling with all the strength she had left. Pulling and tugging, yanking them one way and then the other until she realized the fabric was finally beginning to stretch. It was a small success, but enough to inspire her to pull harder.

Roy couldn't sleep, and he didn't want to be in the same room with Hershel's dead body. He'd done what needed to be done. Or at least he'd thought so until after Hershel was dead, and now he felt weird. Like if he went back in there, Hershel would open his eyes and call him a murderer. Rationally, he knew that couldn't happen, and he thought he'd done his buddy a favor by putting him out of his misery. But right now, he didn't feel so good about it.

Dammit it all to hell, none of this was supposed to happen. And it's all because we turned on Santos.

He couldn't get past the irony of picking a house that was empty when they had desperately needed food. And then finding that woman! The bitch had been hiding here all along. And she'd had a fucking gun! What were the odds of that ever happening? He wanted to think it was all random, but there was a part of him that felt like this was the justice they thought they'd escaped, and he didn't like it. No matter how this turned out, he intended to make sure her life ended here with Hershel.

So he sat in the hall with his back against a wall, his knees pulled up beneath his chin, waiting for sunrise. Whatever he did to Haley Quaid, he not only wanted to hear her scream, but he wanted Hershel to see it. Even if he was dead, Roy needed it to happen in Hershel Arnold's presence.

He got up again and went into an empty bedroom to look out the window. That lull in the storm had to happen soon, and when it did he would be gone— and he was leaving his prison orange behind, even though it meant he'd be wearing nothing but an undershirt and boxers. It was his only chance of really escaping from the law.

The storm was still obviously blasting everything in sight, but the longer he stood there watching it, the more he convinced himself that it didn't seem as intense as it had. Maybe that damn eye was finally moving into shore.

Once the wind began to weaken, Sam walked out to the doorway of the hangar to see if he could get a signal on his cell phone. To his relief, he had a message from Lee.

Got your text. Eye is due to hit land around noon tomorrow. I'll be at the airport as soon as I can drive. It won't take long to get the chopper ready. Is there much damage?

Knowing this was a huge relief. Sam stayed where he was to check storm updates. He learned that the US Army Corps of Engineers had released water from two reservoirs into Buffalo Bayou, knowing if the dams on either one failed, West Houston would be floating corpses by the thousands. And the worst of it was, the house in which Haley was trapped was right in the Energy Corridor, which was quickly becoming the danger zone. And then his phone rang.

Please, please let this be from Haley. But it was Lee.

"Hello."

"Thank God," Sam said. "I haven't heard from Haley since she told me about the escaped prisoners. I'm trying not to think about what may or may not be happening. I just need to see her face."

"Understood," Lee said. "I'll have to do a preflight check once I get there, and make sure the chopper is fueled up."

"I'll help you do anything you need if it'll get us in the air faster," Sam said.

"Be ready," Lee said. "The eye won't be stationary, so the window of opportunity won't last long."

"I'm already ready. See you soon," Sam said.

Haley had been pulling and yanking so long at the ties around her wrists, that when one finally came free she was stunned. Desperate now to get loose, she swung both legs off the side of the bed and was now sitting up, frantically yanking and pulling at the last tie when it suddenly came loose, too. She glanced at the open doorway, listening, but all was quiet.

Oh my God, oh my God.

Trembling from the adrenaline rush, she leaned over and untied her ankles, but stumbled when she tried to stand.

Both of her feet were numb.

She stood there a few moments, trying to think how she could protect herself, and then realized the first thing would be to shut and lock the door. It wouldn't stop him, but it would slow him down, and if she was lucky, he'd waste another bullet on the lock. She hobbled over to the door and eased it shut, turned the lock and then began looking for something to use as a weapon.

With the door shut, the room was in shadows, so she pulled back the curtains. The first thing she saw were some the contents of her tote bag had been dumped on the floor. She dropped to her knees, wincing from the pain, and began sorting through what was there.

She reached for the bottle of water she been drinking the night before and finished it off. Then she saw the screwdriver she kept in her tote bag beneath a small table. It was as close to a weapon as she was going to find. She grabbed it and slid it in her waistband.

Her heart was hammering so hard as she stood up, that it almost drowned out the noise of the wind. She began looking around the room for furniture she might use to block the door, but there was nothing big enough to stop him. Even if she pushed a bed against it, it wasn't heavy enough to keep him from just pushing it away.

She hurried into the adjoining bathroom, still looking for something to use as a weapon. What little was in there was all staging material—lightweight and portable. So she palmed the screwdriver, went back into the bedroom and hunkered down to wait.

Roy was eating the last blueberry muffin, stuffing it into his mouth in huge bites. The wind speed was decreasing, and the rain was hardly more than a normal downpour, which meant he had no time to waste. Time enough to put an end to the bitch— a little payback for the misery he was in—and then go out the broken windows by the front door and out into the flood. It shouldn't be hard to find some floating debris, and ride it out of this nightmare.

He was trying to get up without passing out from the pain when he heard more glass breaking downstairs. He ran to the head of the stairs and looked over the landing, but saw nothing obvious that would have made that sound.

Shrugging it off as nothing but storm-related noise, he headed back down the hall, passing the pallet he'd slept on, kicking an empty water bottle out of his way as he went. He was all the way down to the end of the hall before it dawned on him that he'd gone too far, but he'd been looking for the open doorway, and all the doors were closed.

Frowning, he backtracked, assuming he must have shut the door when he left without thinking. He grabbed the doorknob, but when it wouldn't turn, he frowned.

"What the fuck?" Roy muttered, and this time leaned against the door, trying to get in.

Now he was looking for explanations. He didn't remember shutting it, but he could have. And the lock could have already been turned when he pulled it shut. It never once occurred to him that the woman could have gotten loose.

His side hurt so bad, and the desire to leave her in the room to rot along with Hershel was strong, but he'd promised to end her life before he left. He owed it to Hershel and he didn't want to let him down.

Then he remembered the gun. He could just shoot the lock. He pulled it out of his pocket, aimed it straight at the doorknob and pulled the trigger. Wood splintered as the door swung open.

"That's what I'm talkin' about," Roy crowed, and strode inside with a grin on his face.

She came out of nowhere, stabbing at his arm, and then his neck, drawing blood as she launched herself at him.

He began slapping at her arms, but she wouldn't stay still long enough for him to grab her. She stabbed his forearm deep enough that the gun went flying out of his hand, and he was screaming out in pain and rage, trying to get hold of that screwdriver before she blinded him.

To Sam's horror, the gas pump they needed to put fuel into the chopper wouldn't work. Without re-fueling the chopper, it wasn't going anywhere. Lee worked on the pump for almost an hour before he had it fixed, and then they had to wait while he fueled up the chopper. And all the while, Sam was slowly going out of his mind.

Finally they were airborne, and the knot in Sam's gut was a steady ache. They were moving so fast through the light rain still falling that the landscape below them was a blur. Every thought he had was of Haley, and his head was filled with possible scenarios of what was going on, and what he would find when they got there.

When the rain slacked up even more, seeing what they were flying over was mind-boggling. The water was everywhere and thick like hot chocolate. Debris was floating along with the current or piling up against something below the surface.

There were single-story homes submerged all but the tops of the roofs. In places, stoplights were only feet above the water, and in other places, the water was flowing over bridges.

Sam was in shock. The devastation was far worse than he could have possibly imagined, and thinking of Haley at the mercy of this, in any way, was frightening.

All of a sudden Lee's voice was in Sam's headset.

"Not far now," he said, pointing.

Sam looked down. They were flying over an obviously wealthy neighborhood, marked by the rooflines of massive homes and gated estates. The single-story houses were barely visible, while the two- and three-story houses rose out of that dark water like toad-stools in a swamp.

"She said the house she was showing was a big two-story with attic dormers. If all is well, she'll be watching for us. When she sees the chopper, she plans to climb out onto the roof."

"And what if she's a no-show?" Lee asked.

"Then you put me down on that roof. And if I don't come right back to let you know we're coming out, then get the hell out before you get caught in the backside of the hurricane. You can come get us when it's over."

Lee frowned. "There's no way to predict when the weather will clear up for safe flying time. Sometimes the aftermath of a hurricane spawns tornadoes and thunderstorms. You might be walking into big trouble."

"No, Haley is the one in big trouble. I'm the cavalry," Sam said.

Lee nodded in understanding. Minutes later they were over the house. Lee began to circle the area, giving her time to hear them and exit through one of those windows.

Only she didn't show, and Sam stifled a groan. This was not a good sign, and he couldn't wait any longer.

"I'm going down," he said.

Lee pointed over his shoulder. "Then get in the harness like I showed you. I can put you on the roof near one of those windows. Make sure you can get in, then send the harness back out. I'll pull it up and circle until I can't wait any longer. And remember, those shingles are probably slick from rain, so hang on."

"Understood," Sam said, and took off his headset and harnessed up as Lee had shown him, grabbed his gear, then gave Lee a thumbs-up. Moments later he was out of the chopper and going down, being lowered closer and closer to those dormer windows. When his feet touched shingles, he grabbed at one of the windows, slowly working his way around to the front. When he found it unlatched, he silently cheered. Haley had been prepared for rescue. Something must have happened.

He managed to get the window up, tossed the backpack with all his gear inside, then crawled in after it. He got out of the harness and dropped it back out the window, then dug his weapon out of the backpack and was loading a clip as he heard the chopper moving away from the house.

It was hot and airless in the attic as Sam put another loaded clip in his pocket and headed for the door. He was down the stairs with his hand on the doorknob when he heard a gunshot, and then a heartbeat later, a scream.

The door hit the wall as he shot out of the stairwell and began running down the hall to what sounded like a riot. Things were breaking. Haley was screaming, and he could hear a man cursing and shouting. He couldn't get there fast enough.

* * *

Haley shrieked when Roy grabbed her by the hair. She elbowed him in the ribs. He let out a roar of pain and let her go. Haley was running for the gun she'd knocked out of his hands when he grabbed her by the ankle and yanked her to the floor, knocking over a lamp and overturning the chair at the writing desk against the wall.

"You bitch, you bitch! I'm going to kill you," Roy screamed as he reached for the gun.

Haley was on her belly and trying to get up when the gun went off. Shocked that she was still alive, she rolled over just as Sam stepped over Roy's body and picked her up into his arms.

Haley couldn't believe it! When he pulled her close, she wrapped her arms around his neck and started crying.

"You came! You came! I didn't think you would get here in time!" She looked down at the body on the floor and the spreading pool of blood beneath his head. "Please tell me he's dead."

"He better be. I put a hole in his head. What happened to that one?" he asked, pointing at the body on the other bed.

"I shot him. I shot both of them," Haley said, and then her eyes rolled back in her head.

Sam carried her out of the room and back to the attic. But even as he was hurrying, he heard the wind speed increasing, and the sound of more rain beginning to fall. By the time he got back to the attic window, rain was coming in, and Lee was gone.

He laid Haley down and ran to close the window. Lee would be back, and she was alive. He wouldn't ask for anything more. He knelt down beside her and began checking her body for injuries, but there were so many and in varying stages of bruising, he was almost afraid to touch her.

He pulled his backpack up beside them, then dug out a bottle of water and poured a tiny bit across her lips.

"Baby, wake up. Come on, sweetheart. Come back to me."

Haley heard Sam's voice, which meant she was dreaming again, and then she felt something wet run across her mouth and opened her eyes.

"You're real!" she said, and started to cry.

Sam sat down and pulled her into his lap.

"Yes, I'm real. And I am so proud of how hard you fought to stay alive. When did they find you?"

"I've lost track of time. I don't know, maybe a day ago. I hid from them for a day. It wasn't until I tried to get to the attic that they even knew I was here. I shot Hershel in the shoulder. I shot Roy, too, but it just grazed him and broke a rib. Then Roy knocked me out. I woke up tied to the bed," she said, and then covered her face and went silent.

Sam groaned inwardly, afraid to ask what happened next, and picked up the water.

"Take a drink. I brought food. Are you hungry? Your poor face. Would it hurt you to eat?"

She dropped her hands and then took the water bottle and drank, thirstily, then pointed to the door behind where Sam was sitting.

"There's a bathroom over there. If the water is still potable I want to wash my face and hands. I feel like I'll never be clean again."

She scooted off his lap as he got up and went to go check. She heard the toilet flush, and water running. And then he was back.

"The toilet works okay and the water seems fine. I tasted it. I have stuff in my backpack. Hang on a second."

He unpacked everything he'd brought with him, helped her up and handed her a roll of toilet paper and a bar of soap.

Haley took the roll, and then stood there staring.

"What?" Sam asked.

"Just trying to convince myself you're really here," she said quietly, and then walked away.

Sam watched her body language for signs of injuries she hadn't mentioned, and couldn't help but notice she was limping. Then he looked away and pulled out a large container of wet wipes, the first aid kit and a change of clothing for her. She wasn't wearing shoes. He'd go back down to the room they'd kept her in and see if he could find them.

Haley put the roll of toilet paper on the spindle as she flushed, then turned on the water taps and soaped up her hands. Watching the dirt on them coming off and running down the drain was a relief. When she hobbled back to Sam, she saw that he'd spread out and unzipped a sleeping bag to sit on, and patted the space beside him.

She groaned beneath her breath. Sam reached across the space between them and cupped the back of her neck. "I'm so sorry you had to endure this."

Haley shuddered. "You saved my life. Thank you, Sam. Thank you for coming."

Sam saw the way her eyes widened just before she looked away. She was in shock, and the constant spurt of tears she was shedding was just part of the symptoms.

"Thank you for thinking to call me," Sam said, and then saw all expression fade from her face.

"Oh, Sam, I think of you every day. Calling you was the hard part. After what I did to us, if I hadn't been so desperate, I don't know that I would have had the guts."

Now Sam was the one with a lump in his throat. He had to change the subject or he'd be saying too much.

"I'm still grateful you did. I saw you limping. Is it your leg or your foot?"

"Ankle…the one I turned that made me fall in the first place," she said.

"Oh hell, I knew that," Sam said, and patted her leg. "Let me take a look at it, okay? And then I'm going to clean up all the open wounds so we can get some medicine on them."

"Grateful for whatever you can do," she said.

Sam eyed the swollen ankle, then pushed her pants

up to her knee so he could check for internal problems. What he saw were bruises almost everywhere. You don't get all that falling down stairs. She'd been beaten, and the thought made him sick. It was her right ankle that looked the worst. The whole foot was almost black with bruising, and the cut on her cheek was gaped and oozing.

"Good Lord, Haley. I cannot imagine how much that hurts."

"Not as much as my head," she said, and fingered through the dried blood in her hair, trying to find the cut. I cleaned the cut up the best I could."

Sam got up, then knelt behind her, found the gash and began cleaning it again.

"Tell me if I mash on a sore spot," he said, and then dug through the first aid kit for some butterfly strips. She sat motionless, allowing him full access to her wounds, while the sweat ran out of her hair and down the back of her neck.

The heat in the attic was stifling, but opening a window in a hurricane was suicide. In truth, they should have all been boarded up before the storm ever hit, and Sam wondered what the owners had been thinking, letting a place this elegant weather a hurricane without protection.

He pulled the edges of the cut together as best he could with the butterfly strips, but this should have happened the day of her injury, not days later. It was going to leave a noticeable scar.

As soon as he was finished, he moved around to

clean up her face so he could doctor and butterfly the cut on her cheek. He eyed the torn and bloody clothes she was wearing and rocked back on his heels.

"Uh…we used to wear pretty much the same work-out clothes, and I thought about how long you've been here in the heat in the same clothes, so I brought you some of my gym shorts and some clean T-shirts. If you want, I can—"

Haley's eyes welled. "I want."

He dug out the clothes, then gave her a hand up. "I can't help you out with underwear, but this should feel a little better."

She clutched the clothes to her chest as if he'd just given her a dozen roses.

"Do you need any help getting undressed?"

She shook her head as she dropped the clean clothes onto the sleeping bag and then started unbuttoning her shirt. The moment he saw the bruises on her belly, he grunted, as if he'd been the one who'd been gut punched.

"You didn't get the bruise on your stomach from falling down stairs."

"No, I didn't," she said.

Sam stifled his rage, knowing it would not solve a thing, and shifted focus.

"I know this is going to sound invasive after what you've endured, but technically, this house has become a crime scene. I think we need to photograph your wounds before they begin to heal, so the authorities will see the lengths you fought to survive.

It will matter considering the two dead bodies down the hall."

She took a deep breath and then looked up straight into his eyes.

"If you think that matters, then do it. I'm so far past worrying about propriety it isn't even funny. Where do you want me to stand?"

"It's dark up here, so as close to those windows as we dare."

She nodded and shed all the rest of her clothing down to her underwear, then took her phone out of the hip pocket of her pants.

"If you can get a signal, you can use my phone," she said.

Sam picked it up. "There's a signal, but it's weak. I'll try."

The amount of injuries she'd endured was horrifying, and asking her to do this made Sam feel like he was abusing her all over again. His voice shook, and he couldn't help it.

"Sweet Jesus, Haley."

Haley shook her head. "Don't cry for me, Sam. I'm alive."

He cleared his throat. "Right. I'll make this brief. A couple from the front, a couple from the back, close-ups on your face and stomach, then a few final ones of the rope burns on your wrists and ankles where you were tied."

She lifted her chin and stared at a point somewhere behind him, then opened her arms, holding them parallel to her shoulders. He couldn't get it out of his head that she looked like she was about to be nailed to a cross.

He took the front views first, then the close-ups of her wrists and ankles, then a couple of close-ups of her face and belly, before finishing up with a couple of shots of her from the back.

"That's it," he said. "I'm going to email them to myself, so if something happens to this phone, we still have the evidence."

"Can I get dressed now?"

"Just a minute," Sam said, and grabbed a handful of wet wipes, and very gently wiped down the entire backside of her body.

Hayley was so moved by his thoughtfulness she couldn't speak. When she turned around, he handed her another handful of wet wipes.

"Can you do your front, or do you want me to do it?"

"I can do it."

He nodded and gave her the wipes, thinking again that she was the strongest person he knew.

Five

Sam immediately turned his back as she began wiping up the dried blood on the front of her body, giving her the pretense of privacy.

Hayley sighed. The simple act of being clean. Who could have imagined it would feel like a gift?

After she was through, she put on the clean clothes he'd given her. The T-shirt smelled like Sam's favorite aftershave, and pulling it over her head was almost like being in his arms. The shorts were a little big in the waist and hips, but they stayed up. She took her phone and charger cord out of the pockets of her pants and piled the ruined outfit in a corner.

Sam was on the pallet. "I have some energy bars. Not your favorite T-bone steak, but they're pretty tasty."

"I need to get my stuff," she said.

He frowned. "What stuff, and where is it?"

"Everything that was in my tote bag, including

my purse. He was in my wallet, because he knew my name. Roy dumped it out on the floor. I want my gun back, and my shoes. There was a portable phone charger in it, too. I don't know if they have working phones or not, but I want to let my people know I'm okay when they are. And I need to notify the authorities to let them know about their missing prisoners."

"I'll call the Marshals office when I go get your things," Sam said. "You sit there and eat. It won't take me long."

"Okay. Thanks for going after my things. I wasn't looking forward to going back inside that room."

"Absolutely," he said, and went down the stairs and out into the hall, leaving the door open behind him.

Walking in on two dead bodies was surreal, but he had no qualms about the man he'd shot. There was no choice when it came to Haley. He would choose her welfare every time.

He stared at the man in the bed, at the light reddish hair and whiskers a shade of brown. He found the tote bag and her shoes right beside it. He dropped them in the bottom of the bag, found her purse and wallet, and checked it to make sure he'd left all of her ID and credit cards behind. But they were gone.

He straightened up and turned around, staring down at the man he'd shot. He rolled him over on his back, eyeing the scraggly scruff of brownish gray whiskers on him, and the scar in his right eyebrow. There was only one other place they would be. So he dug through the pocket on the orange jumpsuit Roy

Baker was wearing, and found everything he'd taken. He returned it all to Haley's empty wallet, then began gathering up the things that had been scattered during the fight. It stood to reason anything on the floor was hers, because the house was empty before the storm, and they'd escaped in prison garb and nothing else.

It took him a bit to find the phone charger, then finally spotted it in the corner closest to the door and added it to the tote bag. He paused to look at the empty bed, and saw the ties she'd been bound with, still attached to the headboard. From where she'd been lying, if she turned her head to the left, the dead man was in her direct line of sight.

Then he saw the two bullet holes in the wall above the headboard, and realized she'd been shot at for intimidation and sport. It made him sick thinking about how afraid she must have been. Then he turned his back on the room and shut the door behind him as he left.

He stopped in the hall long enough to put down her things and tried her phone again, scratching his jaw where his stubble had grown. If the US Marshals Office was open for business, he'd get through. He Googled for a number, and then called it. To his relief, he got an answer.

"US Marshals Service. How may I direct your call?"

"I need to speak with someone regarding the escaped prisoners," Sam said.

"One moment please."

Sam walked toward the stairs so Haley wouldn't hear him.

"Marshal Landry speaking."

"Marshal Landry, my name is Sam Quaid. I'm a private investigator out of Dallas."

And then he began to tell the story, right down to the moment he put a bullet in the back of Roy Baker's head.

"What a nightmare for her. Is Mrs. Quaid in need of hospitalization?" Landry asked.

"She doesn't have mortal wounds, if that's what you mean, but I have no idea of internal injuries. She was beaten severely after they caught her and tied her up," Sam said. "I just took photos of her before I cleaned her up and changed her clothes. The clothes she was wearing will be in the attic with us. The bodies are in an upstairs bedroom. As soon as the backside of the hurricane passes, I have a chopper returning to this location to lift us off the roof. You have my info when you want to take an official statement from her, but she'll be back in Dallas with me. If you'll give me an email address, I'll send you the pictures I just took."

"I would consider it a favor if you would go take some pictures of the room where the bodies are as well, before things get too nasty in there. Don't move anything."

"I'll take them if we don't lose service. I've already been in there twice. Once when I carried her out, and once more to get the tote bag with her things.

If you need them, we can leave them in the attic with her clothes."

"What about her gun?" Landry asked.

"She'll be taking that with her, but it will be available at your request for any testing you need to do."

"Then I think that about covers it for now," the marshal said. "Thank you for letting us know. I'll send you the email address for you to send the pictures. My sympathies to Mrs. Quaid. I hope she heals quickly."

"Thank you, sir," Sam said, then disconnected, went back to the room to take more pictures, and when the email address arrived, he sent them and the pitctures he'd taken of Haley, and hurried back to the attic.

Haley was curled up on the sleeping bag when he came back. He put the tote bag aside, took off his shoes and shirt to lay down beside her.

She stirred.

"It's just me, baby. You're safe."

"Safe," she murmured, and closed her eyes.

Mae Arnold was washing the dishes from the noon meal when a breeze stirred the curtains behind her. She stopped and turned, then frowned. The window was shut. Then she felt it again, fainter, but closer to her face, and all of a sudden she dropped to her knees and began to wail.

Her husband, Pete, came running. When he saw

her on the floor, he thought she had fallen, and knelt down beside her.

"Mae, honey! What happened? Did you fall? Where are you hurting?"

"No, I didn't fall. Hershel is dead. I felt his spirit in the room with me! Oh Lord, Lord, Pete. Our boy is gone!"

Pete wasn't going to argue, but he wasn't one for believing spirit visitations really happen.

"Now, Mae, we've been concerned as to his whereabouts because of Hurricane Gladys, and I think you just worked yourself up to—"

"Just stop talking, Pete. I didn't ask you to believe me. You asked if I fell. I told you what I know."

Pete got up, then helped her to her feet. "I'm sorry, sugar. You know how I am. I'm not doubting what you believe. I'm just saying, I've never been shown anything like that, okay?"

Mae nodded, then went to the sideboard to get a tissue and wiped her eyes.

"I'll finish those dishes later. I want to sit outside a spell and come to terms with this. I've been praying for an answer to his whereabouts, and now I know."

"I'll finish the dishes. I want you to know this hurts me as much as it does you, but I guessed long ago that this is how his life would end. You go on now."

"Thank you," Mae said, and took another tissue with her as she went out onto the front porch.

She pulled her granny's old wooden rocker into

the shade, and settled into it, swallowing back a fresh set of tears as she gazed off across the front yard to the purple irises blooming tall against the white board fence.

Pete was right. They'd both known Hershel's life-style would be the death of him. She'd just never thought about a natural disaster being the way he would pass.

She thought about calling the US Marshals Office and then changed her mind. They were all about evidence, not a mother's intuition. They'd likely know soon enough.

Dude Santos had evacuated Houston before the hurricane and gone back home to Mexico. He was in Cozumel, having lunch with old friends, and enjoying the view from the little casa where he'd grown up. Their chatter was full of laughter and teasing as they availed themselves of shrimp ceviche, warm, handmade tortillas and a pitcher of margaritas that never seemed to go dry.

One beauty, a woman named Marigrace, caught Dude staring off into space. She wondered what he was thinking about, and decided he needed to be thinking about her.

He wasn't all that tall, but then neither was she. But he was vain, which explained why his friends always called him Dude, when his real name was Alejandro. Someone once told him that he looked like the Hollywood actor Mario Lopez, which fed into his desire to be important and wealthy, but she didn't see it. She also knew he walked on the shady side of the law, but so did most of the people she knew.

He didn't often come back to his home, and when he did, she suspected it was to hide out, or at least stay under the radar of the US law enforcement, until whatever he'd done calmed down, but he always had money to spend on her, and he always had great parties.

He still had that look on his face, and she wanted attention, so she left the buffet, put her arms around his somewhat ample waist and ran a finger down the side of his face.

"So, my beautiful man, what is it that puts such a frown on your face?"

Dude shifted into party mode and laughed as he pulled her close.

"The fact that you have been ignoring me, of course."

She giggled. He popped her shapely bottom and then let her pull him back to the buffet where she insisted on serving him. He let her choose his food and drink, and even let her lead him to a table out on his patio where his guests were seated and eating their food.

"Look at this view!" Marigrace said. "Cozumel is *muy magnifico*, is it not?"

"*Sí, sí*, Marigrace, but not as stunning as you."

She beamed, then forked up a bite of the shrimp ceviche. "For you, my beautiful man."

He let her put it in his mouth, and winked at her as he chewed, all the while wondering what the hell was going on with Hershel and Roy, wondering why they hadn't tried to call. It was eating at his greedy heart that all that money might have been lost to the flood. If it was gone, then Hershel and Roy better be dead, too, because if they weren't, he'd kill them himself.

Momma, I'm tired.
Daddy's crying. Tell him it's okay.

Haley woke. Her head was throbbing and her belly hurt. When she felt the weight of an arm across her waist she remembered.

Sam has saved her.

But she was hot—so hot. When she moved her head, the room began to spin.

She moaned, and Sam woke and sat up.

"What's wrong, honey?"

"I hurt in so many places…so hot. Feels like I can't breathe."

Sam felt her forehead and frowned. She was hot, but her skin was barely damp. This worried him.

"You need water," he said, and got up to drag the backpack close to the sleeping bag.

Haley eased up into a sitting position to watch him.

"I was dreaming about Robbie," she said.

Sam paused. "I dream about him. I dream about you, too."

Haley's shoulders slumped. "I spent six months

in therapy when I first moved to Houston. I only remember those days in bits and pieces. I had a total meltdown. For the longest time, I blamed myself for losing him. I was as close to the bottom as I ever want to be." She paused, trying to read his expression, then shrugged it away. "She was a really good therapist. She let me scream and cry. She listened to me shouting in anger at God. She held my hand the day I had the breakthrough, and held my head when I vomited up everything in my belly, then sat in silence, watching me as I gave up the fight and finally admitted, both to her and to myself, that what I killed was us."

Sam felt the words like a punch in the gut, and got up to put some distance between them, because what he wanted was her.

He moved toward the window, then stopped and turned to face her. Seeing her in his clothes was just a reminder of before.

"We didn't just lose Robbie. We lost each other. I didn't know how to reach you then. You were so broken."

"I know I was."

He watched her face, wondering how she was going to respond, then said it anyway. "Robbie was our gift, not our loss."

She frowned. "You always saw the rainbow."

"And you always saw the storm," he countered. "But it was your strength that held you together as long as Robbie needed you. And that same strength is what kept you alive through this. You are a warrior, Haley, and I'm grateful that you trusted me enough to call."

Haley held out a hand, and when he moved back to where she was sitting and grasped it, she tightened her grip and pulled him back down beside her.

"Forgive me?" she asked.

"There was nothing to forgive," Sam said. "That was then and this is now. We'll get through this, only this time, it will be together. Understood? You called me back into your life. I won't easily leave you again." He got a bottle of water and opened it for her. "Drink. You're hot, but you're not sweating much. You need to hydrate."

Haley took the bottle and took a big drink while Sam was digging through his things for a bottle of salt pills. As soon as he found them, he shook two out into her hand and made her take them.

Haley kept the bottle of water, continuing to sip from time to time.

"Will the chopper come back when the wind dies down?" she asked.

"It's not all about the wind. If it's still raining too hard to fly, Lee will still be grounded. He will have to be the judge of when that's safe."

"Is Lee the pilot?" Haley asked.

Sam nodded. "He's also a friend. He won't let us down."

Haley glanced toward the little stairwell, and to the door beyond.

Sam saw the fear on her face.

"They're dead, remember?"

She nodded, then looked away.

"I saw the bullet holes over the bed," Sam said.

Haley stared off into space. "I shot two rounds at them. He put two in the wall, and one in the door after I got free and locked him out. There was one bullet left, and I'd just lost the wrestling match to recover the gun when you arrived."

Sam frowned. She sounded so matter-of-fact. Somewhere down the road the shock of what she'd gone through was going to hit hard.

Haley screwed the lid back on the water and then set it aside as she got up. She started toward the bathroom, and then the room began spinning again. She turned toward Sam, but there were two of him.

"Sam, I don't feel good."

He saw the color fading from her face and was up and running, barely catching her before she hit the floor. He carried her back to the sleeping bag, then began checking her vitals. Her pulse was racing. Her forehead was hot, but dry. He feared she was hurt somewhere—somewhere he couldn't see, or sick with some kind of disease brought here by the flood. This was the worst-case scenario he'd feared, and no way to get immediate help.

"Please God, please don't let her die," he said, grabbed some wet wipes and began wiping her face to cool her down, then put the cool wipes on the back of her neck.

She moaned.

"Haley? Honey? Can you hear me?"

"Shot them…caught me…can't get away. Miss my ride."

"You didn't miss your ride, baby. I'm here. We'll leave together."

Haley sighed, then began mumbling.

Sam took the lid off her water and lifted her head.

"Open your mouth, Haley. Water. Drink the water."

She moaned. "Dark water…rising…gonna drown."

Sam gritted his teeth and drizzled a little water on her lips. When she licked it off, he poured more.

"Open your mouth, Haley. There's water to drink."

Her lips parted slightly, but he feared she was going to choke, so he raised her into a sitting position, and poured some into her mouth.

"Swallow, Haley! Swallow the water!"

A little water dribbled back out, but he saw her throat working. Some of it had gone down. He kept pouring it, a little bit at a time until he had most of the bottle in her, then he put the rest aside as he eased her back down.

There were two injuries she had that he was most concerned with. The head wound, and the huge bruise on her stomach.

He grabbed her phone to contact Lee and was relieved to still see it in service.

Lee answered on the first ring.

"Hello?"

"This is Sam. I don't have long to talk. Haley is unconscious. Dehydrated. Not sweating and the attic is a sauna. She'll need a litter rescue. Advise the need for Life Flight helicopter for her. Will you coordinate?"

"Yes. Will send details when the weather clears," Lee said.

Sam lost the signal, and then laid the phone aside and began tending to Haley.

US Marshal Reagan Landry had just finished briefing Deputy Director Bob Richmond of their missing prisoners' whereabouts, as well as what they'd done while on the loose, and Richmond wasn't taking the news well.

"You said you had photos of the woman they kidnapped?"

"Yes, sir. Her ex-husband sent them to me when he called."

"He called you? From Houston? I thought communications were knocked out."

Landry shrugged. "I don't know how he did it, but I had him checked him out. He's a hotshot private investigator out of Dallas. If he hadn't arrived when he did, Haley Quaid would be dead." Then he pulled up the shots from his phone and handed it to his boss. "Some of these old bruises are from when she fell down the stairs. But a good deal of them are from the beating she endured at Roy Baker's hands. These are shots Sam Quaid also took, at my request, of the room where she'd been held. See the bullet holes in the wall above the bed where she was tied? Baker was using her for target practice."

The deputy director's eyes narrowed as he studied the pictures. "You say she shot both Baker and Arnold before they caught her?"

"Yes, sir." Landry pointed to the body visible in the bed. "That's Arnold. She shot him in the shoulder when he was coming at her, and then fired a second time at Baker, and nicked a rib."

"So Arnold died from his bullet wound?" Richmond asked.

Landry shook his head. "No. Haley said Baker couldn't stop the bleeding, so he put a pillow over Hershel Arnold's face and smothered him."

Richmond frowned. "That's cold."

"Baker was a bad one," Landry said.

"And we know where this house is located?" Richmond asked.

Landry nodded. "Yes, sir. And the moment it's safe, we'll have boats in there to pick up the bodies and work the crime scene, although it's gonna be a rough one. The house is a cooker right now with the power off, and the bodies aren't gonna hold."

"So where are the Quaids right now?"

"They're holed up in the attic. As soon as the storm passes, they'll be picked up by chopper. He'll have her checked out medically before they head back to Dallas. She'll be there with him for the time being. I have his contact info. We'll get her statement at a later date."

Richmond nodded. "Looks like you've got as many ends tied up as possible until this storm passes. Good work."

Landry shrugged. "Truth is, sir, if it hadn't been for Sam Quaid's phone call, we still wouldn't know where our prisoners were."

Richmond picked up one of the phones and scanned the pictures of Haley again. "Do you know how hard you have to be hit to get a bruise like this on your belly?"

Landry shook his head. "No, sir, but according to Ms. Quaid's story, she was tied to the bed when he did it."

"We won't be wasting anymore taxpayer money housing Roy Baker," Richmond muttered.

Landry picked up his phone and dropped it back into his pocket. "The way I see it, Baker was a dead man walking after he made his first kill at the age of seventeen. It just took this long for someone to stop him."

"Even though we know it's them, hold off on notifying the Baker and Arnold families until we have recovered the bodies and made positive identifications," Richmond said.

"Yes, sir," Landry said. "Will that be all?"

"Yes, and thank you for coming in," Richmond said.

Night came and Sam still had no answer from Lee.

But he had dragged a full-size mattress from one of the bedrooms into the attic hours earlier, rather than have Haley sleeping on the floor, and had his flashlight out so he could keep an eye on her condition.

She was still talking, but none of it made sense, so he kept pouring little sips of water down her mouth. He'd found a hair band in her tote bag hours earlier and had pulled her long dark hair up into a ponytail to keep it off her neck, but he needed to cool her down.

He needed that fever to break, and the water coming out of the taps was lukewarm. Putting her in a bathtub in one of the bathrooms wouldn't break her fever. It would just be like giving her a bath, which she was too weak to handle. He discarded that idea. He didn't need lukewarm, he needed cold. He paced the floor, trying to think of every survival trick he'd ever heard of, but the obvious need was for water. He jumped as the winds blew a sheet of rain against the window, and that's when it hit him. The rain was water, and coming straight off the ocean, it should be colder than what was in this house. And, until it reached the flood below, it wasn't contaminated!

He looked back at Haley, then at the window.

"If I wait, I take a huge chance of losing her," he muttered. "Oh, what the hell. I can't stand here and do nothing."

He pushed the window back up as far as it would go, and got an immediate blast from the storm. He picked her up and carried her toward the window. The rain coming in was blowing hard enough that it stung his skin, so he could only imagine how her bruised body would feel. But he needed that fever to break.

Afraid the force of the rain would damage her eyes, he turned her face to his chest, and let the storm soak her to the core.

Six

Haley was locked into a bad dream loop that wouldn't go away.

Roy Baker was shooting at her, and every time he pulled the trigger, the bullets came closer and closer to her head.

"Stop! Stop!" Haley shouted. "The gun is empty. Stop shooting!"

Roy laughed. "I don't have to stop until I want to." Then he walked right up to the foot of the bed, aimed the gun straight at her head and shot her.

The pain in her head was terrible, but she was still alive, and where was Roy? As soon as he pulled the trigger, he disappeared.

Still tied to the bed, she felt water all over her body. The flood! The water level was rising and she was going to drown!

Someone was coming to save her. Sam. It was Sam. Hurry, Sam, hurry. Water was everywhere.

Haley woke with a jerk, only to realize she was in Sam's arms, and there was rain coming in the open window. She moaned, and then put her hands over her face.

The muscles in Sam's arms were in spasms from holding her so long, but she was awake, and that was a plus.

"I'm sorry, baby. I'm so sorry. Just a minute."

He carried her back to the mattress, then ran back and closed the window. Quite a bit of rain had come in, but it had run straight across the attic floor to the stairs and then out beneath the door.

"What's happening?" she asked.

He knelt beside her, felt her skin, then opened another bottle of water and helped her sit up.

"Drink as much of it as you can," he said, then watched her fingers trembling as she did what he asked.

The faint light within the attic cast sunken shadows on her battered face, making it difficult to see her within the bruises and wounds. But the eyes were the same. Big and brown, but not as dark as her hair, and set perfectly within her heart-shaped face.

"Why am I so wet?" she asked.

"You have…had…fever. You're dehydrated. I couldn't get you awake enough to drink." He felt her forehead. Her skin was still cool to the touch. "So far, so good. But it may come back up again. Can you tell me where you hurt the worst?"

"My head. My stomach."

Sam nodded calmly, but inside he was still very concerned.

"Do you think you could stand up?"

"I don't know. I'm still dizzy."

"Then never mind," he said, then added, "You do know I'm taking you home with me?"

Haley wasn't going to argue. "Okay."

Then he added, "Are you good with that?"

"Yes. Are *you* okay with an unexpected guest? I mean… I'm not going to be messing up some relationship you have going, am I?"

Sam tossed the meds back in the first aid kit and slammed the lid. His eyes narrowed until they nearly disappeared, and the tone of his voice deepened in quiet anger.

"I don't have relationships. I do, however, have a woman I love who got lost for a while. I want *her* back." Then he leaned forward, their foreheads touching. "If you weren't a walking advertisement for disaster, I'd kiss you senseless."

Sam heard her breath catch, then rocked back on his heels and changed the subject before she could turn him down. "Want to go to the bathroom before I turn the light back out?"

She nodded.

He helped her up, handed her the flashlight and then held on to her all the way across the hardwood floor.

"I'll be waiting out here to help you back to bed."

"Okay," she said, and carried the flashlight in with

her. When she shut the door, the attic was in sudden darkness again, just like his life had been, but this time the loneliness he usually felt was gone.

He was bringing Haley home.

Sam woke just after daybreak. Haley was still asleep. Her skin was fairly warm again, and barely sweating. She had a fever again. He got up to go to the bathroom and then paused to look at himself in the mirror on the wall over the sink.

He had the makings of a pretty good beard going that was as black as his hair. He'd worn beards before, doing undercover work, but he didn't like the way they made him look.

Dangerous, even mean.

He wasn't mean at all, and dangerous only when threatened. He finished what he came to do, then washed up before going back to the windows for enough light to check his weather app. The fact that he could actually see out the attic window was encouraging. The wind didn't sound as strong, and the rain wasn't nearly as heavy.

The weather update was encouraging. Hurricane Gladys had moved far enough inland that she'd been downgraded to a storm. With that report, the skies over Houston should begin to clear by noon.

He glanced over his shoulder at Haley and frowned. She was rolled up in a little ball, like she was trying to become invisible. She never used to sleep like that. He turned all the way around and then leaned against the wall, looking his fill. He used to wake up every morning with her head tucked beneath his shoulder and her arm thrown across his chest, and now he smiled thinking of their second chance at happiness.

He sent Lee a text.

Weather is breaking. Can you give me an ETA and an update on the Life Flight chopper? She's running a fever, and too weak to help herself.

He hit Send, and then carefully opened the window halfway to let in fresh air, taking a chance on not bringing in more rain. The rush of air was more than welcome, and the little bit of rain that came with it cooled the sweat on his arm.

He sat back down on their bed and dug through his food supply. Still a handful of energy bars, and a few days' worth of MREs. Thank God this nightmare was coming to an end. He was still rummaging through his backpack when the phone signaled a text. It was a response from Lee.

If the rain and wind continue to abate, I'm heading your way just after midday. Life Flight is on board. I've given them your GPS. We're flying in together. They'll lower a litter and a team member to help you get her in it. As soon as you get her out of the attic, they'll do the rest. When they leave, I'll drop the harness. You buckle up inside and then climb out.

Relieved that the plan was in place, he sent back the message, text received.

He heard Haley stirring, and reached for her hand. "Morning, honey. Want some good news?"

"Yes."

"The hurricane has been downgraded, the rain and wind are both abating and if the weather continues to upgrade to safe flying, Lee's coming after us around midday."

Haley's eyes welled.

"Don't cry," Sam said.

Haley grabbed his forearm, then wiped tears with the hem of her shirt. "Oh, Sam, you don't understand. The whole time I was tied up, I was absolutely certain I was going to die in this house, and I'd never see you again. And today I'm leaving this house alive with you. It is nothing short of a miracle."

He felt so much regret for what she'd endured. "You break my heart, Haley, and at the same time, I am so proud of how fiercely you fought to stay alive. Now we just need to get you healed."

Haley nodded, but wouldn't let go of his arm. And, now that she was awake, she realized she was breathing fresh air, and the room felt cooler. That's when she saw the window was partially open.

"I'll never take fresh air for granted again. I want to get up."

Sam frowned. "Are you still dizzy?"

"I don't know. I guess I'll find out."

He helped her up, then walked her to the window and raised it all the way up.

Haley spread her arms wide and leaned into the rain.

Sam watched her carefully until Haley finally backed away.

"I feel like I was just baptized. Cleansed of this hell, of the heat, and the pain and the memory of his hands on me. I'm ready to lie back down."

US Marshal Reagan Landry was on the phone, coordinating the arrival of three large boats belonging to the Marshals Service, with all the teams necessary to retrieve two bodies and work a crime scene. He was meeting up with them to head up the recovery, and guessed if things went according to plan, the Quaids would already be gone. He hoped for their sake, they were.

The weather for an air rescue cooperated. A light drizzle was still falling at the airport as Lee arrived. The wind was at ten knots—nothing to be concerned about.

After the preflight check, and coordinating again with Life Flight, it was just after noon when Lee left for Houston.

Once the weather became manageable, inflatable boats, fishing boats with little outboard motors, larger boats with inboard motors—if it floated, volunteers were moving through the floodwaters, looking for anyone in need of rescue, even animals.

News crews from all over the country had commandeered their own boats to be on scene as those rescues were taking place, and in the process, getting B-roll for the stories they would put together.

All of the major networks were set up on-scene, ready to go live, while their on-scene reporters were in boats, looking for the stories to be told.

The Energy Corridor of Houston, which was in the Thornwood area, was already a source of controversy. Once it had become known the Army Corps of Engineers had released water from dams without prior notification, the people who had evacuated the area were furious. Despite the reasons why it had happened, it didn't change the fact that multimillion-dollar homes in an area that was never supposed to flood had been inundated. In a place where money was power, all the money in the world would not have bought them the safety they had expected would be theirs.

A few of the news crews had gone straight to that area of Houston, wanting firsthand information at the depth of destruction, and were already filming when one of them noticed two choppers flying into the area. One was a Life Flight, and one was not. When the Life Flight began circling over a particular antebellum home, the reporters began shouting and pointing. "Get a camera on that," and when they saw a litter being lowered over the backside of the house, they knew they were about to witness a rescue in progress, and started the ball rolling with live broadcasts.

Sam heard the chopper coming and pushed the window up as far as it would go. Unless the litter was oversize, it should fit through this window.

Haley still couldn't get her shoe on her injured foot, so Sam packed both of them for her, along with the few things left in her tote bag. Now that they didn't need to keep refilling water bottles, he was leaving the empties and his old sleeping bag behind. It would be a much lighter pack going back.

"Is it coming?" she asked.

"Yes, the Life Flight chopper is overhead to get you. Lee will pick me up and take me wherever you're going."

"What if you can't get there by car?"

"We're not taking you to a hospital here. They're flying you somewhere else." He glanced out the window and then leaned out and waved his arm until he saw a litter coming down, and right behind it was a crew member who would assist. "There's your ride home, honey. Just stay put."

Danny's job was to stabilize the victim for evacuation. So once they got the litter through the window, he came in next, and went straight to where Haley was lying, introduced himself and began a quick assessment. The wounds and bruises were obvious, but Sam saw him frown when he saw her belly.

"She's keeps mentioning her stomach and her head really hurt," Sam said.

"Duly noted," Danny said. "Okay, Miss Haley, we're going to lift you up and into this litter, then I'm going to strap you down so you'll be safe for transport."

Haley's gaze immediately moved to Sam.

"Are you okay, honey?" he asked.

"I'm scared, but I want out of here bad enough to ignore the fear," she said.

"I love you, Haley. You can do this," Sam added, and kissed her on the forehead.

Without giving her time to respond, he and Danny lifted her into the litter, then Sam stepped back while Danny strapped her in.

"Okay, let's do this," Danny said. "You get one side, I'll get the other, and we'll lift her straight up and send her headfirst out the window."

Sam did exactly what he was told, and moments later they had the litter resting on the sill.

"Easy does it," Danny said, as they began pushing the litter through the opening. It was a tight squeeze, but they made it.

For Sam, watching her going up into that chopper was a huge relief.

"We'll take good care of her," Danny said, then shook Sam's hand before he went back out the window.

Sam watched until Danny was safely inside the chopper, and then began looking for Lee. As soon as the Life Flight chopper left the area, Lee moved into place.

Sam leaned out the window and waved to let Lee know he was ready, and down came the harness. Without the weight of a person in it, the downdraft from the rotors sent it into a swinging arc, like the pendulum on a clock.

Sam was leaning out as far as he could, and when it finally dropped down to window level, he had to try to grab it as it swung past. It took several tries before he finally got a handhold, and the moment he did, Lee let out slack for Sam to pull it into the attic.

Sam was working quickly as he climbed back into the harness and strapped himself in, then grabbed his backpack. He was standing with his back to the open window, so he ducked his head and went out backward, head and shoulders first, dragging the backpack with him.

As soon as he had the backpack clear, he pushed himself the rest of the way out with his feet, until he was swinging in midair. The moment Sam was clear of the house, Lee began hoisting Sam up.

All Sam had to do was enjoy the ride. He glanced down, surveying the vastness of the flood and the devastation it had caused, and as he did, he noticed some people in boats a distance away. When he realized they had big cameras pointing right at him, he guessed that they were part of the media coverage.

He gave them a thumbs-up as he was being rescued. A couple of minutes later, Lee had him in the chopper. Sam put his backpack behind the seats, came out of the harness and buckled himself back into the copilot seat. Lee pointed to a headset, wanting him to put it on so they could talk.

"Where are they taking her?" Sam asked.

"Nacogdoches Medical Center. As soon as I drop you off, I'm going back to the hangar. My son, Brett, will drive your Hummer to Nacogdoches, and I'll be behind him to pick him up."

Sam nodded. "I owe you big-time, over and above the hiring fee," he said.

"We're gonna forget that fee. I'm not willing to profit off saving your lady's life," Lee said, as he turned the chopper and headed north.

The news crews were all filming the Life Flight chopper in hover mode. They'd seen the litter going down, followed by a man in royal blue coveralls. Now that the litter was going up, they had no way to tell who was in it, or in what condition. The man in blue coveralls quickly followed, and as soon as they were safely inside the chopper, it circled the area and headed north.

When they saw the second chopper move into position and lower a harness rig, the news crews kept filming. It wasn't long before they saw a man in harness gear appearing above the roofline as he was being evacuated, too.

"Somebody zoom in on his face!" someone yelled.

All of the news crews on-site had gone live, and

by now, half the country was in on the rescue. As the cameras zoomed in, they caught a clear shot of a big dark-haired man in harness—with the makings of a good beard in the works. When he gave the crews a thumbs-up, they cheered. As soon as he was inside the chopper, they watched it circle, then head north.

Now that the drama was over, the crews were about to move on, when three large boats from the US Marshal Service shot past them, heading right toward the area where the rescue had taken place. And like the bloodhounds they were, the news crews followed them in.

The noise inside the Life Flight chopper was loud, but the medical team working on Haley distracted her. She kept answering questions as one hooked her up to an IV, while another took her vitals, leaving her to explain how she incurred the injuries.

In a way, it all seemed surreal. She'd been so close to dying, and now it was over. Only it wasn't. She had to heal again. The emotion of leaving that house alive was so overwhelming that she broke down in tears.

A nurse put a hand on Haley's forehead, then reached for her hand.

"You're safe now, honey. Cry all you want."

Lee reached the Nacogdoches Medical Center only minutes behind the Life Flight chopper. It was already lifting off as they went in for a landing. The moment they were down, he dug the keys to the Hummer out of his pack and gave them to Lee, and then took off running toward the entrance to the ER.

The clerk at the registration desk looked up as he slid to a halt in front of her.

"How can I help you?" she asked.

"Haley Quaid! Life Flight just brought her in from Houston. Where is she?"

"Are you family?" she asked.

"Yes, I'm Sam Quaid."

"She's in Bay 3. Through those doors," she said, pointing to her right.

"Thank you," Sam said, and shifted from the mad dash he'd made through the parking lot to a rapid stride, with the backpack hanging off one shoulder.

He walked into the room, dropped it against the wall and moved to the foot of her bed.

Haley's anxiety disappeared when Sam walked in. "You made it!"

"I told you I'd be right behind you, baby." He glanced at the doctor and nurse on the opposite side of her bed. "I'm Sam Quaid. What can you tell me, Doc?"

"This is Dr. Trenton," Haley said.

"Doc is fine," Trenton said, and gave Sam a quick smile. "I've ordered several tests…a CT scan and an MRI. X-ray has already been in to take pictures. I'll know a little more after I see them. The lab drew blood. I'm wondering where the fever is coming from."

"Did she tell you what happened to her?" Sam asked.

"She's a Realtor who injured herself in an empty house and by the time she regained consciousness, was trapped due to the hurricane."

Sam glared at Haley. "Really?"

She shrugged.

Dr. Trenton looked surprised, and then looked at Haley again. "So what don't I know?"

Haley's eyes welled. "Sam…"

He put a hand on her leg. "I'll explain. Just don't cry again."

He took a quick breath, and then began by pointing to the rope burns on her wrists, then pulled back the covers on her feet to show the same marks on her ankles.

"She wound up trapped in the upper story of a flooded house with two escaped prisoners. They tied her up, and when they weren't using her for target practice, they beat her. The cut on her cheek and the basketball-size bruise on her belly were not part of the fall. They reinjured the ankle she turned that made her fall, and that happened two days ago. Whatever is wrong with her has been stewing far too long."

Dr. Trenton was momentarily speechless, then turned to his nurse. "Trudy, tell the lab to make space for Haley Quaid. I want that CT scan ASAP."

"Yes, Doctor," she said, and hurried out of the room.

"Forgive me for asking, but what happened to the prisoners?" the doctor asked.

"She shot both of them before they took her down. It put one in bed, and injured the other one. They're both dead now."

Dr. Trenton stared at Haley as if he was seeing her for the first time, and then eyed Sam with new respect.

"How did you get to her… I mean, the hurricane… the flood?"

"He arrived in a chopper, landed on the roof and came in through the attic window while the eye of the hurricane was over Houston. If he'd been ten seconds later, I would be dead," Haley said.

"Freaking amazing," Trenton said. "You two have the same last name. Are you—"

"He's my ex-husband," Haley said.

"Only by law. I never let go of her in my heart," Sam said.

"Obviously," Trenton said. "So you did your part, now let me do mine. I'm going to see if there are any test results ready. I'll be back," and then he left the room.

Sam pulled up a stool and sat down beside the bed.

Haley reached for him, grasping his hand.

"I ache to kiss you, Haley Jo, but you're too damn hurt. The good part is you're finally where you need to be."

Haley was too emotional to do anything but nod, but she was holding on to him with every last ounce of strength she had left.

Less than five minutes later, an orderly walked

in, eyed Sam and checked the ID band on her wrist, then asked her name.

"Haley Quaid."

"Okay, Haley. We're going to the lab for your CT scan. Sir, you can wait right here. I'll bring her back as soon as we've finished."

Sam didn't want her out of his sight, but he didn't argue.

"I'll still be here, honey."

"I know," she said, and then they were gone.

Sam got a text from Lee. He and Brett were on the way with his car.

There was also a text from Marshal Reagan Landry, asking about Haley's condition. Sam replied, saying they were running tests.

He had three messages from his secretary about new jobs. He turned them all down in texts, and told her not to schedule anything new until he let her know.

Once he'd run out of texts to read and answered all his messages, he was beginning to worry, then the orderly brought Haley back. The doctor followed them in and went straight to Haley's bedside.

"Your head hurts because you have a concussion. But the headaches will dissipate as you heal. You have bruised ribs, which is causing the pain in your midsection, and you have an infection likely caught from all of your open wounds. Were you in direct contact with the floodwater?"

"No, but the prisoners who caught me were. They

waded through a lot of floodwater downstairs to get to the stairs."

"How does that heal?" Sam asked.

"We're going to give her some antibacterial meds and monitor her for a day or so. Once the fever is gone, we'll check you again to make sure it's out of your system before you can be released. Someone will be down to take you up to your room."

"Thank you, Dr. Trenton," Haley said.

"You're welcome, Haley. You might just be the most amazing patient I've seen come through this ER in the five years I've been here." Trenton gave Sam a big thump on the back. "And you, sir, are the stuff heroes are made of. You also might want to know that you've already made national news. Just saw an update on the aftereffects of Hurricane Gladys, and there is rather remarkable footage of what I can only assume was the both of you being rescued. Prepare yourself, Sam. They got a really good shot of your face."

"Free advertising at its best," Sam said.

Seven

Haley fell asleep in the ER bay. Sam felt her forehead again and frowned. The sooner they got some meds in her, the happier he'd be.

About thirty minutes later, an orderly showed up, identified himself to Sam, said hello to Haley and began getting her ready for transport. He unhooked her from the blood pressure cuff, took the IV bag from its hook and then hooked it to the small pole on the bed frame.

"Am I allowed to follow you?" Sam asked.

"Sure," the orderly said. "The nurses may ask you to wait until they have her settled before you can go in, but it doesn't take long. Grab your stuff."

Sam gathered up his things and walked beside the bed all the way to the elevator so Haley could see him. Once they reached the third floor, it was as the orderly predicted. He was asked to wait, and directed to the waiting area. His steps were slow from exhaustion, but he was relieved they were here.

The waiting room was empty, so he leaned the backpack against the wall, and then stood in the middle of the floor, at a loss as to what to do next. He hadn't been in a hospital since the night Robbie died, and being here again under these circumstances was nerve-racking.

The scent of fresh-brewed coffee turned his attention to a coffee maker on a nearby table. He poured himself a cup, added sugar and stirred, then sat down. The first sip was too hot, so he set it aside for a bit to cool as his phone signaled a message.

It was from Lee inquiring about Haley's condition. Sam responded.

Haley has been admitted with an infection, which caused the fever.

Lee quickly replied.

After what she survived, you gotta know this is a piece of cake.

The knot in Sam's stomach eased just a little. Lee was right.

He sat back and drank the coffee, then eyed the food choices in the snack machines and opted for another MRE from his backpack.

Fortunately for Landry and his team, their office in the Woodlands-Sugarland area had escaped flooding. After the prisoners' bodies were recovered and on their way to the medical examiner, Landry headed back to headquarters.

Since several news crews had filmed the body bags coming out of the big house in Thornwood, and two people being airlifted from the roof, they had beat him to the office and were awaiting some kind of explanatory statement.

Landry saw them as he was pulling into the parking lot and went in the back door and straight to his office to write up the report. A clerk knocked on his door and then leaned in.

"Sorry to interrupt, but there are several news crews outside, wanting to know what we were doing in the Thornwood area this morning, and if it had anything to do with the missing prisoners."

"Thank you, Kelly."

The clerk nodded and left.

Landry wasn't surprised by their request, but family had not been notified, and they were jumping the gun expecting any kind of comments. He pushed back from his desk, and strode through the building, and out the front entrance.

The moment they saw him, they began shouting out questions.

Landry just shook his head and held up a hand for silence.

"There will be no comments until family notifications have been made. You'll be notified when official comments are forthcoming, so please move along."

"Marshal, can't you at least tell us who was air-lifted out of the house?"

He walked back inside, closing the door firmly behind him as he went, then stopped at the front desk.

"Kelly, I'm not taking calls from anyone in the media."

"Yes, sir," she said.

"Thank you," Landry said, went back to his office. He didn't need autopsies to prove identities because both bodies were still easily recognizable. And there were the prison-orange jumpsuits to verify. It was time to notify families before they began hearing suppositions via the media.

After pulling up the files to get the contact info for next of kin, he got up and poured himself a fresh cup of coffee. No matter how many times he did this, he hated notifying families.

Roy Baker's contact was a sister named Glory Buchanan. He made the call, and then took a slow, calming breath for giving the news.

A woman answered on the fourth ring.

"Hello."

"This is US Marshal Reagan Landry. May I speak to Glory Buchanan?"

"This is Glory. It's about Roy, isn't it? Is he dead?"

"Yes, ma'am. I'm sorry to inform you that he is deceased. The medical examiner will notify you when the body is released. My condolences to you and your family."

"I'm not surprised. We've been expecting this call for years. So, did the hurricane get him?"

"No, ma'am, and I'm giving you these details now, because eventually, it's going to be national news. As his family, you have the right to know everything first. He and Hershel Arnold, the man he escaped with, took shelter in an empty house where a woman, another refugee from the hurricane, had been trapped. As they attacked her, she shot the both of them. Neither died from those wounds, and they took her down, tied her up and beat her until she was rescued."

He heard Glory gasp.

"Oh. My. God. I'm so sorry that happened. Is she okay?"

"Don't know her condition at this time other than she's at a hospital."

"What about Hershel, the man he was with? You said he didn't die from the gunshot."

"It has been reported that Hershel's injuries were worse, and Roy smothered him with a pillow, rather than try to take him along in his plan to escape."

Glory was crying. "Now I have to tell Mom and Pop what he did, and how he died. He couldn't just drown and do everyone a favor. I'm sorry, but he's been the shame of our family since he was a teenager. Thank you for letting me know. I'm at my parents' house. I'll let them know right away."

The click in Landry's ear was abrupt, and he did not envy her the task of giving her parents the news.

He pulled up Hershel Arnold's next of kin, and

then took a drink of coffee before making the call. It rang only a couple of times before it was answered.

"Mae Arnold speaking."

"Mrs. Arnold, this is US Marshal Reagan Landry."

"I've been waiting for your call," Mae said. "I already knew he was dead. His spirit visited me yesterday to let me know. This must mean you've found the bodies. Did he drown?"

Landry was trying to come to terms with the fact that she believed she'd been visited by her son in spirit, when he realized she was waiting for an answer.

"No, ma'am, he did not drown."

He heard a hitch in her breath, and then hesitation, as if she was afraid to ask.

"Then how?"

Landry repeated what he'd told the Baker family, up to the point about cause of death.

"We've been given information that while the woman shot both of them, neither died from her shots. According to the woman they'd taken hostage, your son was killed by the other prisoner, Roy Baker, when it became evident that Hershel was going to be a liability. Roy Baker was killed during the woman's rescue. I'm giving you this much detail because this will eventually be national news, and you deserve to know his fate."

Mae was so silent, Landry thought she'd hung up.

"Mrs. Arnold? Are you still there?"

"Yes, sir. I don't know how to feel, except I'm so sorry for that poor woman."

"Yes, ma'am," Landry said. "One other thing. The medical examiner will be notifying you when the body is released."

"I thank you for your courtesy," Mae said.

"Yes, ma'am. My condolences to you and your family."

He got another disconnect, then hung up. That job was over, but he needed to contact Sam Quaid again, and pulled up the number from his previous call.

Sam was finally in the room with Haley. They were nearing the three-hour mark since she'd been admitted, and about an hour ago they had begun the treatment designed to get rid of the bacteria that was making her sick. Her fever broke earlier and right now she was pale and clammy. He knew this was going to be a yo-yo process until she was well.

When his phone rang and he saw who it was from, he answered quickly.

"This is Sam."

"Sam, Marshal Landry here. Where did they take her, and do you have an update on her condition?"

"She's in Nacogdoches Medical Center. She is recovering from a concussion, has bruised ribs, likely from the beating, and a bacterial infection that entered her body through open wounds, and stitches in a couple of places. If the meds they're giving her work, we should be out of here in a couple of days, maybe less."

"When she's able, and before you head back to

Dallas, I need to talk to her. Let me know when that would be possible."

"I'd say that anytime tomorrow afternoon should be okay for a few brief questions."

"Thank you. For now, just know that this will break in national news before long, so be prepared for the media to vie for interviews with both of you."

"I know it's coming, but she was so hurt I don't think any of that has occurred to her."

"Good enough," Landry said. "So, that's all for now, and I'll see you both tomorrow right after noon unless I hear otherwise."

"Yes, sir, and thank you."

"Absolutely," Landry said, and they disconnected.

Technically, the Marshals Service could close this case, but he was curious, and began reading through the men's files, and realized there had been a third thief in on the original heist who had yet to be identified, and was in the wind. So, Landry thought. They'd been on the run with something over two million dollars for almost two days before they were caught, and the money was not recovered.

He finished off his coffee, and then kept reading. When he was finished, he picked up the phone and called the deputy director's number.

Deputy Director Bob Richmond was on his way out of his office when his phone rang. He glanced at his watch. He still had time until his meeting, and so he went back to answer.

"Deputy Director Richmond."

"Hello, sir. Marshal Landry speaking."

"Yes, yes, Reagan. Good news on recovering the missing prisoners."

"Yes, sir. That's why I'm calling. I know our part of this job is finished. I will still file an interview with the woman they abducted, with details as to their demise, but the federal end of this is still open, because the two million plus that they got away with has not been recovered. I think the Feds should know we have recovered the bodies, and that there is a woman they abducted who might have overheard a conversation helpful to their case."

"Yes. I'll call them on the way to my meeting."

"If they want her contact info, just have someone call me."

"Will do, and again, good job."

"Yes, sir. Thank you, sir," Landry said.

Sam was kicked back in the recliner he'd pushed beside Haley's bed, when someone knocked lightly at the door. "Come in," he said and got up as Lee Tolson and his son, Brett, walked in.

"You guys made good time," he said.

"That Hummer is one fine vehicle," Brett said. "It was my pleasure to get to drive it." He gave Sam the keys and told him where he'd parked it.

"How's Haley?" Lee asked.

"As you can see, sleeping. Fever comes and goes,

but at least they've identified it as a bacterial infection. She should have a good recovery."

Lee nodded. "Good enough, Sam. Is there anything else we can do for you?"

Sam shook his head. "No, and I can't thank you enough. Seriously, Lee. I owe you one."

"That's what friends are for," Lee said. "Give my best to Haley, and safe travels when you head home."

"I will," Sam said, then closed the door behind them.

Haley's fever was back up.

Sam had been listening to her mumbling and crying in her sleep, and he was worried.

All of a sudden, Haley opened her eyes, looking around in total confusion. She saw Sam and reached for his hand.

"Houston drowned," Haley mumbled.

Sam patted her arm. "I know, sweetheart. But you didn't, and that's what matters most."

"Water?" she asked.

He raised the head of her bed up enough so she could drink, poured cold water into her glass and as soon as she drank her fill, he lowered her bed again.

"Sam saved me," she whispered, then dozed off, only to wake up less than an hour later.

People were talking all around her. She was vaguely aware of a lot of machines beeping. Her heart skipped when she heard a man's voice, then she felt his hand. Sam. It was Sam.

"Hey, honey. It's me, Sam. You don't need to talk.

I just wanted you to know I'm right beside you, and I'm not going anywhere. You're safe. You can rest."

"Safe…"

She sighed. Safe with Sam. Her eyes closed.

Sam felt her forehead. Her fever was still there, but being out of that hot attic and in this cool room was a blessing in itself.

He wanted a shower and clean clothes, but right now he'd settle for the change of clothing.

A nurse came in to check Haley's IV.

Sam dug a change of clothes out of his backpack and pointed at the bathroom.

"Nurse, I'm going to change clothes in there, okay? The hurricane trapped us for several days in a really hot attic."

She gasped. "Oh, bless your hearts. Wait and I'll get some bath towels, and you can shower in there."

"Really?" Sam said.

"Of course. I'll be right back," she said, and hurried out of the room, returning shortly with a couple of bath towels, a wash cloth and some liquid bath soap. "Here you go. Sorry there's no shampoo."

"Oh, I have some in my backpack! I sure appreciate this." He dug out the travel pack of toiletries and headed into the bathroom. His unshaven whiskers were turning into a very black beard, and he couldn't wait to get it off.

The bathroom was very small. A toilet and a narrow shower. He turned on the water to get it warm, stripped, then dropped his dirty clothes just outside the bathroom before stepping in the shower. The warm water on his body felt the height of luxury as he squirted a dollop of shampoo into the palm of his hand and then rubbed it into his hair. After the shampoo, he began shaving, and when the whiskers were finally gone, he began scrubbing his skin.

Dude Santos was watching the morning news on CNN as he ate breakfast, thinking about when he would return to the States, when he realized the broadcast was airing an update of hurricane news. When they cut to a live feed of a rescue in progress, he upped the volume to watch a Life Flight chopper circling a house, then saw the rescue in progress as he smeared some more guava jelly onto his toast. He was refilling his coffee when they began pulling a litter and a man back up into the chopper. He assumed the rescue was over until he saw the second chopper rescue a man who seemed in good health.

Both choppers had flown out of sight when the camera cut to a trio of big boats bearing the logo of the US Marshals Service speeding past them. His first thought was what would the Marshal Service be doing there, and then it hit him.

"Ahhh, *madre de dios*!"

It was the US Marshals Service who had been transporting Roy and Hershel to a federal prison. All this time he'd assumed they had escaped before the hurricane, but what if they had not?

His cook entered the kitchen from outside and

began fussing because he had waited on himself, then removed the food and dishes and refilled his coffee as Dude sat back down to watch the rest of the live feed unfolding.

Almost an hour passed, showing repeat footage of the chopper rescues, and then CNN went live again on the same area. The trio of motor boats had been anchored in front of a huge two-story manor, and people in flood gear and hip boots were walking in and out of the open door to the house.

The camera zoomed into a quick view of the inner foyer, showing water several feet up on the stairs leading to the second floor, and then showed four men coming down the stairs, carrying something between them. When he realized it was a body bag, his heart skipped a beat, and minutes later, when they carried out a second body bag, he cursed beneath his breath.

For all his criminal interests, Dude wasn't much of a gambler. He liked sure things. But he would have bet every bit of that missing money that he'd just watched them carrying out their missing prisoners.

Dude walked out the back door onto the patio to the beach below his little casa and stared thoughtfully at the beautiful waters of Cozumel. Usually, he was reluctant to leave here, but there was a big question regarding what he'd just seen that hadn't been addressed by any of the media. Maybe they didn't realize the significance, but Dude did.

If that was really Hershel and Roy in the body bags, then who were the two people airlifted out who were obviously alive? How had they all wound up in that house together? Maybe they were the owners of the house who had not evacuated? But if Roy and Hershel were in the body bags, how did they die? What did the survivors learn about the escaped prisoners during their time together? There was a huge amount of money at stake here. It would be careless of him not to at least investigate this matter further. He obviously couldn't go back to his place in Houston. But he needed answers, and he knew exactly who to call to get them.

Miles Rafferty lived in Waco, Texas, but thanks to technology and the World Wide Web, he was a stringer for several Texas newspapers, and always on the lookout to scoop the next big story.

The fact that he'd become an answer man for Alejandro Santos was pure coincidence. Miles did not run in criminal circles, but he was a pretty decent hacker when the need arose, and had, on occasion, gotten info Santos needed about certain individuals, and was paid handsomely for the information.

He'd caught the same CNN piece about the hurricane and flooding that Santos had seen in Cozumel. Like Dude, his curiosity had been piqued as to who the two people were in body bags, and the identities of the two people airlifted out of the house.

And then Dude had called, wanting Miles to find out the names of the people who were airlifted. Then he wanted Miles to interview them, which was something he'd never done for Santos before, but for five thousand dollars, he was willing to give it a try.

As soon as the call with Santos ended, Miles logged onto his bank account, and waited for the money to show up as a deposit. It took about a half an hour, but once he saw it, he began searching the contact list on his phone. Who did he know who was connected to Life Flight? There had to be someone with inside contacts who could give him a name, or at least a location where the victim had been taken.

After a few minutes of frustrating calls that went nowhere, he suddenly remembered the girl from his twin sister's wedding last month. She worked for Life Flight. Not as medical personnel, but in their office. What the heck was her name? Glenda? Gwendolyn? No! It was Gwyneth, like the actress Gwyneth Paltrow!

He scanned back through his contact list again, and then he found it. No wonder he hadn't connected it first time around. He'd put her in the contact list as Goody Two-shoes, because she wouldn't put out. But he did remember she talked about how she liked to surround herself with "nice things." Maybe Goody Two-shoes could be bought? It was worth a try. Not wanting to waste any time, he gave her a call.

Gwyneth Barrett was inputting costs from a rescue flight into their billing program when the phone rang. It wasn't the work phone, and her boss didn't like employees doing personal business on the clock, but then she saw Caller ID and frowned.

Why on earth would Miles Rafferty be calling me again?

It was curiosity that drove her to answer.

"Hello?"

"Hi, Gwyneth. This is Miles Rafferty."

"I know. Caller ID and all," Gwyneth said.

"Yeah, right. I wasn't thinking." Miles rolled his eyes. This wasn't his best opener. "Listen, I need some information about Life Flight, and it's worth three hundred dollars to me if you can get it."

Gwyneth's eyes widened, then narrowed sharply. "I don't do illegal things," she snapped.

"Oh for pity's sake," Miles said. "Who do you think I am? I'm no crook. All I need is info. Now, are you interested, or not?"

The fact that Gwyneth was actually considering it said something about her spending habits. Three hundred dollars would almost pay off a credit card bill.

"Well, ask the question. If I think it's legit, I'll consider it."

"Great!" Miles said. "I'm working on a story about Hurricane Gladys, covering people being rescued, as opposed to the bodies that are being recovered. Staying on the positive side, right?"

Gwyneth was beginning to relax. Positive was good. "Yes, I suppose. What do you want to know?"

"We all saw the footage this morning of Life Flight rescuing someone from the Thornwood area. They brought the victim out on a litter, and one of the flight crew was with them. I needed the victim's name and location as to where they were taken for medical attention. That's all."

Gwyneth lowered her voice. "That's private information. I can't give that out."

"Seriously? Everyone saw Life Flight pick up someone. It's going to be on the news within hours anyway and you know it. No one will ever know how I found out, and I can even claim that I just happened to be in the area when I saw the chopper landing, and found all of it out by accident."

Silence.

Silence lengthened.

Miles frowned. "Hello? Gwyneth? Are you still there?"

"Yes," she hissed. "I'm still thinking."

"Oh, right. Look, if this is too big a deal for you to consider, too, then I'm sorry I bothered you."

Ire rose in Gwyneth, just as it had the night she'd refused to have sex with him. The fact that he'd been mildly amused by her reticence had irked her. She was used to men begging a bit before she crumbled. I mean…she had her own game to play, right? And he'd ruined that. Now he was being all snarky again.

"How do I know you're going to really give me the money?" she asked. "Considering the fact that I barely know you and all, I have nothing on which to base your truthfulness but a fairly pitiful hard-on."

Miles choked. What the hell? Goody Two-Shoes had an edge he hadn't seen.

"Do you have a PayPal account?" he asked.

"Yes." She gave him the email addy to send her money to, then added, "Deposit three hundred dollars in there, and call me back in an hour. I'm busy right now."

She hung up on him and smiled.

Miles's eyes widened. She'd hung up on him. What the hell, again?

He scrambled to pull up PayPal, logged on and quickly sent the money, then sat there staring at the clock until exactly an hour had passed before he called her again.

Gwyneth was in the ladies' room with her phone, waiting for the call when it came. She checked Caller ID and then answered.

"Hello."

"I sent the money," Miles said.

Gwyneth lowered her voice to just above a whisper. "I know that, or we wouldn't be having this conversation. Her name is Haley Quaid. They took her to Nacogdoches Medical Center. Don't ever call me again."

Miles blinked, wrote down the info and took off out the door. It was a little over a three-hour drive from Waco to Nacogdoches, but he didn't have anything else to do.

Eight

Clean, and in clean clothes, Sam felt human again. He stayed close to Haley, leaving once to get snacks from the waiting room down the hall, and then once to step out of the room to call his neighbor, Louise, who was checking on his house and taking in his mail. With all calm on the home front, he was free to devote his attention to Haley.

She was mumbling in her sleep. Sometimes tears rolled from the corners of her eyes. It was heartbreaking to watch. Once she cried out, "Don't shoot," and then jerked and moaned, as if in fright.

Sam guessed she was reliving her nightmare, and there was no way to stop it from happening.

A nurse came in to check stats and made note of them.

"Is there anything I can do for you?" she asked.

Sam shook his head. "No, ma'am, I'm okay."

She paused, eyeing Haley's condition. "Bless her heart. She had a rough time of it, didn't she?"

"Yes, ma'am," Sam said.

The nurse nodded, and gathered up her things. "Just buzz if you need anything. I'm on duty until midnight."

"Will a doctor make rounds this evening?" Sam asked.

"Most often around 6:00 p.m. or after," she said.

"I'm going to assume it won't be the ER doctor."

"Not likely," the nurse said. "Haley will have been assigned to another physician."

"Okay, thanks," Sam said.

The nurse left, and once again, he and Haley were alone. He leaned over the bed rail and brushed a kiss across her forehead, then whispered near her ear.

"I love you, Haley. You're going to be okay."

He heard what sounded like thunder and went to the window to look out. The sky was darkening again. Thunderstorms were a common aftereffect of hurricanes and could last for days. He hoped that wasn't the case this time. The water needed to go down, not continue to rise.

By the time a doctor showed up in their room, followed by his nurse, it had been raining for almost an hour.

"Good evening. I'm Dr. Wyman."

Sam got up from the recliner to get out of the way as the doctor approached Haley's bed.

"Has she been awake much?" he asked, glancing up at the readouts on everything she was hooked to.

"Three, maybe four times," Sam said. "She doesn't

stay awake long, but she's cognizant when she is awake."

"Good," Wyman said, and then laid a hand on her arm and spoke her name. "Haley, can you hear me?"

Haley opened her eyes. "Yes, I hear you."

"I'm Dr. Wyman. I'll be your doctor until you are released."

Haley managed a slight smile, then looked past the doctor and nurse, searching for Sam.

"I'm over here," Sam said.

Haley turned her head, saw him and blinked. "Just checking," she said, as the doctor began questioning her and examining her at the same time.

"How do you feel? Have you been up yet?" he asked.

"It hurts if I move around much, and no, I haven't been up."

He nodded, checking her over as carefully as the doctor had done in ER, took note of her intermittent fever and made a comment to the nurse. "I want her up once before bedtime. Even if it's just to stand up beside the bed for a minute."

"Yes, sir," she said.

Then he laid a hand on Haley's arm. "Sleep well. I'll see you in the morning during rounds."

The doctor glanced at Sam. "I'd wish you a good night's sleep, too, but I know from experience that's not always easy to do here."

"As long as Haley is getting well, I'll be fine," Sam said.

"It's looking better, but we'll have to keep an eye

on the infection, none the less," he said, and then left the room.

"They're bringing dinner soon," the nurse said. "Since you are new today and didn't have time to choose your own food, they'll give you a regular menu." Then she glanced up at Sam as she worked. "We can bring you a tray, too, if you like."

"That would be great," Sam said.

"No problem," she said, checked the IV drip and left to go order one more tray for this room.

Haley looked around for the controls, and then raised the head of her bed a little.

"I'm so thirsty. Would you please pour me some water?" she asked.

"Absolutely," Sam said, and filled the plastic cup with water from the pitcher on her tray table. She took a big drink, then handed the cup back to him. "How do you feel?" he asked.

She shrugged. "Weird. Hot. Achy. Sleepy."

He cupped the side of her face. "At least you didn't have to have surgery. That takes a while to recover from."

She frowned. "When did you have surgery?"

"About two years ago," he said, and pulled the hem of his T-shirt up over his shoulder, revealing a big scar on his right side.

Haley gasped. "Oh my gosh! Sam! What happened?"

"Caught a guy in the act of robbing my place. We went out a window together."

Haley gasped. "Oh no!" Then her voice softened as her eyes welled with tears. "Who took care of you?"

"My secretary, Deborah Lee, picked up meds and shopped for groceries for me. I used Uber to get around until I was released to drive."

Undone by the shock of him suffering alone, Haley covered her face with her hands, trying to get the sight of that scythe-shaped scar out of her mind.

Sam pulled her hands away from her face. "Don't."

"It's hard to face shortcomings," Haley said.

He frowned. "You had nothing to do with that."

"That's not what I meant," Haley said. "I left and never once imagined your needing help, but the first time I had the need, I called you."

"You already had the invitation to do so, remember? Besides, I think the extenuating circumstances of what was happening to you trumps tenfold what happened to me."

"I'm sorry," she said. "I keep saying that to you, don't I? But I swear to God I mean it."

"Since I still love you as much as the day I married you, coming to your rescue was only natural. Fate put us back together, and I'm not going to stay silent and let you walk away so easily from me again."

"I have this horrible feeling of guilt…and an even bigger belief of not deserving a second chance. But I want it. I want that chance, Sam."

"Then hush," he said, and lifted her hand to his lips and kissed it.

She heard the rumble of thunder and frowned. "Is

it really still raining? The floodwaters will never go down if it keeps this up. I have no idea what's happening in my apartment building, and I don't have a clue as to what happened to my car."

"What about your car?" Sam asked.

"After I was injured and then trapped by the hurricane, I looked out the front window and it was gone. I have no idea when it was taken, because I was already unconscious before the hurricane hit. I thought maybe someone in need hot-wired it and tried to leave the city."

"No worries. You can report it to your insurance company. As for your apartment, when it's safe to go back, I'll take you to get your stuff…"

"But—"

"No buts," Sam said. "Just hear me out. Yes, I am hoping you'll choose to stay in Dallas with me, which means returning to Houston to pack what you want to bring what you want to keep. But if that turns out to be something you don't want, then I will do everything to help you get your life back together here."

Before Haley could answer, a nurse came in carrying a food tray.

"Dinnertime. Are you hungry, Haley?"

"Not really," Haley said, as the nurse set the food on her tray table and then rolled it up to her bed.

"Try to eat something anyway," she said, then smiled at Sam. "Be right back with yours." She returned with a tray and set it on the wide windowsill. "This serves as a pretty fair table, unless you want to hold it in your lap. At any rate, just leave them. We'll pick them up later."

Sam raised Haley's bed enough for her to eat, then removed the covers from the food.

"Baked chicken and rice. Salad and peaches. Not bad, honey. Do you need help?"

"Maybe you could cut up some of the chicken for me? I feel shaky…and I'd rather sleep," Haley said.

He brushed a strand of hair away from her cheek and tucked it behind her ear, then took the cutlery out of the little plastic bag it was in and began cutting up the chicken.

"If you had some food in you, that sleepy feeling wouldn't be so strong."

She lay back against the pillow, watching the way his brows knit when he concentrated, catching sight of the small scar just inside his hairline and remembering he'd been hit with an empty beer bottle when he was in college. There was a faint streak of gray at his temples now, which hurt her heart, but there was no way to change the past.

He glanced up at her and winked, but she was remembering what that sexy mouth felt like on her bare skin, and how fast he could bring her to a mind-numbing climax. That was then. But what about now? It had to still be there. Magic is magic, no matter how long in between before the spell is recast.

"There you go, honey. Open wide."

She came back to her senses to see the food on the

fork he was holding. She took the fork and popped the bite into her mouth, then chewed.

"Not bad. Needs salt...and some red pepper flakes...and maybe a little bit of Tabasco in the marinade."

Sam laughed. "Dang... I'd forgotten all about that Hot Mama Chicken you used to make."

"I'll make it again for you sometime," she said, and pointed at his food. "Eat yours, too, while it's mostly warm."

Sam pulled up a chair beside the bed, balanced his tray in his lap and kept her occupied and awake enough by telling stories. She ate a decent amount of food before she began to fade.

"I can't eat anything more," she said, and pushed the tray table away from the bed.

Sam had already finished, so he let her bed back down, covered her up, then frowned when he saw her move a hand over her belly and wince.

"Are you hurting, baby?"

"Yes...probably just changing positions, but it hurts. A lot."

Sam rang for the nurse, then asked if Haley could have something for pain.

"I'll check her chart," the nurse said.

Sam frowned. That wasn't a yes or a no. When he asked questions, he didn't want information. He wanted answers.

Haley was already drifting in and out of sleep, but couldn't get comfortable enough to properly rest.

Fortunately for her, the nurse appeared in the room within minutes with a drug-filled syringe and injected the contents into the IV. She checked the drip and removed the trays.

"Buzz if you need anything more," she said, and then frowned as she looked out the window at the downpour. "I have to drive home in this tonight. Hope it lets up before midnight."

"Yes, ma'am," Sam said, and when she left, he followed her to the door and closed it.

Haley was already feeling the drug in her system and soon fell asleep. She'd been out for a little less than five minutes, when something crashed in the hall outside her room.

She screamed in her sleep, "Don't shoot!" and jerked, thinking that Roy Baker was shooting at her again. The sudden movement sent a fresh wave of pain rolling through her. Then she heard Sam's voice.

"You're okay, Haley. That wasn't a gunshot. Someone dropped a tray."

She groaned and fell right back into an unconscious sleep. No dreams. No memories good or bad. Just blessed silence in a much-needed rest.

Sam watched her long past the need for concern, thinking of all the days and weeks to come, knowing her body would heal long before her mind ever came to terms with what she'd endured.

Miles Rafferty reached Nacogdoches before the rain began and was already in his motel for the night.

He was downstairs in the bar nursing a gin and tonic when he heard thunder, and glanced up at the television over the bar.

They had a weather report running a crawl across the bottom of the screen. There was a line of thunderstorms moving across this portion of the state, but they should be gone by morning. He tossed some money on the bar for his drink, then picked it up and took it with him across the lobby to the restaurant.

It was far from a four-star establishment, but it was here and so was he, and he was ready to get some food in his belly. He scanned the menu until he saw barbecue, ordered ribs, fries and a beer, then settled in to wait for the food.

The dining room was almost full, and it didn't take long before he figured out that most of these people were Houstonians misplaced by the hurricane. He thought about the woman who'd been airlifted here, and empathized with her situation. He kept wondering why Santos wanted to know where she was, and for a moment, wished he'd never gotten involved with the man.

He was kidding himself about not doing anything wrong. If he was giving Santos information about someone, then the likelihood that someone would suffer for it later was strong. If someone died, he would be an accessory to murder.

Shit.

He was feeling down about himself and the mess he was in—until his food came. By the time he cleaned his plate and had a couple of beers in his belly, his conscience was quiet, and his moment of regretting culpability had passed.

He returned to his room, got out his laptop and Googled Haley Quaid—Houston, Texas. He scanned down the names until he found quite a few new articles in which a woman named Haley Quaid had garnered some Realtor awards. He jotted down the name Truman Realty, which was where she was listed, and Will Truman as owner.

Then he scanned everything he could find about that rescue. To his dismay, the media already knew her name, and it was being reported that she was at an empty property listed with Truman Realty when she was injured, which related to how she became trapped there. There was still no mention of prisoners being accounted for, and he fell asleep watching TV in bed. He woke up hours later, turned off the television and didn't wake up again until morning. The rain had passed. When he went outside after breakfast, water was dripping off everything, and the air was already getting hot and steamy.

He drove around until he found a florist shop called Pots and Stems, went in and bought a potted hydrangea plant laden with huge purple and lavender blooms, got a get-well card and wrote "Love and get well soon, from all of us at Truman Realty."

Pleased with his ruse to get into her room, he headed for the medical center. Less than fifteen minutes later, he was knocking on her door.

Sam was out of the room returning messages to his office. Haley heard the knock, but didn't respond. To her surprise, the door opened anyway, and a thirty-something man came in carrying a large potted plant.

"Haley Quaid?"

"Yes, I'm Haley."

"Delivery from Pots and Stems." He set it on the window sill and then smiled politely. "Would you like the card, ma'am?"

"Yes, please," Haley said.

Miles was still playing it cool as he handed it to her. But as soon as she had it in hand, he shifted focus.

"They said you're the person on TV who was airlifted out of a flooded house. They also said the Marshals Service carried body bags out afterward."

Haley frowned. "I have no idea what happened after I left."

"But weren't you trapped in there with them? I heard it was those escaped prisoners. Did they beat you up like that? What were they talking about?"

Haley grabbed the call button and pushed it. Seconds later a nurse's voice answered.

"Morning, Haley. How can I help you?"

"There's a stranger in my room. I want him gone!"

Miles's lips parted. This wasn't the reaction he needed.

"No need, I'm leaving. Didn't meant to bother you."

He turned on his heel and was heading for the door

when it opened abruptly, and a very big, very angry man was coming at him.

Before he could talk his way out of this, Sam had him pinned to the wall.

Haley relaxed. Sam had this covered.

"Honey, are you all right?" he asked.

"Yes. He started asking me about prisoners and body bags."

"What's your name?" Sam asked.

"Miles Rafferty. I'm a stringer for several different newspapers. I just wanted to talk to her...you know, get an exclusive on the woman who wound up trapped with escaped prisoners."

Sam's eyes narrowed. "What made you say that? No info has been released to the public."

Miles didn't miss a beat. "Hell, man. They've already given her name out through the media. Everyone in Houston knew two prisoners had escaped from a US Marshals van. And the media filmed US Marshals taking two body bags out of the same house from which she was airlifted. Doesn't take much to connect the dots here. It's just logic."

A security guard came rushing into the room.

"What's going on?"

"Some guy calling himself a member of the press walked into Haley's room unannounced and started grilling her. At the least, I want him barred from her room, and preferably the hospital."

The security guard grabbed Miles by the arm,

yanked it behind his back and had him handcuffed before Miles knew what was happening.

"Wait! Wait!" he said. "I didn't do anything illegal. I'm leaving, I'm leaving."

"Stop talking," the security guard said, and yanked him out of the room.

Sam shut the door and then went straight to Haley.

"I was at the nurses' station when you buzzed for help. What was he asking you?"

"If the prisoners were responsible for my bruises, and what were they talking about."

Sam frowned. "What the hell? That sounded like he was wanting information about the prisoners, not you."

Haley shrugged, then looked down at the card in her hand and gave it to Sam.

"He brought those flowers, like he was a deliveryman. Look at the card! I haven't even notified anyone at the realty about what happened to me. Last time I tried to call them, communication was down. I had no reason to believe anything had changed."

Sam read the card. "He did his homework. And he was telling the truth that the media has identified you as the person Life Flight rescued. It wouldn't be hard for him to do a little digging and figure out where you worked."

She frowned. "There's no safe place to be anymore, is there?"

"You're safe with me. I won't leave you alone in the room again. I promise."

He slid his hand up the side of her cheek and brushed a kiss across her lips.

"There are doctors on the floor making rounds. Your new doctor should be one of them. We'll soon find out how you're doing, and get an idea of when I can get you out of here."

Haley leaned back and pulled the covers up to her chin. It was an unconscious act that told Sam more than anything else, how the incident had impacted her.

"Haley, honey, don't be afraid. What you went through just happens to be the latest item to talk about. It won't last long, but in the meantime, they're going to have to come through me to get to you."

Haley looked at him, at the angry jut of his jaw, the glint in his eye, and flashed back on seeing him walking over Roy's body to get to her. She gripped his hand, too choked up to speak.

A nurse entered the room.

"Are you all right? I hear you had an uninvited visitor."

"I'm okay, thanks to Sam," Haley said.

"Do you feel like getting up for a bit?" the nurse asked.

"If it will get me out of here sooner, then yes," Haley said.

Sam was right behind her and the nurse as they walked the length of the hall and back. By the time Haley was in her bed again, she was exhausted. She was almost asleep when the doctor came in to examine her. Another check of her fever, which was down, another good report on her stats and she was, once again, drifting off to sleep.

Sam watched until he was sure she was out, and then called Reagan Landry at the US Marshals Service.

"This is Landry."

"Marshall Landry. This is Sam Quaid."

"Oh. Good to hear from you. How is Haley doing?"

"Recovering from infection. Listen, the reason I called is about the bodies you removed. Has the media been notified of who they were?"

"Not officially. That's forthcoming sometime this afternoon, why?"

Sam proceeded to tell him about the intruder in Haley's room, and mentioned the questions he'd asked.

Landry frowned. "Have you spoken to any members of the FBI yet?"

"No, nobody like that has been here."

"They're the ones who need to know this. I'll give them another call."

"What's going on that we don't know?" Sam asked.

"The prisoners were part of a gang who stole two million dollars of bank money from an armored car, the money has never been recovered, and the third member of the gang escaped and has not been officially identified. And now two of the three are dead. This may be a stretch to suggest this, but Haley was

alone with them for some days. She may have information she doesn't even realize. Someone wants that
money. The question to be answered is who, and what
will he do to find it?"

Nine

Miles Rafferty was escorted out of Nacogdoches by two city police cars, with a less than friendly warning not to come back. He considered himself fortunate that he hadn't been booked and jailed. It was a wake-up call. Before, he'd done most of his snooping for Dude Santos online, and he was obviously not cut out for on-site investigations. He'd notify Dude what happened, and then make himself scarce. If ever there was a time to move on and start over, this was it.

He got back to Waco by midafternoon and let himself into his apartment. He was coming back with his tail between his legs, and still had to tell Santos he'd failed.

Five thousand dollars' worth of failure.

This had never happened before, so he didn't know how to address the fact that he'd been paid for a job he couldn't finish.

He set his suitcase in his room to unpack later

and called Dude immediately just to get it over with. When the call began to ring, he realized he didn't know what time it was there, and then Dude answered, and the question became moot.

"This is Santos."

"Hello, Dude. This is Miles. I do not have a good report."

"Why the hell not? I paid you five thousand dollars for information."

"I'll tell you what I know and then if you are still unhappy, I'll just give it back."

There was a long moment of silence, which made Miles nervous. "Uh…are you still there?" he asked.

"I am obviously waiting for your story. Start talking," Dude said.

"Okay…if you've been watching the hurricane updates, you'll notice they continue to replay the Life Flight piece quite often. The media had her name about the same time I did, but I did find out she'd been taken to Nacogdoches Medical Center, so I drove there. I spent the night and first thing this morning got myself into her room when she was alone."

"Ah…this is good," Dude said. "What did she say?"

"Basically, it was a bomb as far as interviews go. She immediately clammed up and called a nurse to have me removed, but before I can even get out the door, this big guy comes into the room, grabs me by the shirt collar and slams me up against the wall, and it wasn't hospital security. They came afterward and I was handcuffed and turned over to the local police."

Dude was cursing in Spanish. Miles knew just enough of what he was saying to be scared.

"You were booked?" he finally asked.

"No. Fortunately for me, I was escorted out of town with a warning not to come back. So I drove home and now I'm calling you. I did find out one thing that might be helpful, and I overheard it while I was in holding."

"So what *did* you find out?" Dude asked.

"The man with her is her ex-husband, Sam Quaid. He's some well-known private investigator out of Dallas, and he's taking her back to Dallas to stay with him after she's released."

"Did you get an address for this Sam Quaid?"

"No, but I can easily enough."

"So, get me the address and we'll call it even. And next time, we'll stick to info you gather from your computers."

"I'll get right on that, and text you the address the minute I find it, okay?"

"Yes, okay."

Miles hung up, then went into his office and started a search for Sam Quaid. Once he gave Santos this info, it would be the last work he did for him. In fact, it might be time to think about moving back home to Boston. He'd come to Texas because of the endless winter up north, but he hadn't counted on hurricanes and gangsters becoming part of his life.

Dude wasn't any happier than Miles, but for different reasons. Staying in Mexico left him dependent upon other people to get information, and he wasn't pleased with the results. He was at the point of going back to the States, regardless of the risks. Nothing was happening here. All of the action, all of his contacts, all of the money he'd ever made was across the border.

Houston was surely too involved with the devastation from the hurricane, and the two men who could tie him to the armored car robbery were dead. It was time to get back to the action.

Haley's fever had been down for almost six hours when Dr. Wyman and his nurse came in for evening rounds. It was going to be Haley's second night in the hospital, and she wanted out.

Wyman began by reading her chart, then looked up at her. "How are you feeling, Haley?"

"Better," Haley said. "No fever since before noon."

"I see that," he said.

"When can I leave here?" she asked.

He chuckled. "All my patients ask me the same thing. Fortunately, I have a good sense of self, or I might get my feelings hurt."

"That isn't an answer," Haley said.

Sam grinned. "You may as well face it, Doc. When she gets a notion, she doesn't let go."

"I'll make a deal with you, Haley. If your fever

stays down all night and it's still down in the morning, I'll release you."

"Yay!" Haley said.

"So, is your home flooded?" Wyman asked.

"Not my apartment. It's on the fourth floor, but I'm sure the building was to some degree. It's in the flood area. But I'm not going back there…at least, not for a while."

"I'm taking her back to Dallas," Sam said. "She's coming to stay with me."

"Good idea," Wyman said. "So…I'll see you in the morning and we'll go from there, okay?"

"Okay," Haley said.

Sam sat down on the side of her bed after the doctor was gone, and held out his hand. Haley grasped it.

"I need your feedback on something," Sam said.

"Okay," she said.

"It's going to be a long drive back for you. And you're going to be wearing my clothes all the way home. Are you okay with that?"

"I don't see that I have any other option," Haley said.

"Well, there is one option. There's a Walmart Supercenter here in town. I could go grab you a few outfits, some underwear and toiletries this evening. They're open all night, and the weather is pretty good. Then you'd be good to go when we get the okay."

"That would be awesome," Haley said. "You have my things. Hand me my wallet. I have credit cards."

"No way. I'm buying. The thing is…I'm going to

have to leave you alone to go do this. Are you going to be afraid someone else might try to sneak in to get a story?"

Haley shrugged. "I wasn't scared before, just angry. I'll be fine. If it makes you feel better, just tell the nurses you're leaving for a bit and ask them to check on my welfare now and then until you get back."

Sam nodded. "Yes, that would work, and make me feel better about leaving you. As for clothing sizes, are you still a size six?"

"Yes, all my sizes are the same. Do you remember underwear sizes, too?"

"I haven't forgotten a thing about you, Haley Jo. Not even the size of your drawers."

"Would you get me a hairbrush and some pony-tail holders?"

"Yes to that, as well. Don't worry. I remember how high-maintenance you were."

She laughed, and Sam sighed. He'd missed that laugh. God it was going to be good to have her back.

"What if they bring dinner while you're gone? Do you want them to leave a tray for you?"

He glanced at the time. "I'm pretty sure I'll be back, but if I'm not, yes, have them leave it. Take a nap while I'm gone, okay? The more you rest, the less chance you have of that fever coming back up."

"I will," Haley said.

Sam kissed her hand, then leaned forward and kissed her forehead. "I will be glad when you are all healed, so I won't be afraid of where to touch you."

"I'll be glad, too," Haley said. "I'm ready to be touched."

Sam's eyes narrowed. "Is that a double entendre? Did I just get an invitation for sex?"

"I'm still suffering from a head wound, so I can't be sure, either, but it sounded like one, didn't it?" Haley said.

Sam laughed. "I'll be back soon."

"Would you please bring something chocolate? Like a candy bar?"

"Like a Hershey's bar with almonds, maybe?"

"Yessss," Haley said, and gave him a thumbs-up.

"Consider it done," Sam said, and was still smiling when he stopped at the nurse's desk to tell them he would be gone for a while.

He was holding his car keys all the way down in the elevator, trying to remember exactly where Brett Tolson said he'd parked the Hummer. And then he got outside, looked out across the parking lot and grinned. That big silver Hummer stood out like a wart on a hog. He couldn't have missed it if he'd tried. Within minutes he was inside, and it was hot as hell. He'd thought the attic was hot, but this was suffocating. He started it up and rolled down a window. With the air conditioner on high, it would cool it off faster.

A few minutes later he found the address for a Walmart through Google, then drove out the parking lot after entering the address in his GPS.

He'd never been to Nacogdoches before, but it seemed crowded. He was guessing there were a lot of Houston refugees here, waiting go back into their neighborhoods and see what was left of their lives.

When he finally pulled into the parking lot at the Supercenter, he had a mental list of what he needed to get. The day was ramping up to be a scorcher, and he lengthened his stride just to get inside where it was cool.

Once inside, he grabbed a shopping cart and headed straight to the women's section, found shorts in her size and chose elastic waist rather than zippers, soft summer T-shirts and a pair of flip-flops to wear out to the pool.

The next section was pants and blouses. He knew colors she liked, and he knew styles she used to wear. A pair of white pants, a pair of black pants with straight legs and front zipper, a pair of jeans and a pair of blue capri pants.

He sorted through the blouse and shirt racks, picking out tops that looked like what she would wear, making sure they went with the pants and shorts already in the basket, then headed toward the lingerie aisle.

This took even less time. He tossed in a dozen different pairs of panties, a half-dozen bras and a couple of sports bras in case she was too sore to tolerate regular ones for a while. The last items of clothing he chose were socks and nightgowns. If it was left up to him, she'd be buck naked and curled up in his arms, but they had three years of abstinence to consider, and he wasn't about to rush a good thing. He chose four gowns in different styles, but all knee-length, sleeveless and low necklines for comfort.

He met a man coming down the same aisle and pushed his cart aside for him to pass. The guy nodded at Sam, then saw the clothing in the cart and looked at him again.

"Flooded out?" he asked.

Sam nodded.

"Hell of a deal, ain't it, buddy?" the man said, and moved along, on his way to somewhere else in the store.

Sam headed for makeup and immediately cornered a sales lady for help. After explaining what he was doing, the woman began gathering up basics: moisturizer, eye makeup and lipsticks, then aimed him toward the pharmacy for toothbrushes and whatever else he might want there.

It took another fifteen minutes for Sam to settle on what he thought she would be needing, grabbed a pair of tennis shoes in her size, and then thought of a suitcase and slid it onto the shelf beneath the cart before heading to check out.

He had everything on the conveyor at the checkout stand, and then grabbed a couple of Hershey's bars with almonds from the display and added them to the stack.

He was quietly waiting as the checker began scanning the items, when the woman in line behind him said, "Hey, mister. You're the guy from TV, aren't you? The one they rescued by air."

"Nope, nope, that wasn't me," he said, and began digging out a credit card, hoping that would speed up the process.

"You look just like him, except the beard is missing," she said.

"Really?" Sam said, and began putting the checked and bagged items into the cart.

She kept staring. "Was that woman they rescued your wife?" she asked.

"Nope. No. I'm not married," he said, and finally slid his credit card into the chip reader.

The woman frowned, but she wasn't giving up.

"Well, if you happen to see that woman you don't know, tell her we've been praying for her ever since we found out she got trapped with them two escaped prisoners."

Sam paused, stunned that he hadn't known that announcement had been made. He tossed the last of his purchases into the cart after he'd paid, with the suitcase on top.

He paused, then turned around. The woman was still staring.

He saw the earnestness in her eyes and couldn't walk away.

"I'll give her your message, and thank you for the prayers," he said softly, and was gone before she had time to react.

Sam drove back to the hospital in a solemn mood, worrying about the ramifications that might occur now that the public knew about her. At the least, there would be more journalists wanting to talk to her. At the worst, there would be the bottom-feeders who would pass themselves off as journalists and then hammer her for details—all of the salacious details they could imagine that might happen to a woman taken hostage by two very bad men.

They couldn't get out of Nacogdoches fast enough to suit him.

As soon as he reached the hospital parking lot, he pulled up a news app on his phone and began searching for any updates on the prisoners. He found them, listened to the briefing held at the Marshals office and groaned.

They didn't go into all of the details, but they did reveal that she'd shot both of them in self-defense when first attacked, which likely saved her life. It was made clear that her shots were not mortal to either of them, she was not responsible for either death and had been hospitalized for multiple injuries. It wasn't good news, but it wasn't exactly bad news, either. Just news she would have wished had not become public knowledge.

Satisfied that he was as up-to-date as possible, Sam grabbed all of the purchases and hurried back into the hospital out of the heat. A few minutes later, he stepped off the elevator on her floor and started down the hall, letting the nurses know he was back on his way to her room.

She was asleep, so he quietly put everything but her candy bars up out of the way. Those, he put on her tray table, then went into the bathroom, washed up and went back to check on her.

Her arms felt cool, so he pulled the lightweight covers up to her shoulders and settled into the chair by her bed.

The hall outside her room was busy and occasionally noisy, but her room was fairly quiet. He leaned back in the chair until it reclined, then closed his eyes.

The first thing that popped into his head was that woman at the checkout register, telling him they'd been praying for Haley. He took a slow, deep breath and then exhaled, letting go of all the nerves and tension he was feeling.

She mumbled something in her sleep. He waited to make sure it wasn't going to be a dream that led up to a nightmare, but when silence followed, he closed his eyes again, and he fell asleep.

Mae Arnold was going through the clothes that Hershel had left in the closet in his old room, and his old suit in particular. He'd worn it to her mother's funeral some years back. It was out of style, but if it still fit him, it would serve the purpose.

She and Pete had talked at length about the funeral, and both of them agreed it should be graveside services only, with no public notification that it was happening. She wasn't up to the scrutiny she knew they'd get, and Pete wanted what Mae wanted. That's how they'd begun their life together, and that's how he planned for it to be until they were gone.

She took the suit out of the closet to look it over. It was still in the plastic bag from the local cleaners, so it wasn't dusty, but she couldn't guarantee there wouldn't be moth holes.

She removed the bag and the laid the suit out on the bed to give it the once-over. It was a dark gray, double-breasted suit with a faint pink pinstripe. He'd looked so handsome when he'd put that on, but she doubted he would have held his looks after ten years of living a life of crime. It was also a winter suit, made out of a heavier fabric, but seeing as how he was dead now, it wasn't like he was going to be bothered by the heat.

She had decided it would do, and was hanging it back in the closet when Pete came into the room.

"There you are, sugar. I've been looking for you."

"What's wrong?" she asked.

"Nothing is wrong. At least I don't suppose it is, but I just remembered something. That box Hershel mailed here to himself months ago. Remember? We don't know what was in it, but I reckon we ought to at least go see."

"Well, I'll swan… I clean forgot about that," Mae said. "Let me get my sun hat. It's hot outside, and I don't want to get overheated and give myself a headache."

"It's hanging by the back door," Pete said.

Mae followed Pete to the kitchen, and grabbed her hat on the way out, tying the ties beneath her chin as she went. They walked toward the old smokehouse hand in hand, talking about the garden, and what needed hoeing, and what needed picking and wishing for a good rain. Talking about anything but the fact that they would be burying their only child before the month was out. Burying him in shame.

Pete opened the smokehouse door and walked in first, just in case that dang raccoon happened to be messing around in there again. They didn't use this building for much of anything anymore, and it had become something of a warehouse for stray critters passing through.

"There's the box up on that back table beneath that tarp, right where I left it," Pete said. "Let me carry it to the light."

Mae stepped back as he came toward the open doorway, then set it down near the threshold. The box was large, and she couldn't imagine what was in it. She ran her fingers over the mailing label, recognizing Hershel's handwriting, then blinked away tears.

Pete pulled out his pocket knife, and then cut through all the shipping tape so he could open the box. The first thing they saw was wadded up newspaper.

"Likely used it for packing," Pete said, as he grabbed it all with both hands and tossed it on the smokehouse floor.

And then they gasped, looking at each other in disbelief.

"Lord, Lord, would you look at this," Pete muttered.

Mae's jaw set into instant disapproval. "If this is what they stole from that armored car, then there's blood on this money, Pete. One man's dead and the other crippled for life because of Hershel and his running buddy."

Pete nodded. And then, even though they were the only humans within a five mile radius, he began to whisper.

"What are we gonna do, Mama?"

Mae reached for his hand, touched that he'd reverted back to what he used to call her when Hershel was a boy.

"First thing is pack it back up and get it to the house before some pack rat breaks into the box and chews up a few thousand."

"Right, right," Pete said, and quickly stuffed all of the newspaper back into the box. "It's too heavy to carry all that way. I'll get the pickup to move it."

Mae was sick to her stomach. "I'm not gonna like knowing that blood money is under our roof. As soon as we get to the house, I'm gonna look up the phone number of one of those federal agents who called back when they first stole the money. 'Course that US Marshal called, too, after the marshal's van was wrecked and they were on the run."

Pete knew Mae was really upset. She was just talking to keep from crying, and was pale and shaky as he took her by the elbow as they returned to the house. Once inside, he took her to the living room.

"Honey, you sit right here in the recliner where

it's cool. I'm gonna get you something cold to drink, and then take the pickup to haul the box back to the house. It won't take me long."

He hustled out of the room to get Mae some water, and then came hurrying back, the ice cubes clinking against the glass.

"You drink this slow and cool off. I won't be long."

"You are such a sweet man, Pete Arnold. Smartest thing I ever did in life was marry you," Mae said.

Pete was beaming as he gave her a quick pat on the head, and then ran outside again, letting the back door slam behind him.

Mae took a few sips of the cold water, and then set it on the table beside her. She heard the pickup start up, and rolled her eyes when Pete gunned the motor.

"It's not a race. Slow yourself down, old man," she muttered.

She drank some more water, and was feeling more like herself when she heard him drive up. She got up to go open the door for him, but when she saw him struggling with the box, she ran out to help him. Together, they got it all the way into Hershel's old room, and then pushed it in his closet and closed the door.

Pete was red-faced and puffing for air when he turned around.

"Woowee…that box is some heavy."

Mae took him by the elbow. "Now you come sit and cool off."

He nodded, too winded to argue, but as they

started down the hall, Pete suddenly grabbed his chest.

Mae saw the fear on his face, and her heart nearly stopped.

"Mae... I think I'm havin' a heart attack," he mumbled, and then dropped to the floor.

Mae screamed, dropped to her knees beside him and rolled him over onto his back, trying to find a pulse.

"Pete! Pete! Don't do this!" she begged, and shook him, then weakly pounded on his chest, without knowing what to do.

The phone! She needed to call the ambulance!

She pushed herself up, and ran, stumbling all the way to the landline in the kitchen. The number to the police station and the ambulance were the same, and posted right there by the phone. She punched in the numbers with trembling hands, and then waited for someone to answer.

"Oh please, please, please," she whispered.

"Carytown Police Department."

"Hello, Will! This is Mae Arnold! I need an ambulance to my house! Pete just had a heart attack. I think he's gone. Help me, Will, help me."

Will Dawkins grew up with their son, Hershel, and had known them all his life.

"Yes, ma'am, I'm dispatching them right now. Stay on the line with me, okay?"

But she had already hung up the phone and was running back to Pete. Mae dropped down beside him again, then realized his need for her had passed. She stared at his face—at the features frozen in pain—and screamed.

She was still wailing when the ambulance arrived some time later. Distance from any kind of medical help was the downside of living in the backwoods of Kentucky, although a speedy arrival would not have changed Pete Arnold's fate. He was gone before he hit the floor.

Haley woke up to all of the new things Sam bought for her at Walmart and went through each bag as if it was Christmas. She finally picked out a pair of pull-on shorts, a soft blue T-shirt and the flip-flops to wear home, because her ankle was still slightly swollen and tender.

She also kept out the brush and ponytail bands for in the morning, and then as their dinner arrived, she became oddly silent and ate without comment.

Sam wasn't the kind of man who let a question go unanswered, and asked Haley point-blank, "What's wrong? Is it something I said or did?"

Haley looked up at him, startled he would even think that.

"No, you didn't do anything wrong."

"Then what is this sudden silent treatment?" Sam said. "Are you second-guessing going back to Dallas with me?"

"No. But I feel weird about it," she said.

He frowned. "Explain weird."

"I quit you, Sam. It was a cruel and heartless thing to do, and I had finally come to terms with what I'd done. Now this happens, and you not only save my life, but want me back in yours without question. I know this sounds stupid, but I feel like there should be some kind of parole, or some sitting on the bench time before I get to be happy again. I walked out, and now I'm walking right back in as if I owned the place."

Sam stared at her as if she'd lost her mind all over again.

"Oh, bullshit, Haley. That sounds like psychobabble. I want to be happy again. You make me happy. You said you wanted a second chance. So do I. Why do you feel the need to put yourself in time-out? You already did that, and we lost three years of our lives together. So you feel like you need to punish me again? Because it sure as hell sounds like you're trying to back out."

Haley stared at him as if she'd never seen him before. "You only say *bullshit* when you're really pissed off. So, are you really pissed off at me right now?"

"I'm gonna be, if you start down this 'I don't deserve you' road," he said.

A tiny grin came and went so fast on Haley's lips that Sam might have thought he had imagined it. And then he heard laughter in her voice.

"If I retract my statement, and actively readjust my misplaced emotions, would we be cool?"

"As a cucumber," he drawled.

"Consider it done. I think I would like a bite of that Hershey's bar with almonds—now. To take the bad taste out of my mouth."

Sam pointed to her tray table and the candy bars he'd left there.

She eased herself around and took one, opened it and broke off a bite. She started to put it in her mouth, then offered it to Sam instead.

"Is this a peace offering?" he asked, as he took it from her fingers.

"I thought it might take away the taste of that bullshit," she said.

He grinned and put it in his mouth.

"You eat the rest of it. You're already eating crow about what you said, and that's a skanky bird, even if you're starving."

Haley grinned. "Skanky?"

"Skanky," Sam said.

Haley broke off a piece and popped it in her mouth, then closed her eyes in a rush of chocolate ecstasy.

"Mmm, this stuff is so good."

Sam laughed, and for a few moments, it felt like it used to be between them.

Ten

The night at Nacogdoches Medical Center was long. There had been a wreck sometime between midnight and 2:00 a.m. out on a highway, and six people were brought into the ER. Two died en route, one went straight to surgery and the other three were finally brought up from ER and admitted to the fourth floor.

As word spread between family members of the survivors, visitors began arriving. Between the crying and the constant stream of frantic conversation up and down the halls, no one was resting, and certainly not the nurses.

Haley woke up the first time to people crying, and saw Sam was wide-awake.

"What's happening?" she said.

"From what I could hear, I think some people were in a bad wreck, and they didn't all survive. They admitted some to this floor. That's what the noise is about. Family arriving."

"Oh, bless their hearts," Haley said. "We know loss, don't we, Sam?"

A sudden wave of emotion welled up in Sam, turning into a hard, burning pain in his chest. He let down the bed rail on her bed, and took her in his arms. He kept trying to talk, but words wouldn't come, and when Haley tucked her head beneath his chin and started to cry, he cried with her. Three years of loneliness and heartache came bubbling up into the room. Tears for the child they'd lost. Tears for the years they'd lost.

Long after the tears had ended, Sam still held her. Sitting in the recliner now with her in his lap, the IV tubing carefully draped over his shoulder and the covers from her bed swaddled around her. She slept with her hand on the heartbeat beneath his chest.

Mae Arnold had stopped crying when they took Pete out of their house. The ambulance was driving away when she washed her face, changed out of her everyday shoes and took herself into Carytown. The EMTs and the driver all knew he was dead, but they transported him to the hospital anyway. Someone had to officially state that Peter Wayne Arnold was no longer of this world.

Just as Mae was passing the city-limits sign outside of town, a cloud passed in front of the sun, slightly darkening her view. She took it as fair warning that her day was going to get only worse.

One of her friends from church was coming out

of the pharmacy as Mae drove past. She smiled and waved, but Mae didn't acknowledge the greeting and just kept driving.

When she finally reached the little hospital, she parked in the back near the emergency entrance, and then stumbled and nearly fell as she got out. Once she got her legs under her again, she couldn't make herself move any closer. She was still standing at the hood of the pickup when a nurse who'd seen her there came out to get her.

"Come inside with me, Mrs. Arnold. It's hot out here." Then she looked around for other family members and frowned. "Are you here by yourself?"

"I'm the only one left," Mae said, and welcomed the arm to lean on.

They led her straight back to the bay where Pete's body was resting, and told her she was welcome to stay with him until the funeral home came to pick him up.

Mae stared at the sheet-covered body, and then finally walked over to the gurney and pulled back the cover from Pete's face. The fear she'd seen in his features was gone. The muscles had relaxed, leaving him in peaceful repose. She reached out and patted his cheek.

"I'm here, Pete. I don't know why this awful thing is happening, but I'm going to have to gather up the courage to put you in the ground, and then figure out how to live the rest of my life without you." Tears were rolling now. "I love you, and I am gonna miss you something fierce."

Then she took his hand and held it until the undertaker from the funeral home arrived. He gave her a few instructions, then took the body away, leaving her with his condolences.

It was the longest trip home Mae had ever made. A few hours ago she'd been readying clothes in which to bury their son, and now she was going to have to do the same for Pete.

And in all the ensuing drama, she had completely forgotten about that box of money, and with its status still listed as missing, Haley Quaid's life was still in danger.

Haley was sitting on the side of the bed, digging through what passed for breakfast, trying to find something she was willing to eat. Even Sam, who usually ate what was put in front of him, had set his aside and was trying not to laugh at the look of disgust on Haley's face.

"Oh my Lord, whoever cooked this morning had to have been suffering a hangover," she muttered.

Sam chuckled.

She looked up. He was laughing at her. "Well, it's awful."

"I know, baby. But if the doc releases you this morning, I promise to take you through a drive-thru for your choice of breakfasts-to-go."

"Deal!" she said and pushed the food and table aside.

A few minutes later, Dr. Wyman entered the room, all smiles and energy.

"Good morning, Haley. How do you feel this morning?"

"Except for sore muscles, I feel fine. Are you going to release me?"

His smile widened. "See, you're just like all my patients. Really happy to see me when they're sick, then they start feeling better, and I become the jailer who won't let them leave. But today, I am going to be your best friend. I've already signed off on your care, so as soon as they get release papers ready for you to sign, you are free to go."

"Thank you, Dr. Wyman, for everything," Haley said.

"You're very welcome," he said, and then included Sam in his goodbye. "Safe travels to the both of you… and take good care of your girl."

"Definitely," Sam said. "And thank you."

"It's what I do," Wyman said.

Haley was buzzing the nurse's desk before he got out the door.

"Good morning, Haley, what do you need?"

"I need to be unhooked from all this stuff so I can get dressed. Dr. Wyman says I can go home."

There was laughter in the nurse's voice. "We know. Someone will be there shortly to remove your IV."

"Thanks," Haley said, and then looked at Sam. "A

sausage-and-egg breakfast burrito from McDonald's, hot sauce and a Dr. Pepper, to go."

Sam nodded. "I knew that's where you'd want to go. It's already entered in my GPS."

The nurse finally arrived to remove Haley's IV, and as soon as she was gone, Haley got out of bed to get dressed. Sam had already removed the tags from the clothing, and Haley was so ready to be gone that she stripped without caring who was watching.

Once again, Sam could only wince at the sight of the battering she had endured.

"Need help?" he asked.

"I've got this," Haley said, as she started with underwear, but it was more difficult than she had imagined to put weight on her bad ankle, so she leaned against the bed as she stepped into panties, and then the shorts, and finished the rest of it easily.

"What did I do with the hairbrush?" Haley asked.

Sam took it out of her tote bag, along with one of the stretchy bands to put up her hair. But instead of handing it to her, he pointed to the bed.

"Sit. I'll brush it for you."

"Don't forget the cut on my head," she said.

"Not likely, since I'm looking straight at it," Sam said.

Haley sat sideways on the bed as Sam began to brush, working out a few tangles.

"That feels good. I could almost go to sleep," Haley said.

"You can sleep on the way home," Sam said.

"After McDonald's," Haley said.

Sam grinned. "You are as addicted as Robbie was to those sausage-egg burritos. Remember?"

There was a quick tug of sadness, and then Haley let it go. "Yes, I remember. He was such a fun kid, wasn't he, Sam?"

Sam stifled a sigh. Like Haley, there was always a pang of longing that came with remembering.

"He was the best."

Haley stayed within the silence that came afterward without feeling dismay, and by the time they came with papers for her to sign, her hair was up and her flip-flops were on her feet.

"Since you have a long drive to get home, Dr. Wyman sent this one-day supply of pain meds to take with you, and then a prescription you can get filled at your convenience."

"Thank you. That's very thoughtful of him," Haley said.

"He's a good guy, besides being an awesome doctor," the nurse said. "Safe travels. An orderly is coming with a wheelchair to take you down."

Haley sighed. More waiting.

A few minutes later, an orderly arrived with the wheelchair. Sam settled Haley in it, then put her tote bag in her lap. He had his backpack on his shoulder, and was carrying the suitcase with her new clothes.

As they started out the door, the orderly paused and pointed to the potted plant still sitting on the windowsill.

"Aren't you going to take your flowers?"

Haley shook her head. "They weren't really for me," she said, and wrapped her arms around the tote bag to keep it from toppling over.

Sam stayed beside her, going down in the elevator, then through the lobby to the front exit.

"We'll wait in here where it's cool until you bring your car up. Then I'll bring her out," the orderly said.

Sam glanced around the lobby. "Okay, but make sure she isn't approached by strangers. We've already had one reporter scare her, trying to get an interview."

The orderly frowned. "I'm on it. No worries."

"I'm fine," Haley said. "Go."

Sam was out the door in seconds.

Haley watched him running, and then momentarily closed her eyes. This entire experience had been a nightmare from start to finish, but it had also brought Sam back into her life. The reward was greater than the sum of all she had endured.

"There he is," the orderly said.

Haley blinked. "It's a Hummer."

"A really nice one, too," the orderly said, and wheeled her through the doors and out into the Texas heat.

Sam took the tote bag off her lap and put it in the floor of the front seat.

"That is one big vehicle," she said.

"It was the size and weight of it that got me through Hurricane Gladys and here to you," he said, then helped her up into the front seat, and fastened her seat belt.

The cool air was already blasting in Haley's face as Sam got inside and shut the door.

"May I say how beautiful you look sitting in the seat beside me?" he said.

Haley grinned. "You can say it, but we both know I'm a far shot from beautiful right now."

"Temporary stuff," he said, and drove away from the hospital, straight to the nearest McDonalds.

They left Nacogdoches, eating breakfast burritos with hot sauce, and washing them down with big cups of Dr. Pepper.

Santos was walking back to his casa from the marketplace when he received a text from Miles Rafferty. He sat down on a bench in front of a jewelry store catering to tourists to read it. It was the information he'd asked for regarding Sam Quaid, which made him happy, but then his smile ended as he read the rest of the text. Miles was moving shortly, he appreciated working for him, but he would no longer be available for source work.

Santos wasn't particularly happy about that, but Miles was only a worker bee, and there were hundreds more just like him, willing to do anything for the right price.

Now that he knew how to locate the private investigator in Dallas, he was putting a professional on the job. He wanted a face-to-face with Haley Quaid.

That meant going back to Texas, which was risky. He didn't know if the Feds knew anything about his identity, But Dude was a risk taker, and two millions dollars was a worthy prize.

Some of the roads Sam had taken to get to Houston were no longer open due to flooding. He had to back-track more than once to find safe travel, and in the process, Haley had seen all of the storm damage she ever wanted to see firsthand, and kept nodding off.

As soon as Sam noticed, he pulled over to get a blanket out of the back of the Hummer, then showed her how to recline her seat before he covered her up.

"That feels wonderful," Haley mumbled. Lulled by the sound of the wheels on pavement, the weight of the blanket and the cool air in her face, she was out.

The farther Sam drove away from the surrounding areas of Houston, the more traffic he encountered. Evidence that life was slowly returning to normal.

He was two hours down the road before the fuel gage on his second tank prompted him to stop. He was almost at the truck stop he'd used on his way down, so when he came up to that exit, he took it.

The change in speed roused Haley as Sam pulled up to the pumps. "I assume you need a restroom," he said, and she nodded. "As soon as I refuel, I'll drive us closer to the station, and we'll both go in."

He got a credit card from his wallet and got out to refuel. A man on the other side of the pumps glanced at him and nodded, then did a double take.

Dammit. Sam wondered how long it would take for people to forget his face, and he hadn't shaved but once since they reached the hospital, so the black beard from the film clip was more or less back in place. It would help if the media would quit showing that footage.

Determined not to let it bother him, he ignored the guy, who finally finished and drove away, and as soon as his tanks were topped off, he drove up to the station, and then got Haley out the same way he'd put her in.

When her feet touched the pavement, she groaned.

"Are you okay?" Sam asked.

"Just stiff," she said.

"Then hang on to my arm until you loosen up."

She didn't hesitate to take him up on the offer.

Haley's appearance was already drawing stares, and Sam was getting a few dirty looks. Haley overheard a comment about wife beaters as he was walking her back to the bathroom.

When Haley stopped, the woman who'd said it looked defiant, as if daring Haley to dispute the obvious.

"Look, lady, Sam didn't do this to me, but he saved me from the people who did, so shut your mouth."

The woman flushed. "I'm sorry, I just thought—"

Haley interrupted. "No, ma'am, you weren't thinking...you just opened your mouth and started talking, and it was so far off the truth that I was insulted for him, okay?"

Sam slid an arm across her shoulders. "Come on, honey. It doesn't matter, okay?"

"Mattered to me," she snapped, and then as quickly as her anger flared, her energy waned, as they kept walking toward the back of the store.

The restrooms were side by side. Haley glanced around the area before she went inside.

Sam guessed she was remembering that damn reporter.

"I'll be out here waiting for you," he said, and as soon as she went into the ladies' room, he darted into the one for men. As soon as he was out, he resumed his wait near the door.

She came out pale and shaky.

Sam was worried. "Honey…?"

"I'm okay. Just weak. Maybe if I get something cold to drink…with ice?"

Sam cupped the back of her head and pulled her close. "Want me to take you to the car, first?"

"No, no, I'm not that weak."

"Just hang on," he said.

Haley was picking out some snacks, and Sam was right behind her getting their drinks, when she heard someone say, "Hey, ain't you the guy who was rescued outa that flooded house?"

She turned. Sam hadn't answered and was putting lids on their cold drinks and stuffing straws in his shirt pocket as fast as he could, but the man was persistent.

"I know it's you, because I seen that video a lot."

"I'm ready," Haley said.

"I've got the drinks," Sam added, and as they

started toward the register, the man saw Haley, put two and two together, yanked the baseball cap off his head and lowered his voice.

"Ma'am, ma'am, are you Haley Quaid? I'm right sorry what happened to you, but in my house, we all think you're a real Wonder Woman. God bless you. Hope you heal up soon."

Haley didn't know what to say and just nodded, and kept following Sam up to pay.

By now, almost every patron near the front of the store had heard what was being said, and Sam could tell by the looks on their faces that they were all curious. A couple of people had pulled out their phones and were even videoing them. All he could do was get them out as fast as possible.

The clerk was staring at Haley when she put their snacks up on the counter. Sam leaned across it and lowered his voice.

"Lady...for God's sake, just check us out."

She blinked, then hastily did as he asked.

When they headed for the door, yet another patron jumped ahead of them.

"I'll get that door for you," he said, and held it open as Haley walked past.

"Thanks," Sam said, and unlocked the doors of the Hummer with the remote, set the cold drinks in the console cup holders, then helped Haley back up into the passenger seat.

"I need a ladder to get in and out of this," Haley said.

"You don't need a ladder, baby. You have me," Sam said.

He was already inside and starting the engine when Haley glanced up. The storefront was lined with people watching them.

"Sam! They're all staring at us. Are you kidding me?"

He grinned. "Fame is fleeting. As soon as your bruises fade, you'll be good to go." Then he backed up and drove right back onto the interstate, still Dallas-bound.

A little over two hours later, they were driving on a Dallas freeway, headed for Sam's house. Everything they passed was familiar, street exits, restaurants, businesses and the familiar skyline of Dallas. Haley felt like she'd been away on a long, long trip, and was finally coming home.

"So, is it weird being back here?" Sam asked, as he maneuvered a lane change.

Haley shook her head. "It just feels…normal."

"That's how it feels having you in the seat beside me," Sam said. "It will be even better waking up in a house with you in it again."

Haley hesitated, then asked. "Do you still live in our old house?"

He shook his head. "Too many memories. I sold it right after you left. I live in a different area of the city now. Even though it's nothing like our old house was, I think you'll like it."

"I'll like anything with you in it," she said. "I wish I knew what was happening with my apartment, like is the power still out? Did any windows break? Everything in the refrigerator will be a disgusting mess."

"One thing at a time, baby. We'll deal with it all when it's safe to return, okay?"

She nodded. "I've been trying off and on to reach Rhoda Bates. She's the secretary from the realty office, and the one I called after I regained consciousness in the house."

"If she's had any access to media at all, she's bound to know what happened to you," Sam said.

"That's what I keep telling myself," Haley said. "She's really nice, and so is Mr. Truman, who owns the realty company."

"Will you be afraid to continue in that job?"

"You mean because of being hurt, or the men who broke in?"

"I don't know, honey," Sam said. "I would think it's all one in the same for you right now."

Haley sighed. "I haven't thought about it like that, but I do like the job itself, and whatever hang-ups I might have at first will be temporary. Maybe because I don't feel like a victim."

"That's because you fought back, Haley. You didn't roll over and quit. You kept fighting to live."

Tears quickened, but Haley blinked them away. "I did, didn't I?"

"Yes, ma'am, you sure did," Sam said, and then took the exit to their right. "It's not far now. We're almost home."

* * *

Dude Santos was making plans to cross the border back into Texas, but a little uncertain as to where to go. He'd always maintained his stateside headquarters in Houston, but at the moment, that wasn't possible, and the woman he wanted was in Dallas. It was only logic that led him to begin a search there. He'd been online for two hours, looking for a property to lease in an upscale area of the city, when his phone rang. He glanced at Caller ID and then smiled. Finally, his Dallas contractor was returning his call.

"Buenos dias."

"Same to you, Dude. It's been a while. What can I do for you?"

He began outlining what he wanted, and that he would be in the Dallas area within the week. The caller listened, then clarified the request.

"You want me to snatch this woman, Haley Quaid, and bring her to you?"

"Yes, but I'm not settled there yet. Stake out the location. Get a feel for their routine. You know how it goes. I'll let you know when I'm ready. I'll give you an address. You bring her to me," Dude said.

"What do you want me to do with her once you're done?"

"I don't leave witnesses," Dude said.

"Understood."

Eleven

Mae Arnold had just finished ironing Pete's good shirt and sewed down a button on his suit coat that was about to come loose. The undertaker told her she wouldn't need to bring in the clothes until tomorrow morning, but she wanted it all done and ready to go when she woke up.

She guessed word must be getting around about Pete's death. Their home phone kept ringing, but she wasn't of a mind to answer it yet. Whoever it was could call back if it was important.

She wandered through the house, at a loss as what to do next. Without anyone to care for, she was a woman without purpose. While she was standing in the kitchen thinking about making herself a glass of sweet tea, the grandfather clock in the hall began to strike. Six o'clock. It was too early for evening chores, but she needed something to do.

"I reckon I'll go put the chickens up," Mae said,

and took her sun hat with her as she went out the back door.

The hog they were fattening up to butcher grunted as Mae walked past the lot.

"I hear you, but you're gonna have to wait your turn," she said.

She moved about the barnyard, doing the chores Pete usually did. Chickens got fed and shut up for the night. The old milk cow was dry, but came up to the barn every evening out of habit and went right into the milk stall for a scoop of grain.

On the way back to the house, Mae stopped to feed the hog. He was big, as duroc hogs were inclined to be. Her daddy had always raised the big red pigs, and when Mae and Pete got married, her daddy had gifted them with a boar and two sows. They'd had durocs ever since.

She mixed up the hog feed and poured it in the trough, then stood listening to him grunt and chomp, making a mess in true pig fashion. As she stood watching him eat, a big chicken hawk flew over the back of the hog lot.

"Too late!" she shouted. "You don't get any of my little biddies tonight."

When she began to shout, the hog stopped eating and looked up at Mae.

"I'm not yelling at you," she said, then leaned over the fence and scratched behind his ear. "Pete's dead," she said, her voice trembling from the horror of her predicament. "I thought you'd want to know."

Then she straightened up and wiped her hands on her apron, before making her way back. She paused at the back gate and stared at the house. She'd never slept one night without Pete in the bed beside her since the night they were married. The pain in her chest was incessant, but it was a sad pain, not one that would take her to Jesus. She took a deep, shaky breath.

"I don't know if I can do this without you, Pete, but I have been given no other choice. I sure wish it had been me instead of you."

"We're here," Sam said, as he pulled up into the driveway of a long, single-story ranch-style house.

"Oh, Sam, it's beautiful, and I love these big trees," Haley said.

"I think you're going to love the interior, as well," he said, and pressed the remote to open one of the two garage doors. He pulled into the garage, and then killed the engine and gave her hand a quick squeeze. "I left here in a cold panic, afraid I would not get to you in time, never dreaming we would be coming back together."

"It was a close call, wasn't it?" she said.

"I don't want to think about how close it was. So, let's get you inside out of this hot garage. I'll come back and get the bags in a few minutes."

Haley was just glad to have reached the destination, and waited for Sam to help her out. When he opened the door, the smile in his eyes said it all. All she could think was how lucky she was to have been given this second chance.

Once she was standing on two feet, Sam led her into the house, pausing to disarm the security system.

Haley watched him punching in a sequence of four numbers. "Hey, isn't that my birthday?"

"Yep, seven, three, eighty-four, so you shouldn't have a problem remembering it." He swung the door inward. "After you."

Haley walked into a laundry/utility room, then straight into an open-concept area with a living area at one end of a long room, a dining table at the other end, and a large updated kitchen and island between them. The lower cabinets were gray, the upper cabinets were white. The backsplash was white subway tile with black quartz countertops that looked like marble. The stainless steel appliances were top-of-the-line, including a gas stove with two ovens.

Sam watched her eyes widening as she took it all in and smiled to himself. *She likes it!*

"You can explore the whole house to your heart's content, but I want to show you the bedrooms. There's a master and three other bedrooms, all with walk-in closets and en suite bathrooms. You can take your pick."

It was an immediate gesture to Haley that she was going to be the one to set the tone for renewing their relationship. Part of her appreciated his thoughtfulness, and part of her wished he'd taken the decision out of her hands. Instead, he took her on a tour, leaving the master bedroom for last.

"And this is the master," he said.

Haley's heart skipped a beat as they walked in. "It's our bedroom suite from before!"

He nodded.

She moved around the room, running her hands over the carvings on the bedposts, on the night stands and then the dresser, while Sam stood near the doorway, watching—waiting.

Haley turned to face him. "Why did you keep this?"

Sam told nothing but the truth. "Because this is the last place I slept with you, and I didn't want to lose it, too."

Haley shivered. "So, I get to pick where I want to sleep?"

He nodded. "Totally your choice."

"Then I choose this and I choose you," she said, and walked into his arms.

Sam hugged her. "Thank you, darlin'. And when you're well, we can change the sleeping together to revisiting our honeymoon."

"It will be the beginning of the new us," she said.

He grinned. The chemistry between them had always been there. For them, some things never changed. "I'm going to unload our stuff from the car. Why don't you go check out the rest of the house while I'm doing it."

He headed back to the garage as Haley went into

the living room, and straight to the fireplace. She loved gas fireplaces and always considered them a plus in houses she was showing, although Houston rarely had need of extra warmth to heat a house.

There was a flat screen television in a cabinet above the fireplace and recliners placed strategically for prime viewing. She sat down in one and raised the footrest to try it for comfort. It felt good to be where it was quiet. She could hear Sam moving through the house and closed her eyes, secure in the knowledge she was safe.

Sam found her a few minutes later, sound asleep in his recliner, her flip-flops on the floor where they'd fallen off her feet. Her ankle didn't appear to be as swollen as it had been, her bruises were in different hues and fading, some faster than others. The cut on her cheek still had the stitches, but it was already in a state of healing, as was the cut on her head. Even though she looked like she'd been in a riot, all he saw was his girl.

"My poor sweetheart," he said, and got an afghan from the back of the sofa and covered her up just as the air conditioner kicked on.

He glanced out the window in time to see his neighbor Louise coming toward his house. She was somewhere in her fifties, graying hair and a little on the short and stocky side, with a tendency to go overboard when it came to sunbathing, which explained the nut-brown hue to her skin. But she was a great neighbor, and he liked her.

He slipped out the front door so as not to wake Haley with their conversation and met her on the porch.

"Hi, Louise, thanks for bringing in the mail," he said.

She frowned. "You're welcome. I'm glad to see you still in one piece. That was quite a sight you made, swinging from that harness beneath a chopper."

He grinned. "You liked that, did you?"

She snorted. "The thumbs-up was a nice touch." Then she added, "Without being nosy, which we both know I am, how is the Haley Quaid who was rescued out of that house related to you?"

"She's my ex-wife. I brought her home with me to heal."

Louise's eyes widened in surprise. In the whole three years she'd known him, she'd never even seen another woman in his house. "Is she staying?"

"Lord, I hope so," Sam said. "Right now, it's all systems go for that to happen, but she's pretty battered, and went through some terrible stuff before I got to her."

Louise shook her head. "I'm really sorry she was hurt. If there's anything I can do…like stay with her if you're going back to work, or whatever…just let me know."

"Thank you. That's really sweet of you, but I don't plan to go back to work just yet."

Louise nodded. "Okay, then, but keep me in mind if you have the need. The offer stays open." And then she turned around and went back the way she'd come.

Sam slipped back inside, carefully relocking the door. With Haley fast asleep, he decided to get all the dirty clothes out of his backpack and put them in to wash. One task led to another, and then another, and before he realized it almost two hours had passed and he thought he heard the television turn on, so Haley was awake.

"Hey, sleepyhead," Sam said, as he saw her getting up.

"I can't believe I slept so long. What have I missed?"

"This," he said, and gave her a hug. "So what sounds good for dinner tonight? We'll need to order in because I'll have to shop before there's food to cook."

"You pick," Haley said. "The only decision I'm capable of making is that I want to take a shower."

"You know where the master bathroom is. I put your stuff in the bathroom and hung your clothes up in the closet. Your undies are in the third drawer down in the dresser. You have a small bottle of shampoo in the stuff I bought you. Do you need any help?"

"No, I can manage, but thank you. I'm not used to being babied."

"You're due a little babying, honey. Go do your thing. It will take a good hour or more for the food to get here anyway. You sure you don't care what it is?"

"I'm sure," she said, then trailed her finger down the side of his jaw, before leaving the room.

Sam watched her leave, and then went to the cabinet and pulled out a stack of menus from different eating places in the area and began shuffling through them, trying to decide if he'd order pizza, barbecue or Chinese.

As Haley moved through the house, seeing all the bits and pieces of Sam's world, she could see her absence in his life. The places where she might have added a little bit of color or warmth to enhance it for her were unnecessary to him. It was a reminder that she hadn't come back to jump into their old life. He was offering her residence and love within the world that had become his.

And then she walked back into the master bedroom and paused, smiling. She was still present in here. This was the part of their life together that had meant enough to him to keep.

Even when love broke, it didn't die.

She shed her clothes beside a hamper and then walked barefoot into the bathroom, gathering up things as she went. The water was almost instantly hot, so she adjusted the temperature to suit herself and stepped into the shower with shampoo and a wash cloth. The showerhead was huge, showering her all over as she stepped beneath the jets. As soon as her hair was thoroughly drenched, she poured shampoo into her palm, then began gently scrubbing it into her hair and down the long, dark length of it, washing and rinsing, then washing and rinsing it again, removing every vestige of what she had endured.

When her hair was finally clean, she twisted it into a rope and clipped it to the top of her head so she could shower her body. Again, the simple act of cleansing her skin was a release of the degradation she felt every time she saw her face in a mirror, even though none of what had happened was her fault.

First she'd had an accident.

And then she was attacked.

If it hadn't been for Sam, it would have been the end of her life. She would never take safety or comfort for granted again.

By the time she was out of the shower and drying her hair, she felt human again. Her hair was still damp when she put the dryer away and hurried to get dressed. At this point in her healing, the soft fabric of shorts and a tee were the height of comfort, and going barefoot beat trying to squeeze her sore foot into a shoe. She left the bedroom, curious as to what they were having for dinner.

Sam looked up as she passed his office. "Hey, honey, I'm in here."

Haley backtracked and then paused in the doorway.

"I have never appreciated clean hair and a shower as much. I finally feel human again."

Sam grinned. "I can tell. You smell delicious."

"It's that lemon shampoo. You have yummy tastes, Sam Quaid."

"I always thought so," he said, admiring her leggy, clean-scrubbed beauty. Then his phone signaled a text. He glanced down. "You timed your entrance perfectly. Our food has arrived. The delivery service is on his way to the front door."

"What are we having?" she asked.

"It's a surprise," Sam said, and then loped through the living area to answer the door. He returned with two sacks and a smile. "Follow me, Haley Jo. You won't regret it."

She could smell the barbecue from where she was standing, and when he headed into the kitchen, she was right behind him.

Dude Santos was packing. He'd leased a townhome from a Dallas Realtor and already wired the money, with the understanding that all of the utilities and amenities would be on and ready for him to enjoy. He'd flown from Houston to Cozumel, so he was flying back into the States as well, but couldn't get the flight out he wanted for another day.

He'd checked with his Houston lawyer to make sure there were no pending arrest warrants in his name. To his knowledge, no one knew he was the third man connected to the heist. Once he was certain he wouldn't be arrested upon entering the US again, he was itching to get there.

He'd gotten one text from Ledbetter, the assassin he'd hired, stating the target had arrived, and a stakeout was in progress. Now all Dude had to do was get there.

Realistically, he had accepted that this subterfuge might all be for nothing, because if the Quaid woman heard nothing, then she was useless. It was a chance he was willing to take.

Since he still had to kill time here for another day,

he called Marigrace and invited her to dinner. Her appetite for food was matched only by her appetite for sex. All he had to do was wine her and dine her, and she was good for an all-nighter in the sack.

As the dinner hour neared he jumped in his car and drove away from his casa, making his way through the city into the old part of Cozumel where Marigrace lived.

She was obviously watching for him, because she came out without waiting for him to come to the door, strutting toward the car with a sway in her hips that promised much in the hours to come.

Dude took a deep breath, then exhaled slowly. "Pacing," he muttered. "She's going to be hot out of the gate, and quick to fire…just like I like them."

Then the door opened, and Marigrace leaned in, smiling as she took her seat, then leaned over to give Dude a slow kiss, sliding her hand up Dude's leg all the way to his crotch as she greeted him.

"I am so glad you called," she said, admiring the contrast of a white shirt against his darker skin.

"And I'm happy you were free to join me," Dude said.

"Always," Marigrace said. "Anything for you."

Dude shivered with anticipation.

Mae Arnold was making herself a glass of sweet tea when she heard a car coming down the driveway. She set it aside and went to the living room to peek out the window. When she recognized the car, she groaned. Preacher Riley and his wife, Pearl. She wasn't in the mood to be prayed over, but that's what was about to happen. They parked and got out, each wearing an extremely pious expression. Mae groaned again when she saw Pearl carrying a pie. Nobody liked Pearl Riley's cooking.

She waited until they knocked and then smoothed down her hair and opened the door.

"Preacher… Pearl… Come in."

"We're real sorry about Pete. Pearl brought a pie," Preacher said.

"Thank you on both accounts," Mae said, as Pearl put it in her hands.

"It's peach, and the crust is Mama's recipe."

"The one with vinegar?" Mae asked.

Pearl nodded.

Oh, Pete, be glad you're not gonna have to eat this. "Thank you again," Mae said. "Please come in and take a seat. I'll just put this in the kitchen."

They moved right to the sofa as Mae left the room. She put the pie down on the counter, took a deep breath, and then went back and sat down in a chair across from where they were seated.

Preacher leaned just the tiniest bit forward as he shifted into his preacher voice. It was soft, kind and a tiny bit condescending.

"What can I do for you, Mae? I know you must feel overwhelmed about all you've been called to face."

Mae clasped her hands across her middle. "I don't really need any help, except in burying my man."

"Of course," Preacher said. "Have you chosen a day for the services?"

"He hasn't been gone even eight hours. I've been getting his clothes ready to bury him in. I'll take them in to the funeral home tomorrow and work all that out."

Preacher Riley flushed. "Of course. The main reason Pearl and I are here is to express our condolences and to pray with you."

Mae sighed. He was gonna make her cry and she didn't want to, not in front of people. Sure enough, he and Pearl stood up and walked behind the chair where she was sitting. She felt hands on both her shoulders. Preacher cleared his throat and raised his voice.

"Lord, Lord, shine your healing light upon this poor widow woman and ease her aching heart," he began.

Mae bit her lip and bowed her head.

Special Agent Jack Gordon and his partner, Special Agent Lloyd Townsend, were at their desks late, finishing up paperwork on a federal case they'd just closed.

Jack was going through a stack of messages, while Lloyd was saving his report to File. Jack noticed a message from the US Marshals Office and set it aside, and then noticed a second one from one of the marshals at a later date.

"Hey, Lloyd, do we know why a US Marshal

named Landry would be calling us? I have two different messages from their office," Jack said.

Lloyd signed off his computer and got up. "No, but it's late. Won't it keep until tomorrow?"

Jack frowned. "One message, maybe. Two messages, not likely."

He quickly punched in the phone number, then leaned back in his chair, thinking about prime rib from his favorite steak house for dinner when his call was answered.

"Hello. This is Landry."

"Marshal Landry, this is Special Agent Jack Gordon returning your call. We've been out on a case for a couple of days and are just now back in the office. Sorry for the delay."

"No problem," Landry said. "Just wanted to give you some new info. You are aware our Marshals Service was transporting Roy Baker and Hershel Arnold when they escaped."

"Yes. I heard you lost one marshal and another one was crippled. That's a real tough break. And like everyone else, I saw the Marshals Service carrying two body bags out of a flooded house. I assume they were your escaped prisoners?"

"Yes, but that's not the reason I called. What you may or may not know is that a woman, a Realtor, had also become trapped in the house they sheltered in. She was already injured when they found her. She shot both of them before they caught her and tied her to a bed. Then they beat and terrorized her until she was rescued."

"We saw the Life Flight rescue on TV. So she was the one in the litter?" Jack asked.

"Yes. They were all in the same room together, and one of the men was dying. She could hear any and everything they were talking about. I just thought you might want to interview her and see if she overheard anything about money or where they hid it."

"That I did not know," Jack said. "And yes, we would be extremely interested in talking to her. What's her name and where did they take her?" Jack asked.

"Her name is Haley Quaid. They took her to Nacogdoches Medical Center, but she's already been released. Her ex-husband, Sam Quaid, is the man who rescued her and took out Roy Baker. He took her back to Dallas with him."

"Do you have contact info?"

"Yes, you want to do this old-school and write it down, or do you want it in a text message so it'll be in your phone?"

"Text it, and thanks for the heads-up, Marshal. It would be a plus to recover that money."

Lloyd was still there when Jack disconnected.

"What was that all about?" he asked.

"Confirmation that the two bodies in the body bags were our missing prisoners, Baker and Arnold."

"Didn't we already know this?" Lloyd asked.

"Pretty much. And we also knew they took a

woman hostage while they were in the house, but what we didn't know is that they were all three together in the same room until she was rescued. Landry suggested we might want to talk to her and see if she overheard them ever talk about money or hiding money."

Now Lloyd was interested. "We are going to talk to her, right?"

"Absolutely," Jack said. "But she's been taken to Dallas to recuperate. I have contact info. How about I call this evening, and see if she'll talk to me over the phone. It'll save us a trip if she's able. I'll let you know details after we talk."

"Works for me," Lloyd said. "But if we have to go up to Dallas, don't make it tomorrow. It's Trey's eighth birthday. I missed the last one because of work. I don't want to disappoint him again."

"Understood," Jack said, and took a twenty dollar bill out of his wallet and handed it to Lloyd. "Tell Trey that Uncle Jack says Happy Birthday, and to eat a piece of cake for him, too."

Lloyd smiled. "Will do, and thanks, partner. Expect a thank-you card. His mama is big on social graces."

"Too bad her manners didn't rub off on you," Jack said, and then punched Lloyd on the arm as they headed out the door.

Sam knew when Haley went back for a third rib that barbecue had been the right choice, but he couldn't tease her because he had just finished number six. They'd eaten most of the French fries, and made a big dent in the container of coleslaw.

"You sure made an inroad in that hot barbecue sauce."

Haley wiped a bit of barbecue sauce from the corner of her mouth.

"You hooked me on hot," she said, and then smirked at the pleased grin on his face.

"I need something cold to drink after that remark," Sam said. "Want some more ice tea?"

Haley nodded. "Yes, please, and more ice?"

"You got it," he said, and got up to refill their glasses. He was on his way back to the table with them when his cell phone rang.

"Hello."

"Hello, my name is Special Agent Jack Gordon of the FBI. To whom am I speaking?"

"I'm Sam Quaid."

"Is Haley Quaid at your residence?"

"Yes, she is," Sam said.

"Would it be possible for me to speak with her?" Gordon asked.

"Just a moment," Sam said, and handed his phone to Haley. "Special Agent Gordon of the FBI. He wants to talk to you."

An instant knot of anxiety rolled through Haley so fast it made her shudder. She put down her fork and pushed her plate aside and took the phone.

"This is Haley Quaid."

"Ms. Quaid, I first want to express my regret as to

what you endured at the hands of Roy Baker and Hershel Arnold. I hope you are on the road to recovery."

"Yes, I am, and thank you," Haley said.

"I also understand that for the length of time you were taken hostage, you were in the same room with them."

"Yes, I was. The room had twin beds. Hershel was in one of them, incapacitated by the bullet I put in his shoulder. Roy tied me up to the other bed.

"Did they talk among themselves much?"

"Not a lot. Roy couldn't stop Hershel's wound from bleeding. Hershel was mostly out of his head."

"Do you remember anything of what they were talking about?" Jack asked.

"Um…a lot of muttering from Hershel about someone needing to call his mama."

Jack sighed. This wasn't what he'd hoped to hear. "Can you remember anything else? Even the smallest details?"

"Once before they found me, I heard them arguing in the hall. One said something about having hid money, and the other said Duke…no, it was Dude… Dude Santos was going to kill them if he found out they'd betrayed him."

Jack's pulse kicked. They'd just gotten the name of the third man. Hot damn!

"Did they say what they did with the money?"

"Umm, I don't— Oh wait. Yes, one of them said something to the effect that it was at his place—at home."

"Could you tell which one said that?"

"No. I was hiding. I couldn't see them. I only heard them," Haley said.

"Can you remember anything else?" Jack asked.

"Hershel said he was going to die. He wanted to call his mama and he said something about his things. I don't remember anything else," Haley said.

"I really appreciate this, Haley. If you do remember anything else, give me a call, and thank you."

"You're welcome," Haley said.

"Could you please hand the phone back to Sam for a moment?"

"He wants to talk to you, again," she said, and gave Sam the phone.

"This is Sam."

"There's something you need to know. There were three men in on the armored car robbery. One got away and we had no idea who he was, and the money has never been found. Haley just verified for us the name of the third man. So, if we thought Haley might have overheard something that would help us find the money, then there is a possibility that this Dude Santos might be thinking the same thing."

"Is she in danger?" Sam asked.

"Maybe," Jack said.

Sam frowned. "You mind sending me a picture of Dude Santos? I prefer to know what my enemies look like."

"Sure thing," Jack said.

"Okay, thanks for the heads-up," Sam said.

"Haley gave us some good tips. If we can find the money, then the pressure is off her for good."

"Then get after it," Sam said. "She's been through enough already."

"Agreed," Jack said. "I'll be in touch."

Twelve

Haley could tell by the look on Sam's face that whatever the agent said had upset him. "What's wrong?"

Sam didn't hesitate. "He suggested you might be in danger. There was one other man in on the robbery and they double-crossed him, remember? There is a slight possibility that this Dude Santos might want to find you, too."

Haley gasped. "To see if I overheard where they hid the money?"

Sam nodded, and watched Haley's face lose all expression.

"Should I be afraid?" she said.

"I would say we should be cautious until that money is recovered or at least until the other man is arrested."

"Oh my God, I thought this was over," she muttered.

"Come here," Sam said, and pulled her up from her chair into his arms. "Do you trust me?" he asked.

"Yes."

"Then know that I've got this. Remember what I do for a living, baby. I can spot the bad guys and fakes a mile away."

Haley felt the calm within him and relaxed.

"I remember."

"Then let it go. The Feds will go to both men's addresses and search…they'll find the money and when it hits the news, you'll be off the hook."

"Yes, you're right," Haley said.

"So, let's finish doing the dishes. If you want, we can go out by the pool for a while, or stay inside where it's cooler and watch TV."

"Maybe the pool would be nice for a little while."

He cupped her face, looking past the fading black eyes and the healing cuts to the woman he loved beneath.

"Anything you want, Haley Jo, and when you get tired, we can have an early night. I don't know about you, but I am really looking forward to sleeping in our own bed, in an air-conditioned house."

"Agreed. I don't ever want to feel that hot and suffocated again."

Dude Santos was flat on his back in bed and spread-eagle nude, watching the black curls on Marigrace's head bobbing as she gave him a blow job. He was rock hard and throbbing—the sensation of wet, warmth and tongue was a high all its own.

She'd been at it for less than two minutes and he

already knew he couldn't make it to three. Muscles were tightening down in his belly, and the blood-rush to his groin was racing through his body at white-hot speed.

Never one to deny himself any of life's pleasures, he closed his eyes and came in a rush, the climax washing over him, one spasm after another.

When he was done, Marigrace gently cleaned him and herself, then crawled back into bed with him with a smile on her face.

She was good and she knew it.

Haley sat at the shallow end of the pool with her feet dangling in the water, watching the moon come up. Somewhere in the neighborhood she could hear the shrieks of children playing.

Sam sat beside her, holding her hand without talking. It was a comfortable silence that comes from knowing someone so well that words aren't always necessary.

Right now, Haley felt like she had been walking in a wilderness, searching for a way to be happy again. She would never have imagined that it would take a hurricane to bring Sam back into her life, but she was forever grateful.

The far-off wail of a siren broke the ambiance of the night. Haley sighed and leaned against Sam's shoulder.

"What are you thinking?" he asked.

"How easy this is," she said.

He pulled her closer.

"It's because there is love still between us," he said.

Haley nodded, letting the words settle safely in her heart.

Sam gave her a quick hug. "What do you want to do tomorrow, sweetheart?"

"Nothing. I want to do absolutely nothing until I can go out among people without causing a scene."

Sam chuckled. "Good idea, since you are such a rabble-rouser."

She grinned. "You know what I mean."

"Yes, I do. It just struck me as funny…you causing a scene."

Haley shivered suddenly. "I have changed some, Sam. Six months of therapy dug me out of the victim mode forever. But for the dark hall in which it happened, I came close to shooting two people dead."

Sam nodded. "You're right. You are capable of causing a scene."

She pushed out from under his arm and turned to look at him. "Are you laughing at me?"

"Not *laughing* laughing," Sam said, as a wide grin spread across his face.

Haley grinned.

"See, you think it's funny, too," Sam said.

"Ah, Sam, I had forgotten how easy it is to love you. I had forgotten how much fun you are."

His smile slid sideways and then disappeared. "That's because there was damn little to laugh about the last couple of years with Robbie. It's no one's fault. It just happened. And before you get all sad and guilt-ridden again, want a nightcap? I have Bourbon Pecan Pie, and Urban Bourbon."

"That's Ben & Jerry's ice cream," she said.

Sam shrugged. "So I like my whiskey cold and sweet. What can I say?"

"Can I have a little bit of each?" Haley asked.

"Trying to drown your troubles, are you?" Sam said.

Haley shuddered. "Don't mention the word *drown*."

"My bad," Sam said. "So are we on or not?"

Haley grinned. "We're on!" she said, and took her feet out of the water and got up.

Sam led the way into the house, then got out two pints of the ice cream and two spoons to eat with, and put them on the kitchen table.

"No bowls?" Haley said.

"Heresy," Sam said, scooping up the first bite from the Urban Bourbon and aiming it at her mouth. "Open wide."

Long after they'd gone to bed, Sam was still awake watching Haley sleep and worrying about how the hell he could keep her safe from some faceless enemy willing to do anything asked of him for the right price.

She moaned in her sleep. "Don't shoot," and then jerked as if she'd been hit and woke herself up.

"You're okay, baby. It's just a dream."

"Dream," she mumbled, and then sighed.

Sam scooted closer to her until her entire body was resting against him, and pulled the lightweight covers up over her shoulders. As if complicit in the need to give her comfort, the air conditioner kicked on. He felt the tension in her muscles, but as she fell deeper asleep, her body went limp, until her entire body was resting against Sam, right where she belonged.

Ledbetter had become an assassin because it was easy. The Santos job was straightforward. Study the routine in the Quaid house, and when the opportunity arose, snatch the woman and take her to him. When he was finished with her, make her disappear.

But in this Dallas neighborhood, there was no way to stake out the house without being out of place. This called for removing a resident from one of the houses, and then taking up temporary residence as a house sitter. Nothing out of the ordinary about that. But which house? One next door to the Quaid house, or one from across the street?

After a bit of reconnoitering, the houses on either side were ruled out because of too many kids. So who in the area lived alone? It didn't take long to figure out that Louise Bell, the middle-aged woman from across the street, was divorced.

Target identified.

Next step: removal.

Haley woke up in bed alone, but she could smell fresh coffee, so she knew where to find Sam.

She threw back the covers and headed to the bathroom, emerging a few minutes later with her hair and teeth brushed. She got dressed all but for shoes and headed to the kitchen.

She heard Sam's voice before she saw him, and shivered with sudden longing to make love with him again.

Sam heard her footsteps in the hall and quickly ended his conversation with his secretary, Deborah, then turned just as she appeared in the doorway.

He grinned. "Good morning, sunshine!"

Haley smiled. "Morning, Sam. I had a little sleep-in, didn't I?"

He wrapped her up in a hug, and then went in for a kiss.

"Yum, you taste minty fresh," he said. "I was just about to scramble some eggs. Do you want toast or a toasted bagel?"

"Umm, toasted bagel, but I can do that if you do eggs. Just a couple for me."

"Add four for me and we're cooking. I'll take two toasted bagels, and orange juice is in the fridge, glasses in the cabinet over the dishwasher."

They worked in unison, each tending their own tasks, until they sat down to eat.

"Hey, honey, want to take a ride to my office with me after we finish breakfast?"

When she hesitated, he added, "Only one employee besides me, my secretary, Deborah. She knows all about what we've both been up to and is super nice."

Haley didn't even hesitate. "I'd love to see where you work."

"Good…right answer, because I don't intend to leave you alone until this missing money thing is over. If you go looking for your phone, it's plugged in on the side table in our bedroom."

"Thank you. I want to try calling Rhoda again. She might have a handle on the flood situation. I'm hoping she's okay and her home escaped flood damage."

"Did you have a large circle of friends in Houston?" Sam asked.

Haley shook her head, and reached for the jelly to spread on her bagel.

Sam knew that look. "Did you have any friends you hung out with?"

"Not really. I was all about the job. I won several regional awards for most sales," she said.

"Congratulations!" Sam said. "Does your realty company have a branch office here in Dallas?"

"Yes. When I can, I want to go back to work. I'm actually good at that job."

"Honey, I am not the least bit surprised. You've always been good at everything you did."

"Thank you, Sam. That means a lot to me," she said.

"Want some more coffee?" he asked as he got up for a refill.

She shook her head. "No, thanks, I'm good."

A short while later, Haley was changing the shorts she'd put on for a pair of jeans, and got out her red flats to see if the swelling in her foot was down enough to wear them again. To her delight, she could.

She went through her purse to reorganize what Roy Baker had done to her things. Thanks to Sam, who'd gathered up everything from that room, she had all of her credit cards, a small amount of cash, her driver's license and her debit card. Cash was accessible from any ATM.

Sam breezed into the bedroom. "You beat me," he said. "I have to change my shirt, then I'll be ready, too."

Then he pulled the T-shirt he was wearing over his head and laid it on the back of a chair before going into the closet.

Haley flinched as she eyed his bare torso. The sight of that scar on his side was still shocking. He came out wearing a knit shirt in cranberry red, and was checking his wallet, counting cash.

"If you're going to an ATM, I need to get some cash," Haley said.

Sam gave her a thumbs-up. "Easy request to fill. There's an ATM in the lobby of my office building. Are you ready to go?"

She nodded, grabbed her purse and followed him out into the hall.

Sam could tell she was a little nervous, and paused in the hall to clasp her hand.

"What's wrong?" Haley asked.

Sam smiled. "Nothing's wrong. It's all good. It's

me. You. Together. It's like the first year we were married, all over again."

Haley slid her arms around his neck and this time, she was the one instigating the kiss. The warmth of his mouth against hers was intoxicating, and then he groaned, and deepened the kiss. They were both breathless when it ended.

"I love you so much," Sam said softly.

Haley sighed. "I love you, too."

They walked hand in hand into the garage, and then Sam opened the door of the Jeep Bronco.

"This is more your size, and yours to drive if you want it," he said, as she slid easily into the seat.

Haley beamed. "Really?"

"Absolutely. In my mind, I am still the stud I always imagined myself to be, and yet I never figured out how to drive two cars at once."

Haley laughed as he got into the driver's seat and hit the remote to open the garage door. They backed out into the sunshine of a new day, and then drove away, unaware of the car parked at the curb a couple of houses up.

Ledbetter watched them leaving, then started up the car and drove down the street, pulled up into Louise Bell's driveway, got out and rang the doorbell.

Louise was sitting at the kitchen table making a grocery list when she heard the doorbell. She was friendly with her neighbors, but they didn't socialize at all. Maybe it was Sam.

She opened the door. It wasn't Sam.

Her visitor was in the house before she realized her storm door was unlocked.

"What's the meaning of this? Who are you? Get out of my house—this instant!" she cried.

"That's no way to greet a guest," Ledbetter said, then karate-chopped her in the neck, which silenced her screams, whipped out a nylon stocking so fast Louise never saw it coming and wrapped it around her throat.

One fast kick to the back of Louise's knees and she fell face-forward onto the floor. Ledbetter rode her down, then straddled her butt, making it far easier to strangle the life right out of her.

Louise quit fighting almost instantly as the ligature began crushing her larynx, but Ledbetter wasn't satisfied until the hyoid bone had cracked. Now that the house was free to be used in the stakeout, all that was left was to get rid of the body.

After a quick recon of the house and exterior buildings on the property, Ledbetter chose a garden shed. The eight-foot privacy fence made it easy to get the body out of the house and into the shed unseen. Once that was accomplished, it was time to set up shop.

Sam and Haley arrived at the office building, used the ATM, then got into the elevator and rode up to the seventh floor. The frosted glass front of his office was the first thing Haley saw when they exited the elevator, and the black lettering of *Sam Quaid, Private Investigations* was big and bold. The crowning touch was the URL to his website posted in smaller lettering below.

"Wow, Sam. What a great location!" Haley said.

Sam had been waiting for her reaction, and hearing the excitement in her voice delighted him.

"Thanks," he said, and then opened the door and stepped aside. "Ladies first."

Haley walked in just as the woman behind the front desk looked up and smiled. She was short and thin, pink hair in a flashy upsweep. She reminded Haley of a miniature flamingo.

"Hey, boss, you're back!" Then she stood up and came to greet them. "This must be Haley. I'm Deb Lee, the secretary."

Haley smiled. "Nice to meet you, Deb."

"She's the hub that holds this place together," Sam said. "Thanks for all the shuffling you had to do to keep clients satisfied."

"It was just days on a calendar, boss. When they want the best, they're always willing to pay the price and wait their turn," Deb said. "I put that file you wanted on your desk, and uploaded a copy of it to your laptop, as well."

Sam gave her a thumbs-up, and then took Haley down the hall and into his office.

Haley gasped. "Sam! What a view!" she said, and

walked past him to the wall of windows overlooking the city.

He walked up beside her. "This is where I was when I got your first call. All the while we were talking, I was looking out these windows and thinking of the distance there was between us, and trying not to panic."

Haley turned to face him, but words wouldn't come, and so he held her. It was his phone ringing that ended the moment.

"Hello, this is Sam."

"Sam, it's Special Agent Jack Gordon. Just checking to make sure you got the picture and info I sent you about Santos."

"Yes, I'm in my office now."

"I just wanted you to know that we have located Alejandro Santos, aka Dude. He is back in the States. Supposedly, he left Houston because of the approaching hurricane, but his stay in Cozumel has ended. We know he flew commercial into Dallas this morning, so be aware. It could mean nothing. He can't stay in Houston because it's a disaster area and will be for months, so Dallas might have just been second choice."

"Well, hell," Sam said, as he sat down at his computer and opened the file. He was looking at a mug shot of Alejandro, aka Dude, Santos. "Thanks for calling. I'm on it."

"I have no doubt about that," Jack Gordon said. "My best to your lady."

"I'll pass it on," Sam said, and disconnected, then turned to Haley. "Special Agent Gordon sends his best."

Haley nodded. "Okay, but what did he tell you that got the 'well, hell' comment?"

Sam turned the monitor around so that Haley could see the photo. "This is a picture of the Dude Santos you heard the prisoners talking about.

Haley scanned the mug shot. "And...?"

Sam sighed. "He did evacuate Houston back to his hometown of Cozumel, Mexico, before Hurricane Gladys began causing trouble, but he left Cozumel this morning, and landed in Dallas."

Haley's stomach rolled. "Today?"

Sam nodded.

"Dammit," Haley said. "So what's the plan?"

"Wherever you go, I go, and vice versa. He may be no threat to you at all."

"But he could be?" Haley asked.

"I won't lie," Sam said. "Yes, he could be."

Haley took a deep breath. "So what do we do now?"

"We live our lives, honey."

A thousand questions were begging to be asked, but Haley sensed she'd get the same answer from Sam for all of them.

Whatever happened, he had it covered.

"Okay, then. Where do we go from here?" she asked.

"How do you feel about hitting Whole Foods?"

She shrugged. "Like we might be causing a scene, but I'm game if you are."

Sam grinned. "Then let's go shopping. I want to buy some rib eyes. I think we'll be grilling tonight."

Thirteen

Special Agent Lloyd Townsend was going through the info they had on both Roy Baker and Hershel Arnold at the time of their arrest, looking for last known place of residence. Both men had Pasadena addresses at the same apartment complex, but different room numbers. He paused, then looked around for his partner, and saw him coming back into the office.

"Jack, I have last known addresses to add to our search warrants, but I don't know how this is going to play out. They were both residents in an apartment but in different rooms on the sixth floor. It's been months since they lived there and no way to tell how many have lived there since. If there was money stashed, what are the odds that it's still there?"

Jack shrugged. "The sixth floor would not have been flooded. They wouldn't leave it lying around. It would be well hidden, and it's unlikely renters occupying an apartment in that part of the city are into cleaning and redecorating. So get the search warrants. This is the first good lead to recover the money since their arrests, but we may have to wait until the flood-waters recede before we can search."

"I'm on it," Lloyd said, and added addresses to the search warrants. All they needed now was a judge's signature.

Dude arrived to his newly leased condo within an hour of landing in Dallas. A short time later, he had his clothes unpacked and was already ordering in some food. He had no reason to hide, so he felt no threats from the law.

He was kicked back watching TV and waiting for his food delivery when he received a text. It was from Ledbetter.

Am in place and on stakeout.

"Good," Dude muttered, and then felt obliged to reply.

Whatever you do, don't bring her here. Once you have her, secure her someplace and let me know where. I'll come to you.

He got a thumbs-up emoji for his trouble and frowned. He hated that crap.

A short while later, his food arrived, and he settled down to eat.

* * *

Mae Arnold brought Pete's burying clothes in to the funeral director, then sat down as he turned to leave.

"Um, Mrs. Arnold, there's no need for you to stay. We'll call you when your husband is ready for viewing."

"How long?" Mae asked.

"Likely right after lunch."

A lone tear rolled down Mae's face. "He could dress himself in ten minutes."

"Yes, ma'am," the director said. "We just want to make sure he looks his best."

Mae nodded. "Then I'll be home waiting for your call," she said.

She went straight to the feed store to buy chicken feed and hog feed. Everyone who saw her had to stop and express their sympathies for Pete's passing, and all of them vowed to pray for her. By the time she got her purchases loaded and drove off, she was mad at Pete for dying and leaving her. Prayers weren't going to be any kind of comfort alone in the house, or tending to livestock.

Her last stop was at the local grocery store, and she knew before she went in that it was going to be more of the same emotional upheaval, and it was. She shopped quickly, paid for her purchases, then headed home.

Once she caught a glimpse of herself in the rear-view mirror and thought she'd aged ten years in less than twenty-four hours. She already looked like an old widow woman.

A couple of miles from her house, she stopped at the river bridge to let a truck pulling a cattle trailer pass. The driver waved his appreciation. She nodded.

A cardinal flew across her line of vision as she started over the bridge. She'd always heard cardinals were good luck, but the bird had showed up too late to help the situation.

When she got home, she drove straight to the feed shed to unload. The sacks were heavy, but Mae didn't have options. She was hot and mad and crying by the time she managed to get them inside the shed, and she still had to carry in the groceries, so she headed back to the house.

By now, it was nearing noon, but Mae didn't want to cook. She opened the refrigerator to see what was there ready to eat, which amounted to milk for a bowl of cereal, or cheese to go with crackers in the pantry.

Pearl Riley's peach pie was sitting on the cabinet, so she got a spoon and took a bite, crust and all. It was short on sugar in the filling, and long on vinegar in the crust. Mae made a face and washed away the bad taste with a drink of water.

"No matter," she said. "Fattenin' hog can have it. I'll settle for the cheese and crackers."

She washed up and sat down to eat, twice catching herself from calling Pete to the table, and made herself two little cracker sandwiches with some cheese she'd cut off the block. She poured herself a glass of milk to wash it down, and looked up at the rooster clock on the wall to check the time.

Ten minutes to twelve. She watched the minute hand going around the clock face, thinking how her life had come to a halt, and yet time kept ticking. She had a whole new appreciation for the phrase "time's up."

A crumb fell off the last cracker as she took a bite, and she looked down to see where it had fallen, and realized the whole front of her dress was filthy.

The feed sacks!

The phone rang. Mae got up to answer, still brushing at the front of the dress.

"Hello."

"Hello, Mrs. Arnold. This is George, from the funeral home. Did you intend to bring a tie with your husband's suit and shirt?"

"No, I did not. Pete never wore a tie. I won't bury him in one."

"Of course, no problem," George said. "Just checking. We want everything to your liking, you understand. And since you opted out of a tie, your husband is ready for viewing. However, we will not open it to the public until you see him first and give us the okay."

Mae's stomach knotted. "I'll be in shortly."

"Yes, ma'am," George said, and disconnected.

Mae stared at the receiver, wondering why funeral directors spoke in a near whisper. Did they think the dead could overhear what was being said about them?

She replaced the receiver and then remembered

her dress. She had to change to look good. She was spending the afternoon with Pete.

Ledbetter cleaned and straightened up what had been displaced during Louise's struggle, and then sprayed some lemon-scented air freshener. It always made it appear as if a house had just been cleaned, and to make the house sitter story work, the house needed to stay neat.

It would have helped to know Louise's daily routine a little better, in case a neighbor saw lights on at night that never were, or saw too many lights in a house usually dark. There was no way to tell if shades were normally pulled down, or curtains drawn. But the purpose of being here was to keep an eye on the house across the street, and the quicker Ledbetter snatched the woman, the better.

From the front window, Ledbetter could see a black Jeep slowing down in front of the house with two people inside, and when the garage door went up, it seemed apparent the woman was inside. The back end of a Hummer was also visible before the doors went down. So two vehicles to keep track of.

A timer went off in the kitchen.

The frozen pizza was done.

Ledbetter's steps bounced on the way to get the pizza out of the oven. This was nice. A great house, plenty of food and a front row seat. It damn sure beat sitting in a car and peeing in a cup to go to the bathroom.

* * *

Haley carried in the shopping bag with bread and eggs, while Sam carried in the heavy bags and put them on the counter. He noticed how Haley's steps were dragging.

"Honey, are you okay?" he asked, as he took the bread bag out of her hand.

"I'm just a little tired. Probably too much running around first time out," she said.

Sam glanced up at the clock. "We ate breakfast late. Unless you're hungry, why don't you go lie down for a bit. We can always eat later."

"Are you sure?" Haley asked.

"I'm positive, and as soon as I get the groceries put up, I'll come check on you."

Haley nodded, then paused. "My phone should be charged by now. I'm going to try and call Rhoda again before I lie down, and I also need to call my insurance agent about my missing car."

"That's not resting," Sam said.

"Yes, it is. I'll be sitting down, then I'll be lying down."

"Then go do your thing."

She walked out of the kitchen carrying her shoes, but she wasn't limping, which was a plus.

Haley put her shoes beside the bed, and then sat on the bed and reached toward the charger for her phone.

Rhoda was in her contacts, and she pulled up her name and hit Call. It rang to the point Haley thought she would be leaving a message when Rhoda answered, breathless and excited.

"Haley! Is this really you?"

Haley smiled. "Yes, it's me. How are you? Are you okay? Did you stay in the city or did you evacuate?"

"We drove to my sister's house. We've been there all this time, so we didn't suffer a bit, but I still don't know what's left of our house. It did flood where we live. But enough about me. What in holy hell happened to you, girl? The last thing I knew, you were injured and trapped. Then we see that Life Flight rescue and found out a couple of days later it was you, and the men in the body bags they carried out were the escaped prisoners."

Haley sighed. It was wonderful to hear a familiar voice, and so she retold her tale.

"You shot them? Haley! Girl… I am stunned. Have you talked to the boss? He'll be so relieved to hear from you, too."

"No, I haven't. I'd rather not have to tell this twice, so would you call him for me?"

"Yeah, sure," Rhoda said. "So you shot both of them before they caught you. That probably saved your life, right?"

"No. Sam saved my life. Literally. If he had arrived five seconds later, I would be dead."

"Sam? Who's Sam?" Rhoda asked.

"My ex-husband. He's a private investigator in Dallas. I knew if anyone could save me, it would be him."

"But how did he get to you? The whole area was flooded."

"A chopper pilot dropped him on the roof, and he came in the same attic window that I went out of later. After I was released from the hospital, I came back to Dallas with him."

Rhoda gasped. "As in, he's taking care of you until you heal?"

"No, as in, I'm staying with him and do this love and marriage thing all over again."

Rhoda squealed. "I am so happy for you. Oh wait! That means you're not coming back."

"Only to get my stuff out of my apartment. I'll miss you guys so much, but I am so blessed to have been given this second chance."

"There's a branch office of Truman Realty in Dallas. Want me to ask Will if he'll write you a glowing letter of recommendation?"

"That would be awesome," Haley said.

Haley disconnected. One more call to make and she could rest. So she dug through her wallet until she found her insurance agent's card, and called her.

"State Farm, this is Edie."

"Edie, this is Haley Quaid."

"Oh my Gawd! Haley! Girl! I have been frantic wondering if you are all right. I mean… I saw that Life Flight rescue and was thinking to myself, Gawd…I'm so glad that isn't me, and then a couple of days later I find out it was someone I know!"

"I'm good. Healing a little slow to suit my taste.

Listen, I called to let you know my car disappeared during the hurricane and I don't know what happened to it. I don't know if someone stole it, or if it blew away. It was parked up by the house, so I know it didn't float away, because the floodwaters were only in the streets at the time I realized it was gone."

"No problem," Edie said. "I'll report it as lost in the hurricane. Everything else damn sure was. We'll send you a check in the mail."

"I'm not home now. Just send it to this address. Are you ready?"

"Yes, go ahead," Edie said, and took it down as Haley gave it, then read it back.

"Yes, that's it," Haley said.

Edie sighed. "I'm just sick about our city…and all the surrounding burbs…you know?"

"Yes. I haven't been back to my apartment yet, but I'm on the fourth floor. I don't expect flood damage, but I have no way of knowing if any windows were broken…or if there is water damage from that."

"So you're not in Houston right now," Edie said.

"No, I'm in Dallas, staying with my ex-husband."

Edie giggled. "That sounds promising."

"It's more than a promise," Haley said. "As for my car, if you have further questions, you have my cell number and mail everything here to Sam's house."

After they disconnected, Haley laid down the phone and stretched on the top of the bed. The cool, quiet room was so comfortable, like a hidden den to keep her safe. With Sam between her and trouble, she was hanging on to the hope that the missing money would soon be found, and remembering Hershel begging to talk to his mother.

Haley knew what it was like to lose a child, and even though Hershel Arnold had been a grown man with a dark heart, once upon a time he was some woman's little boy. That mother would still grieve the loss of a child, despite what he'd grown up to be.

She fell asleep, unaware that Sam had come to bed and was lying beside her. She was dreaming of Robbie at the age of six, when they'd gone to beach in Galveston. Robbie was holding a seashell and talking about the wind inside it, and Sam was carrying him on his shoulders.

Haley could still see the look on Sam's face when Robbie wanted to put the shell back in the water, so the little crab that had been in it could find his way home again.

They held hands, watching as Robbie took those seven steps to the water without them to return the shell to the sea.

"He is such an awesome little guy," Sam said. "I can't wait to see what he does when he grows up."

Haley moaned in her sleep, and Sam heard her.

"You're okay, baby. You're safe," he whispered.

Haley sighed, and then she was still.

Sam heard his phone vibrating, and rolled out of bed, picked it up and left the room to answer.

"Hello. This is Sam."

"Sam, this is Mildred, Louise Bell's bridge partner. I'm sorry to bother you, but you're her contact in case of trouble, right?"

Sam frowned. "Yes, I am, Mildred. What's wrong?"

"Louise never showed up for our weekly bridge game, and she didn't call. I've called her phone a dozen times in the past three hours and she hasn't answered. I don't know what to do."

"I'm actually working from home for a few days. I'll run across the street and check on her for you, okay?"

"Yes, yes, thank you. And let me know what's going on, will you?"

"I sure will," Sam said, and disconnected. He went back to the bedroom to check on Haley. She was still sleeping, so he headed out the door and across the street, wondering as he went whose car that was parked in the drive.

Ledbetter saw the man come out the door, and when he started walking across the street toward this house, there was a quick moment of concern. This wasn't supposed to be happening. Fuck.

The doorbell rang and Ledbetter was not armed. *Fuck. Fuck. Fuck.*

The doorbell rang again, and it was now or never.

Sam was worried enough when he came over here, but not getting an answer at the door was making him worry even more.

He was just about to go back home and get the spare key he kept for her, when the door swung inward.

It wasn't Louise.

"Hello? Can I help you?" Ledbetter asked, and smiled.

Sam frowned. "Where's Louise, and who are you?"

"Um, I'm the house sitter. I would imagine Mrs. Bell is almost to Wyoming by now."

Sam's frown deepened. "I didn't know a thing about that, and she always tells me when she's leaving town. What's in Wyoming?"

"Sir, I have no idea. And if you're Sam Quaid, she said you might be over, and for you not to fuss. That you had enough on your plate as it was."

Sam began to relax. That much made sense. But Wyoming? And, if she was on a plane, she wouldn't be answering calls.

"Okay. Sorry to bother you," Sam said. "Her bridge partner was worried when she didn't show up and asked me to check on her."

Ledbetter smiled. "Ah, well, that makes sense. So no worries here. I'm getting in mail and tending to business until her return. In three or four days, she said."

"Thanks," Sam said, and went back across the street to his house.

Haley was wandering through the house, looking for him when he came in the front door. She smiled.

"I couldn't find you."

"Checking on a neighbor," Sam said, then kissed her. "Are you getting hungry?"

"For many things," Haley said. "Not the least of which is you. I missed you, Sam."

He cupped her face, and kissed her again, then again, and then backed her against the wall until she could feel how much he missed her.

"This would hurt you, baby. I carried you away from that hell you were in and was afraid you would die before I could get us out of that house. I can't bring myself to cross this line yet."

Haley sighed. "I know you're right. I guess I should be grateful that at least one of us has good sense."

Sam hugged her. "So, will you trade sex for a sandwich?"

Haley laughed. "That is a sad substitute, but yes… for you…anything for you."

Ledbetter was not celebrating. This job was going to get dicey. It needed to be over now. But now she was thinking shooting Sam Quaid first to get him out of the picture might not be a good idea. By the time she had him down, it would have given Haley Quaid all kinds of time to get away…or fight back. Didn't she hear on the news that she shot both intruders before they took her down? The man didn't look like anyone's pushover, and she knew the woman wasn't, but letting Santos down wasn't going to happen, either. Ledbetter had a reputation to consider and didn't want it tarnished. It was a good four hours before dark.

Plans were made to be changed.

Rules made to be broken.

Ledbetter was a master at both.

* * *

Mae Arnold sat quietly in a chair beside Pete's casket, as visitors came and went. Carytown was a small community, and by now, almost everyone knew what had happened. They'd all been braced for Hershel's funeral. His reputation was well-known, as was his recent demise. But no one had expected this. No one knew what to say to Mae, and there was nothing to say to Pete.

When the first floral spray showed up in the viewing room, George turned the card so that all of the visitors could see the sender's name. It was from Preacher Riley and the church, nothing out of the ordinary.

But when multiple flower arrangements began to arrive, and the deliveryman from the florist wouldn't look at her, and didn't read aloud the names on the cards, she felt something was wrong.

As soon as he left, she got up and looked at the cards for herself. They were all addressed to Pete and signed "With love."

Two of them were from ladies at their church. One was from the redheaded checker at the grocery store, and one was from a woman who lived less than five miles from Pete and Mae. And the one thing they all had in common? They were single.

Mae felt the world tilting at her feet. This couldn't be happening. It wasn't enough that her son had turned into a criminal, but all signs were pointing to Pete being a philanderer.

She walked to the coffin and looked inside. Pete looked innocent enough, but he was dead, and she wasn't a woman who assumed, so she left to verify the facts.

The first place she went was to the grocery store, then straight to Millie's register. Millie was checking someone out when she felt a tap on her back. She was smiling as she turned, and then she saw Mae. A red flush ran up her neck two shades redder than her hair.

"Uh…my condolences, Mae. Pete was a good man."

"Just how good was he?" Mae asked.

Millie's eyes widened, and she began looking around for help, but the whole front of the store had gone silent.

"Uh…why, I'm sure I don't know what you mean!" Millie cried.

"Don't lie. How much did you charge?"

Millie gasped. "How dare you? I'm no prostitute."

Mae's heart was beating so fast she thought she might die.

"So you just gave it away for free," Mae said. "Well, I hope you didn't love him, because you're just one of four."

Millie's eyes widened in disbelief. "You lie! He said I—" And then she stopped. She'd just given herself away and Mae Arnold was already out the door.

"Well fuck," she muttered, and went back to scanning groceries.

Mae's next stop was one of the women from

church. The woman usually sat with them at church dinners, and not once had Mae ever suspected it was so the bitch could sit close to Pete. She knocked on the door, heard footsteps and then the door opened.

"Evening, Rita. I got your flowers."

Rita tried hard to find something to say that wouldn't give herself away, but she suspected from the look on Mae's face that she already knew.

Mae stared, trying to figure out what Pete saw in this little dried-up thing. She rarely smiled and her lips were in a perennial moue of disapproval.

Finally Rita got herself together. "You know how fond I am of you two. Of course I sent flowers."

"Addressed to Pete, signed 'Love, Rita.' I'm thinking you were fonder of Pete than you were of me."

Rita's eyes welled. "I didn't mean for it to happen, but I know in my heart we were meant to be together. I'm sorry."

Mae sighed. "Just so you know, Pete was poking his prick all over town. There are four of you. I hope you all get SIDS."

Rita frowned. "Sudden Infant Death Syndrome?"

"Maybe I meant STDs," Mae muttered.

Rita grabbed at her crotch as Mae walked away, then closed the door and ran to check herself out.

Mae was in so much emotional pain she couldn't focus, but the anger in her was stronger as she drove straight for the house of the third woman on her list, Doris Wakely, who liked to be called Miss Doris.

Doris was on her knees in the front yard, weeding her flower bed when she heard a car pulled up in her drive. She looked over her shoulder just as Mae Arnold exited her pickup and was so startled by her appearance that when she tried to get up, she fell sideways.

"Don't get up on my account," Mae said. "I just came to tell you I got your flowers. And Millie's flowers. And Rita's flowers. And Connie's flowers."

Doris gasped. "What? What are you saying?"

"Why, Miss Doris, I am saying that you shouldn't have wasted your money...or your time with my husband, because he was screwing all of us. You might want to have yourself checked for psoriasis."

Doris was pale and shaking...then confused. "For a scaly skin condition? What on earth?"

Mae cursed. "Obviously, I am not current with hooker diseases. I suppose I meant to say syphilis. Pete was plowing a whole lot more than the rows in my garden."

"Oh my God," Doris cried.

Mae shook her head. "And you, flat as a button. Pete always liked boobs. You must be hot to trot in bed."

Doris pressed her hands over her flat chest at the slight about her lack of woman parts. Then she heard the words *hot to trot*, and the world began to spin. She tried to put her head between her knees to keep from passing out, and instead went headfirst into the ground.

Mae drove away as Miss Doris was picking grass

out of her nose. Three down and one to go. But before that last stop, she had one more visit to make.

No one was more surprised than George when Mae strode back into the funeral home. Everyone was talking about the scandal, and no one had expected Mae to come back, yet here she was.

Mae sailed past George with her nose in the air, and went straight into Pete's viewing room. She looked down into the coffin, then jabbed Pete's chest with her finger.

"You better be glad you're already dead, Pete Arnold, or I would have killed you myself. Someone else is going to have to see you to your grave, because I've seen all of you I ever care to see."

Then she spun on her heel and stomped out.

"Oh my," George said. "Oh my, oh my, oh my."

Mae drove out of Carytown as dry-eyed and mad as she'd been the day Hershel was first arrested, and when she left the blacktop and hit the many miles of dirt road between Carytown and home, she stomped the gas, leaving a rooster tail of dust in the air behind her as she went.

She was five miles from home when she took the turn going down to Connie Hibbard's house. Gravel was rattling in her hubcaps and there was a wild look on her face when she stomped the brakes just shy of the front gate.

The ruckus set the dogs to barking, and Connie came out to see what was happening, yelling at the dogs to be quiet. They slunk away as Connie walked to the edge of the porch and shaded her eyes.

She recognized Pete Arnold's pickup. But since Pete was dead, she could only assume it was Mae. Then Mae got out, and when Connie saw the look on her face, she knew that Mae knew, and started screaming and shouting.

"Don't you hurt me! Don't you dare! I'll sue you!"

Mae stopped at the bottom of the steps, her hands fisted, her gray hair wild, windblown and standing up all around her face like the puff on a dandelion.

"Hurt you? You're the one who caused hurt, you horny heifer."

Connie gasped, but Mae wasn't finished. "I came to tell you I got your flowers…or I should say, Pete got your flowers…but he didn't get the message because he's dead!"

Connie blustered her way down to the second step, which put her within striking distance, and then waggled her finger at Mae.

"You don't know what you're talking about!" she snapped.

Mae's pale green eyes widened, and then they narrowed in a snaky kind of way.

"No, you're the one in the dark. Pete had women all over town. He was pokin' women faster than he could fart. Likely that's what caused him to drop dead at my feet. I'm going to the clinic tomorrow to get tested for diseases. Fucking all you hookers, then sleeping with me in our bed. Lord only knows what I might have caught."

Connie was still trying to absorb the fact that Pete hadn't been true to their love, when Mae just accused her of having the clap. Then it dawned on her that she might. If he was poking other women, there was no telling what he left behind.

She burst into tears as Mae Arnold drove away. This was a fine mess she'd gotten herself into.

Fourteen

The little one-doctor clinic in Carytown opened at 8:00 a.m. sharp, just as it had for the last thirty years. They'd seen all kinds of illnesses and injuries during that time, and everyone in Carytown, including the employees at the clinic, was talking about what had happened yesterday, and how Mae Arnold had called out every one of Pete's women and put them to shame.

There were mixed feelings about what Mae had done publically by facing down Pete's harem, but they all agreed the fallen women should be ashamed. Then as the clock on the wall chimed eight times, a billing clerk left the conversation to open up the clinic, and strode through the lobby to unlock the door.

Before the clerk could get out of the way, five women marched over the threshold and straight up to the check-in desk, with Mae Arnold in the lead.

The receptionist had just taken her seat and was fumbling for her glasses when Mae leaned across the counter.

"I need to see Dr. Irick."

"What is your illness?" the receptionist asked.

Mae glared at the four women behind her. "I had a cheating husband. I need to be tested for STDs."

The receptionist gasped.

"So do I," Millie said, glaring at the other three.

"So do I," Rita said, and then started crying.

"So do I," Doris whispered.

"I guess I do, too," Connie said, then slunk into a chair in one corner of the room, while the other three also chose to sit alone.

Mae chose not to sit down in a room with any of them, and tapped on the counter.

"Someone take me back to an exam room now. I don't want to breathe the same air as these whores."

The receptionist buzzed the nurse. "First patient is ready," she said.

"I'm not ready for her," the nurse snapped.

"You need to get that way fast, before all hell breaks loose up here," she whispered.

The nurse came up the hall with a frown on her face, then read the room, grabbed Mae Arnold's chart and gently took her by the arm.

"This way, Mrs. Arnold, and please accept my condolences," she said, as she put Mae in a room and closed the door behind her.

Haley was curled up on Sam's sofa, watching television in the living room when he came in from outside.

"Hey, honey, I'm through checking the chlorine

levels in the pool. I'll be down the hall in my office. I won't be long, okay?"

Haley was riveted to the ongoing updates about Hurricane Gladys and nodded. It was the first time she'd seen the footage of her own rescue and was horrified at how high up in the air she'd been before they got her inside the chopper. And then she saw the footage of Lee Tolson rescuing Sam, and grinned at the now famous "thumbs-up" he'd given the cameras trained on him at the time.

Down the hall, Sam was at his desk reading email. The one he'd been waiting on wasn't there, so there was no way to proceed further on one of his open cases until it came.

He thought of Louise again, and knew she had to be in Wyoming by now, but the PI in him needed confirmation. So he pulled up her number in his contacts, and made the call.

It rang and rang, and with every subsequent ring, his concern grew. Something was wrong. Despite what that house sitter said, something was wrong with Louise.

Without knowing what airline she'd chosen to fly, the only starting point he had was her morning departure, because the house sitter was already in place when he went over just after lunch. But that didn't stop him. He wasn't going to bed tonight until he knew where Louise was, so he used a little trick a hacker once showed him, and began going through passenger lists on flights going anywhere in Wyoming before noon of this day.

It took a little over an hour for him to find out that no women by the name Louise Bell boarded any flight to Wyoming today, and the realization dawned that the only explanation for this would be the house sitter lied. And if the house sitter lied about where Louise had gone, then it stood to reason that person might not have been house-sitting at all.

Sam got up from the desk and then peered through the blinds in his office. From where he was standing, he could see Louise's house. As he was watching, the garage door went up, and he saw the house sitter come out, get something out of the car, then go back into the house through the garage. Just as the door was coming down, Sam caught a glimpse of the back end of Louise's BMW.

It was still in the garage!

Why wouldn't she have taken herself to the airport? Another question without a satisfactory answer.

And that's when Sam remembered Special Agent Gordon's warning about Santos. What if he'd hired someone to snatch Haley? Sam's thoughts were spinning. What the hell was Santos even doing in Dallas? It's understandable that he might be unable to get back to his place of residence in Houston, but if that was the case, why come back into the States at all when he was in his home in Cozumel? And why come to Dallas only a day or so behind Haley, unless he was still chasing that money?

This was getting scary. But he wasn't ready to put the fear in Haley just yet. He scanned through his contacts again until he came to Special Agent Jack Gordon, then made the call.

Jack answered on the third ring.

"Hello, Special Agent Gordon speaking."

"Jack, this is Sam Quaid. I have a question."

"Hi, Sam. Ask away."

"Do you have anymore intel on Dude Santos that would lead you to believe he might have hired someone to get to Haley?"

"Not right offhand, but it wouldn't take me long to find out. What's going on?" Jack asked.

"My neighbor Louise Bell, who lives across the street from me, seems to have gone missing, and there's a house sitter in her place. I found out all this when I was making a welfare check on her at the request of her friend, when Louise didn't show up for their weekly bridge game."

"A house sitter? Is this a regular thing for Louise to do?"

"Not in the three years I've known her," Sam said. "She doesn't have pets, and we water each other's plants and get each other's mail when one of us is out of pocket on a regular basis. So I circumvented proper procedure and did a little digging and found out there was no woman named Louise Bell listed on any manifest, on any airline flight from Dallas, to anywhere in Wyoming this morning. And the house sitter came out of the house through the garage a few minutes ago. I saw Louise's BMW still parked in the garage, and no, that's not like her, either. I can't completely rule out her traveling by other means, but I was going by what this house sitter said."

"I don't like this scenario," Jack said. "Let me make a few calls and then we'll talk more. We are building a case to issue an arrest warrant for him, but we need more than Haley overhearing Baker and Arnold talking about betraying him."

"Thanks," Sam said, and then dropped his phone in his pocket.

He made a side trip into the kitchen for cookies and cold drinks, came back into the living room and plopped down beside Haley.

"Dessert, if you're in the mood," Sam said, and set her cold drink on the end table near her elbow.

Haley hit Mute on the remote and took a couple of cookies from the jar. "What's going on, Sam? And don't tell me it's nothing, because I've known you too long."

"Right now, it's just a case of someone missing."

"Oh…related to your work," Haley said.

"No. It's Louise, my neighbor across the street. She's gone missing, her car is still in the garage, there's a house sitter on duty, which she's never had before. Louise's friend called me this morning while you were asleep and said Louise never showed up for their weekly bridge game, and she couldn't contact her. That's how I even found out about the house sitter."

Haley frowned. "This doesn't sound good. Where did the house sitter say Louise went?"

"She *said* she flew to Wyoming this morning, but

I did a little digging, checking all of the airline manifests with flights going to Wyoming and she wasn't on any of them."

Haley put the cookies down and sat all the way up.

"The house sitter is lying. We had a house listed a year or so back that the client was still living in. One day we called to set up a showing, and he didn't answer, but when we went by the house some woman came to the door. We told her she needed to be gone from two to four for the showing and she had a fit, told us she wasn't leaving and not to come."

Sam was interested now. This was too eerily similar to what he was afraid had already happened to Louise.

"So what did you do?" Sam asked.

"My boss, Will Truman, called the cops asking for a welfare check on the old man, and when the cops showed up, they found the old man in bed. He'd been murdered, and the house had been robbed."

"Oh hell," Sam said, and then his phone rang. It was Jack Gordon.

"I need to take this. Hang on, honey."

Haley nodded, then picked one cookie back up and took a bite as she listened in.

"Hello. This is Sam."

"Sam, it's Jack. So here's what we know. He has known associates who we suspect of being hired killers. Also Santos himself has taken a year's lease on a very nice town house here in Dallas, and is making himself at home."

"Do the Feds have pictures of these people?" Sam asked.

Jack chuckled. "I figured you'd ask that question. What I'm sending is not for public use. Ever."

"Deal," Sam said. "You have my email, right?"

Jack repeated it.

"Yes, that's it," Sam said. "If I recognize anyone, I'll be calling you back, because if they're sitting in the house across the street from me, then Louise is either in serious danger, or already dead, and they're after Haley."

"Understood," Jack said. "I'm sending them now."

Haley was big-eyed and pale. "Sam?"

"Come with me, baby. I need to get to my office."

She took his hand and followed him down the hall.

Sam sat down behind the desk, and Haley stood right behind his chair, her chin on the top of his head as she watched his fingers flying over the keyboard. Then he opened an email and pictures began to emerge in lineup fashion.

"Who are these people?" Haley asked.

"Suspected assassins."

"Oh my God," she whispered, and put both hands on his shoulders, needing contact to keep from losing it again.

All of a sudden, Sam gasped, then pointed. "That's Louise's house sitter. I need to call Jack."

"Am I in danger?" Haley asked.

"Yes. We both are, because whoever tries to get you has to come through me, and they know it."

Haley moaned, then walked away. She got as far as the doorway before Sam caught her.

"No, honey, no. This isn't going to be a rerun of Houston, I promise. I need to call Jack. I'm going to put this on speakerphone so you can hear, too, okay?"

She couldn't stop shaking, so Sam wrapped her up in his arms as he returned the call.

"Talk to me," Jack said.

"You're on speaker, Jack. I'm here with Haley. She's not very happy with the situation right now."

"That's fine, I'm listening," Jack said.

Sam tightened his arm around Haley and started talking. "Ledbetter…the one listed as Ledbetter. That's Louise's house sitter. What do I do?"

"You do nothing," Jack said. "But be on the lookout for at least a dozen agents dressed in black to come knocking on your back door within the hour."

"Are you serious? To do what?" Sam asked.

"Ledbetter isn't the patient kind. The move to grab Haley will likely happen tonight. We let Ledbetter get all the way into the house, and then turn on the lights. We will be happy to take Ledbetter out of the picture for you, and then we'll do a search of Louise Bell's house."

"To look for her body?" Sam asked.

"Yes. That's the most likely scenario. People like Ledbetter don't leave witnesses," Jack said. "Just wait for my guys to show…let them get in place and they'll tell you two what to do. Good work, Sam. I'll stay in touch."

Sam disconnected. "Dammit."

Haley hugged him. "I'm so sorry. Maybe Louise is just tied up like I was?"

Sam shook his head. "Your assailants were two escaped prisoners. This is a different situation. You heard Jack. Assassins don't leave witnesses."

"I'm sorry. I'm so sorry," Haley said. "If I hadn't come back here, this wouldn't be happening."

Sam took her by the shoulders. "No! You don't think like that! The truth is, Ledbetter or someone similar would have found you wherever you were, and whoever stood between them and you would be taken out. It's the fault of killers, not of victims, that people die. Understood?"

Haley saw the grief on Sam's face, but it was the rage that was going to keep her safe.

"I understand."

"So we wait for the Feds."

"Where? Now I feel vulnerable, no matter where we sit."

"Let's go to the kitchen. We can watch TV in there while we wait."

She nodded, and when they went back through the living room they picked up their snacks to take with them. For something to do, Sam put on a pot of coffee to brew, then moved the kitchen table so that when they sat down, they were out of sight from the windows.

"Better?" he asked, as Haley settled in.

She nodded.

"Want some ice cream?" Sam asked.

"We ate all of the Bourbon ones," Haley said.

"I have a whole pint of peanut butter cup."

Haley nodded. "Yes, then I want ice cream."

Sam tilted her chin with the tip of his finger and kissed her. "It's going to be okay, love. And we'll raise a spoon to Louise when we begin. She'd love that."

And so they did.

Sam had just gotten up to toss the container in the trash when there was a single knock at the back door. He moved the curtains aside to look.

"Reinforcements have arrived," he said, and opened the back door, letting in at least a dozen armed Feds in SWAT-team black. They closed and relocked the back door, then one separated from the others.

"Special Agent Delvecchio," he said, and shook Sam's hand.

"I'm Sam Quaid, and this is Haley Quaid. What do you want us to do?" he asked.

"It's almost eleven p.m.," Delvecchio said. "Start turning out the lights, going room to room in your usual fashion, then show me your master bedroom."

Sam turned out the kitchen lights, then the living room lights, then headed down the hall to their bedroom.

"This is it," Sam said.

The agent looked it over carefully, then looked out the bedroom windows to the large hedge of shrubs along the outside wall of the house.

"This will not be a good entry point. Too hard to get to the window and come in unobserved. Stay in here."

"There are three entry points into the house," Sam said. "From the garage, the front door and the sliding doors you guys came in."

"That's why we brought so many men. We'll have all of them covered by multiple agents. My best guess is the sliders. They're the easiest. You have a security system?"

Sam nodded.

"Then activate it. We'll take care of it from here."

"What if Ledbetter doesn't come tonight?" Sam asked.

"Assassins work fast. In and out, leaving bodies. In this case, you would be the body, and likely, Haley would be taken. It will happen tonight."

This was way out of Sam's league, and he wasn't going to argue with men who did this for a living.

"I can set the alarm from the hall," Sam said.

"Then do it," Delvecchio said.

Sam stepped out of the room. Moments later, he was back.

"It's done."

"Keep the lights off in here, but you can leave a night-light on in the bathroom. That would not be out of place."

Sam nodded.

Delvecchio pulled the bedroom door shut behind him.

Haley turned on the night-light as Sam turned off the lights in the room.

Haley took one look at the bed in the shadows, and turned around and walked into the walk-in closet and sat down on the floor against the back wall.

Sam grabbed a flashlight from the bed table and followed her.

"What's wrong?" he asked.

"Bullets go through walls," she whispered, and then scooted as close to Sam as she could get. "This feels like being in the attic all over again."

Sam pulled her close.

"But it's not. The house is full of Feds. There's no flood and it's cool."

She leaned against him, too terrified to think past the imminent danger they were in.

Ledbetter didn't like it that Sam Quaid knew the the woman who lived in this house was missing. And Quaid was a private investigator. If he was nosy enough, he also already knew she hadn't landed in Wyoming. So tonight had to be the night to make the move. It would eliminate Sam the witness, and fulfill the contract with Santos by grabbing the woman.

As soon as the lights went out, Ledbetter began watching the clock. 12:45 a.m. was go-time, and Ledbetter took a Taser along with the other weapons, got in the car and rolled it across the street backward, straight into the Quaid driveway, making it easy to get the woman inside. However, the house had a security system, so the plan was to enter from the sliders at the back of the house. It would alert to a break-in, and Sam Quaid would come running. One shot would take him out, then getting to the woman would be simple. One shot with the Taser and she'd be unable to fight and still remain unharmed, like Dude Santos wanted. Ledbetter got out of the car, ran to the back side of the house, then popped the lock on the slider. The moment it began to move, the alarm began to sound.

Ledbetter started toward the hall, with the handgun aimed, expecting Quaid to show at any moment. Ten steps later, the lights came on in a blinding flash, followed by armed men from every direction, all of them yelling the same thing.

"FBI! Drop your weapon. Drop your weapon, or we'll shoot."

"Oh, mother-fucking hell," Ledbetter said, and hit the floor knees first, then slid the handgun away.

Seconds later, one of the agents had a knee in her back as she was flattened facedown to the floor, handcuffed. Then they grabbed her arms and yanked her back up to her knees.

"Amy Lynn Ledbetter, you are under arrest for breaking and entering."

She smirked. "All this for a B&E?"

"Tip of the iceberg," Delvecchio said before turning to one of his agents. "Go get the Quaids. I want a positive ID that she's the house sitter, before I drag her ass out of this house."

The agent turned on house lights as he went down the hall and then knocked on the bedroom door.

"All clear!" he called. "Delvecchio wants you in the kitchen to ID the perp."

Sam was at the door with Haley at his side.

The agent escorted them back, then paused in the doorway. "Witness accessed, sir," he said, then stepped aside.

Sam Quaid stared Ledbetter down.

"Yes, that's her. That's the woman who said she was house-sitting."

Ledbetter still couldn't believe this was happening. Thirteen years with a perfect record, and now this.

Then she saw the woman in the shadows behind Sam Quaid. *Damn. Beat all to hell and the famous Haley Quaid is still staring me down.*

"There's a van on the way to take her to booking," Delvecchio said to the SWAT team. "As soon as she's on the way, I want three of you to stay with me and the rest of you to escort that van all the way to lockup."

The other agents nodded, their guns still trained on Ledbetter, as Delvecchio pointed.

"You three, follow me."

"Are you going to search for Louise?" Sam asked. He nodded.

"Then wait, I have a key to her front door," Sam said. He opened the top drawer of the sideboard and gave him a purple key on a Snoopy key ring.

"We'll return it shortly," Delvecchio said.

"The van is here," someone shouted.

Nine armed Feds escorted Amy Ledbetter through the house and out the front door.

Amy saw the irony in her exit point. She hadn't gone through a front door on a gig in years, and then when she finally did, it was to take her to jail. And once they found that old woman's body, jail would morph to a Texas prison. Never a good place to be.

Mama always said I wouldn't amount to a hill of beans. I guess the old bitch was right, she thought, then lifted her chin and was joking with an agent as they shoved her into the back of the van with two more armed guards.

Drivers pulled up to pick up the agents, forming a three-car escort to get Ledbetter to jail.

All of a sudden, Sam and Haley were alone. Sam went to the sliding doors, saw where the lock had been jimmied, so he got an iron bar out from behind the washer and wedged it into the sliders. No one was getting in without breaking glass and making a whole lot of noise.

Haley hadn't moved, and she hadn't said a word, but she didn't miss anything that Sam was doing. He was calm, and the danger had momentarily passed.

As soon as Sam was satisfied they were secure for the rest of the night, he turned around, then focused on Haley's face. The wide-eyed expression wasn't something he was used to seeing.

She'd thought everything was over when they pulled her out of that attic, and now the threat had followed her to Dallas. *So it's time for me to shift her focus.*

"What happens next?" she asked.

Sam slid his hand along the back of her neck, feeling the weight of her hair against his skin.

"I think this is where you finally seduce me. Somebody turn out the lights," he said, and swept her up in his arms.

Haley flipped the switch as they passed it, and then turned off the light switch in the hall. There was a light still on in the master bedroom, and she turned it off as well, when they crossed the threshold.

Sam set Haley on her feet, locked the door and then began to undress her.

"I've lived this in dreams, and now it's our reality. I've been waiting for you to come back. Welcome home, Haley Jo. Welcome home."

Fifteen

Haley was naked beside him, watching the way the night-light sculpted his body with shadows, and Sam was lying on his side, looking past the fading bruises to the woman beneath. He ached to be inside her.

"How are we going to do this?" Haley asked.

"Very carefully," Sam said, as he leaned over her, tracing the shape of her mouth with the tip of his tongue.

Her breasts were warm in his hands as he stroked them and then the valley between. He couldn't keep his hands off her, and she hadn't taken her eyes off him.

Time to change focus again, he thought, and reached for one hard pink nipple, rolling it between his thumb and forefinger until she moaned and arched her back toward the pressure.

Sam knew that turned her on. It's why he'd done it. He leaned down and whispered in her ear.

"You like that, don't you, baby?"

"Yes…so much," Haley said, but when she reached for him, he stopped her.

"Let me," he said softly, and swept his hand down her belly, then points south.

It took only seconds to find the sweet spot with his finger, and when he heard her breath catch, he began to stroke. At first, they were long, even strokes, but he was waiting for her cheeks to flush and her eyes to flutter shut, and when he saw the heat coming on her face, he took her nipple into his mouth and nipped hard enough to make her shudder.

All of a sudden, her hand was fisted in his hair and she was pulling him down. One moment he was lying beside her, and then he was at her feet and working his way up the soft inner skin between her thighs, kissing, running the tip of his tongue against her skin, then between her legs.

Haley's heart was pounding, and when his warm wet tongue found the sweet spot she lost her mind. Time stopped. There was nothing but the sensation and the heat deep in her belly.

One moment she was begging him for more, and in the next heartbeat she was gone, lost in the shattering blood rush of a climax, the likes of which she hadn't felt in years. She didn't even know she was crying until Sam wiped the tears off her cheek.

"Don't move, baby. Just feel," Sam whispered.

Even as the aftershocks of the climax were still rolling through her, Sam covered her, holding his upper body above her without touching and sliding his rock-hard penis so far in, that she came all over again.

After that, he was chasing a high of his own, rocking against every trigger point she had, and pushing himself closer and closer to climax. It was if the last three years had never happened. Nothing had changed. She still turned him on like no other woman before her, and waiting for this had been worth it.

When he finally came in a burst of white heat, it left him weak and shaking. He'd given away everything he was for that heart-stopping climax, and he still had to move. Reluctantly, he gave up their connection to ease away, then lay back down on his side so that he could see her.

Haley's skin was still tingling from the aftershocks, vibrating like a high wire humming in the wind. She hadn't moved so much as a foot, was still on her back, and yet her heartbeat was hammering in her ears, like she'd been running for miles.

"Sam?" she said, reaching toward him.

"I'm here," he said, then caught her hand and kissed it. "I love you, Haley."

Haley turned onto her side so she could see him face-to-face. "Love you more," she whispered.

Sam's phone was on mute, but when it began to dance across the bed stand, he thought of the ongoing search across the street and grabbed it.

"This is Sam."

"We found her," Jack said. "It's going to turn into a three-ring circus in front of your house by the time the police are notified, and the ME arrives. At this time, there is no need for you to show your face."

"Where did you find her?" Sam asked.

"In a garden shed out back, but you proved to Louise Bell what a good friend is all about. You knew something was wrong and followed up. Louise is in good hands now, and we will make sure justice is served."

"I guessed this would be the way this night ended, but it's still a sad thing to know," Sam said.

Haley gasped, and then sat up in the bed beside him.

"Louise?" she whispered. When Sam nodded, she immediately felt sick.

"Would you happen to know her next of kin?" Jack asked.

"To my knowledge, there was no immediate family. But there is a black address book in the desk near the fireplace. I do have contact info for Mildred, her bridge partner. It's possible she would know more of Louise's personal side. I'll text it to you as soon as we hang up."

"Appreciated," Jack said. "And thank you."

"What about Santos?" Sam asked.

"Right now, I can't hazard a guess," Jack said. "Maybe we'll get lucky and Ledbetter will give him up."

"We need to stay informed here, as you know."

"Yes. We're on it. And we'll be searching for the money in Baker's and Arnold's old residences as soon as the water in Houston recedes enough for us to get there. Rest well. You've both earned it."

"Thanks for calling," Sam said, and disconnected. Then he pulled up the phone number from Louise's bridge partner, texted it to Jack, then set the phone aside.

"Talk to me," Haley said.

Sam turned around. Haley was sitting up in bed, her legs crossed, her hands fisted in her lap.

"They found her in the garden shed behind her house. He said the street between our houses is going to get crazy. They will have to rope off Louise's house as a crime scene."

"This is the saddest thing," Haley said. "I wish to God someone would find that damn money so people wouldn't keep dying."

Sam reached for her. The sexual connection between them was as strong as it had ever been. But it was the emotional one that was going to heal her.

"I don't think I'll be able to sleep just yet," she said.

Sam nodded. "Me, either. Maybe we can just lie in bed and watch a little TV and drown out some of the noise I hear coming."

Haley tilted her head. He was right. She could already hear sirens.

"Sweetheart, would you like something cold to drink?"

She nodded.

"Be right back," he said, and left the room, moving through his house without turning on lights.

Haley went to wash up, pausing in the glow of the night-light to look at herself in the mirror. The stitches needed to come out of her cheek, and the darkest bruises were finally turning lighter shades of purple and green.

"Sexy," Haley muttered, and turned away.

When she came out she made a little nest of pillows against the headboard for the both of them to lean against, then got in bed.

She could see flashing lights between the cracks in the shades, and could hear voices calling back and forth to each other out in the street.

Sam came back carrying two cold bottles of water and a little bowl of Hershey's Kisses.

"Thank you for the TV seating," he said, as he handed her a water and then put the candy bowl in the bed between them as he settled in.

She leaned across the chocolate and gave him a quick kiss.

Sam winked, then peeled the foil off of one of the candies. "It's a selfish pleasure," he said. "Here's another Kiss, from me to you," and popped it into her mouth.

He glanced at the play of lights on the ceiling and the wall of the room, then toward the windows.

"Cops and emergency vehicles galore outside. I cannot imagine what the neighbors are thinking, but we're all going to regret losing Louise."

Haley let the chocolate slowly melt on her tongue, watching as Sam turned on the TV and began scanning for movies, but knew the truth of that death was that it wouldn't have happened if not for her presence.

"You want to pick a movie?" Sam asked, offering the remote.

"No, you can do it," she said, and then took a drink of her water to keep from crying.

But Sam saw the tears anyway. "Aww, honey, please don't."

Haley shrugged. "I think about how scared she must have been. I know how I felt. The worst part of it is being helpless."

"Don't forget that a man named Santos sent Ledbetter. He's the one who caused Louise's death. He turned a stone-cold killer loose in Dallas."

"I wonder what he's going to do when he finds out she failed?" Haley said.

"Special Agent Gordon hopes Ledbetter gives Santos up," Sam said.

Haley frowned. "What would she have to gain by doing that? They already know she killed someone."

"There are some really tough state-run prisons in Texas. She might barter her information in return for being sentenced to a newer one," Sam said.

"Oh."

Sam peeled another Kiss and handed it to her.

She put it in her mouth without thinking and pointed to the screen. "Find a funny movie, okay?"

"I already scrolled past a classic. Give me a sec to backtrack." He scrolled back, then stopped and clicked. "Remember the first time we saw this?"

Haley's eyes widened, and then she grinned. "Oh my God...yes! *Me, Myself & Irene*. Jim Carrey is the best in this! Yes, this please."

Sam clicked on the movie, then peeled a chocolate Kiss and winked at her as he dropped it in his mouth.

"Good and sweet, aren't they, baby? But not as sweet as you."

All the while Amy Ledbetter was being booked, she kept thinking of Santos. He was expecting her text, and likely wondering why she hadn't contacted him. She didn't know what was going to happen when he found out she had been arrested. Even though she'd never even come close to being caught before, she knew how all this went down.

She would get a lawyer, and it would be his job to get her the best deal she could get. There was no question she was going to prison. Did she keep her mouth shut about who hired her and wind up in some shit hole, or give Santos up for a better one.

Dude Santos sat by his phone waiting for that text from Ledbetter, and channel surfing television way up into the wee hours of the morning before finally falling asleep.

It was nearing 10:00 a.m. when he woke. Bright sunlight was coming through the shades, and the television was still on. He turned it off, then checked his phone again, but still no word.

It never crossed his mind that Ledbetter would

fail. Her reputation as a hired killer was spotless. She'd never once failed to deliver. Something obviously delayed the snatch, but he knew it would happen. All he could do was be patient. It was a new day and time to get started. He'd slept through breakfast, but there were any number of good places in the area to do lunch, which meant a shower and clean clothes were in order.

Mae Arnold had no intention of going back to the funeral home again. Pete was paid for. They could plant him without her there.

But she had yet to decide what she was going to do now that Pete was dead. She didn't want to stay all the way out here in the woods alone. Pete had ruined whatever sentimental ties she might have had to the land, and she wasn't moving into town and seeing those four hussies every day for the rest of her life, either.

She was humiliated, pissed off and stunned that she'd never seen this coming. Pete had taken out a one-hundred-and-fifty-thousand-dollar life insurance policy on himself, naming her the sole recipient. If she sold the farm to add to that, and had Pete's social security benefits as his widow, her financial situation would be solid. Years ago, she and Pete had once talked about retiring somewhere warm. Just because Pete was now absent didn't mean she couldn't do that.

She got up to go look for their old atlas. It had a

map of the United States, and then a separate map for each state. Time to start eliminating possibilities.

She finally found the atlas in a bookcase and was on her way to sit down with it when the phone rang, so she hurried to answer.

"Hello, Mae Arnold speaking."

"Mrs. Arnold, this is the Office of the Medical Examiner in Houston, Texas. Your son's body has been released."

Shocked by the sudden spate of tears, Mae pinched the bridge of her nose to keep from crying.

"You're calling me here in Kentucky, to tell me to come to Texas to claim his body?"

"No, ma'am. You can have the body transported wherever you want it taken. I can give you a number to call. They'll help you get it set up, if you want."

"Yes, I do. Let me get a pen and paper," she said, and grabbed the pad she made grocery lists on and the pen beneath it. "Okay, I'm ready."

The man gave her a woman's name and a phone number to call, then expressed his sympathies for her loss and disconnected.

Mae put down the phone, ran her fingers through her hair until it was in total disarray, then strode out of the house and out into the backyard.

Rage was burning her gut.

Tears were burning her eyes.

She stood staring off into the green belt of trees surrounding the back barn lot, remembering how she used to stand out here to call the men in to eat—

remembering how Hershel's short little legs would churn as he tried to outrun his daddy, and how right at the last minute, Pete would always let him win.

All Mae could think was how precious those years were, and where the hell did those two people go? Hershel turned into a monster, and Pete, a deceitful whoremonger.

Where did she go wrong? Maybe it was in choosing Pete that the mistake was made. He had not been an honest man, and neither had his son. Mae raised a fist to heaven.

"Why, God, why?" she cried, then began walking in circles and kicking up tufts of grass and dirt with the toe of her shoe. "Answer me, dammit! What awful thing did I do wrong to justify this happening to me?"

But God didn't answer, and anger served no purpose. Exhausted and getting too hot, she staggered back to the porch and into the shade. When she looked down and saw dirt and grass on the end of her shoes, she kicked them off, before carrying them into the house.

The house was quiet, like it was holding its breath until Mae gave a sign she was okay, but she was through waiting for help. She stood at the sink to wash her face and hands, then went back to retrieve the phone number she needed to get Hershel's sorry ass sent home.

She couldn't count the number of holidays she'd waited for a call, or the years that had passed waiting for him to come visit. She'd offered to pay for his flight, if he would just come, and he'd made excuse after excuse. Now he had no say in the matter. She was shipping him home all right. He and his father were two of a kind, so she sat down to make the call. The sooner she got all this over with, the quicker she would be gone.

Haley woke to the sound of running water. Sam was in the shower, and she was naked as the day she was born. She shivered, remembering how the night had started out a nightmare. From the FBI team storming into the house and then setting a trap for Ledbetter, to hiding with Sam in the closet, just like they'd waited in the attic in Houston—both times waiting to be rescued.

And the aftermath…making love with Sam, finding out another body had been added to the growing list of victims connected to the two million dollars of missing money, to making love with Sam, again.

Then she heard the shower stop. Did she get up and go make coffee, or wait for Sam to come back to bed?

The bathroom door opened, and Sam came out dripping wet, with a towel wrapped around his waist. He saw she was awake and smiled.

"Good morning, sweetheart. The bathroom is all yours."

Haley got up, wrapped her arms around his waist.

"I'll get you all wet," he said, and carefully tunneled his fingers through her sleep-tousled hair, kissing her long enough that his hands were all the way down to her butt cheeks when he stopped.

Haley ran her finger down the middle of his chest, drying a little path through the droplets. "The look is good on you."

Sam grinned. "I'm a little partial to your fashion style, too."

Haley looked down at herself, and then shrugged. "What…this old thing? I've had it for years."

"Go, before I take your teasing ass back to bed, woman."

Haley grinned. "It won't take me long to shower," she said, and shut the bathroom door behind her as Sam went to get dressed.

Sam was nursing a cup of coffee and reading the news on his laptop when Haley entered the kitchen. She poured herself a cup and joined him at the table.

"Is there any good news in that? I only want good news today," she said.

Sam glanced up, then smiled. "My good news is waking up to you. So what do you want to do today?"

"Oh, that's not news in my world. It's nothing short of a miracle," Haley said. "And while my luck is holding, I really want to get the stitches out of my cheek."

"I can do that," Sam said.

"I was hoping you'd say that," Haley said.

Sam got up to get a closer look, and then nodded in satisfaction. "Sit tight and I'll be right back."

Haley took a sip of coffee, testing it for heat, then

stirred in a spoonful of sugar and tasted it again. Just right.

She was half a cup down when Sam came back with a small white hand towel and unrolled it onto the table, revealing a tiny pair of manicure scissors, a pair of tweezers, cotton balls and alcohol.

"I've already doused the scissors and tweezers in alcohol. You've healed really well, so pulling out the stitches shouldn't hurt."

Haley locked into his gaze. "I trust you. You should know that by now."

"I know. It was the trust that made you call me, and for that I am grateful." He tilted her chin just enough to give him a better angle, and kissed her because it was too tempting not to.

Haley sighed, and closed her eyes.

Sam made himself focus. "Okay, honey. Here we go."

He reached for the tiny scissors, snipped a stitch, then eased it out with the tweezers. She didn't flinch, so he cut the next, and then the next, until they had all been removed. After swabbing the site with alcohol, he eyed the doctor's work.

"He did a really good job stitching you up, honey. That scar is barely noticeable, and will disappear even more in the months to come."

"Thank you for doing that," Haley said. "It was beginning to itch."

"Anything else?" he asked.

"I can't see the cut that was on my head, but it

feels okay when I wash my hair. Would you check it out, too?"

Sam looked. "Looks pretty much healed."

"Awesome," Haley said. "And when I lose the bruises, I'll be just another face in the crowd."

"Not to me you won't. Now what do you want for breakfast?"

"I'm fine with just a bowl of cereal."

"Works for me, too," Sam said. "And if there's anything you need, or you just want to get out of the house, let me know. I am here for you."

Haley looked away, knowing she wouldn't be able to ask this if she was watching his face when she asked.

"Um… Sam? What are the odds of us going to the cemetery this afternoon? I would like to put flowers on Robbie's grave."

"Pretty much one hundred percent in your favor," Sam said, and hugged her.

Haley lingered within his embrace a little longer than normal, but she was fine when they moved apart. She went to the cabinet to get bowls as Sam got cereal from the pantry. Then she got flatware as Sam got the milk and a bowl of blackberries from the refrigerator.

Haley saw the berries and went back to the cabinet to get the sugar bowl. Finally they were ready to eat.

Sam had just poured cereal into his bowl when someone knocked on the door.

"Ah…that will be the repairman coming to fix the lock on the slider," he said. "Be right back."

Haley had forgotten about the iron bar in the door, and turned around to look. It was still there. Sufficient for one night, but definitely needing the lock fixed.

Sam came back into the kitchen, accompanied by a short guy with a purple-and-green Mohawk buzz on his head. His coveralls stated he worked for Carey Lock and Supply, but his piercings said he was, at the least, an independent thinker.

He saw her and grinned.

Haley smiled back.

Then Sam introduced them. "Haley, this is Elton. Best locksmith in Dallas."

Elton beamed. "Thanks, Sam. Nice to meet you, ma'am."

"I'm pleased to meet you, too," Haley said.

Elton saw the bowls on the table and waved Sam away.

"Y'all go on ahead having your breakfast. I won't bother you none," he said.

"Okay, but if you need something, just ask," Sam said, then he sat back down with Haley, his back to the door, and blew her a kiss. "Pass the cereal, please."

Haley grinned, shoved the box of Frosted Krispies across the table, then went about adding berries and milk to her own bowl.

With Elton in the room, there wasn't much conversation, but Haley didn't mind, and by the time they were finished eating and had the kitchen cleaned up, Elton was replacing the tools in his box.

"I think I got y'all fixed up," he said. "Sam, you come test it out a couple of times, to make sure you're satisfied."

So Sam opened and closed, locked and unlocked, opened and closed, locked and unlocked until he was satisfied it was as good as new.

"Works great, Elton. Want me to pay you now?"

"Naw, the boss will invoice you, but you can sign the work order for me."

Sam signed his name. Elton picked up his toolbox. "Nice to meet you, ma'am."

"Nice to meet you, too," Haley said.

Sam walked him to the door and then came back at a lope.

"What's the rush?" Haley asked.

Sam wrapped his arms around her and gave her a quick hug.

"You're so cute this morning in your gym shorts and that pink tee, I just felt the need to hug you," he said.

Haley laughed. She hadn't been flirted with in years, but it made her feel good—made her feel like a desirable woman again.

Sixteen

Special Agents Gordon and Townsend, along with their search crew, were winding their way through the streets on the southwest side of Houston, heading to the Houston Arms Apartments, the last addresses for Roy Baker and Hershel Arnold before their arrests. The water had receded enough in most places to get through, and the lingering pools in all the low places were shallow enough not to cause concern.

They had the address and apartment numbers, but no info on whether or not the apartments had been rented again. In an ideal world, they would still be empty, but law enforcement rarely encountered ideal situations.

The three-car convoy of black government-issue vans turned more than one head as they passed through the neighborhood. It was a low-income area of the city, and a place where the law in any capacity was a cause for concern.

When they finally reached the apartment building and pulled into the parking lot, it was nearly empty. The only vehicles still left had obviously been in the flood, because they were all piled up against a chain-link fence at the end of the lot. According to the number of vehicles, it appeared most, if not all, of the renters had evacuated the city, and had yet to come back. The good news was the water had receded from the building and parking lot. The bad news was the muddy water line they could see on the outside of the building.

They all parked side by side nearest the entrance and when they got out, the scent of mud, sewage and rot hit them full in the face.

Jack Gordon put a hand over his nose and frowned.

"Smells like a damn swamp. Don't anyone forget gloves, masks and flashlights. In this heat, every disgusting thing that will make you sick is likely growing inside this building."

The agents masked up and put on their gloves. Jack had already gloved up, and held the door for everyone else to enter.

The building was dark, except for what light came in through the lobby windows. After a brief search, they found a handwritten sign on the wall about halfway up the staircase, stating that the apartment manager was on the fifth floor in temporary housing, and listed the apartment number. With the power still out, they began walking the stairs, and the higher they went, the worse the stench and the heat became.

"Wonder why it smells so bad up here?" one of the agents asked. "All of the water damage is on the first floor."

Jack pressed his mask tighter across his face. "Multiply the number of apartments, times the number of floors in this building, and then count how many refrigerators lost power during the hurricane, and estimate how many pounds of ruined food in refrigerators and freezers there might be…and add up the possibility of a dead resident here and there who stayed behind, and then died."

"Damn, I'll bet you're right," the agent said.

Lloyd Townsend was just ahead of his partner and paused on the next landing.

"This is the fifth floor." They went in through the doorway taking them out of the stairwell. Except for one window at the far end of the hall, it was in darkness. Everyone turned on their flashlights and readjusted their masks.

"Room 501," Lloyd said.

Jack paused a moment and aimed his flashlight to look at the room numbers, then pointed left.

"It would be this way," he said and they started walking.

When Jack reached 501, he got out his badge and pulled down his mask.

"We don't want to be shot because we scared the crap out of some guy who thinks he's about to be robbed," he said, and then knocked.

"This is the FBI. Open up!"

There was an immediate noise inside the room, which sounded like someone scrambling to move furniture away from the door. Seconds later, the door swung inward, revealing a heavily bearded man holding a lit candle. His clothing was drenched in sweat, and there was a wild, hunted look in his eyes that made Jack want to reach for his weapon. But he did not.

"Are you Vernon Winkler?" Jack asked.

"Yes! That's me!"

"I'm Special Agent Jack Gordon of the FBI, and this is my partner, Special Agent Townsend. The men who are with us are field agents."

Vernon's eyes welled. "Looters were here. It's not safe out there. Are you part of the rescue teams?"

"No, sir, we're not, but when we're through here, we'd be happy to take you to one of the emergency evacuation centers."

"Then what the fuck could you possibly want here?" he muttered.

Jack handed him the search warrants. "Some months back, there were two renters here occupying two separate apartments. We have warrants to search both apartments, so we need to get inside them."

Vernon took the search warrants, saw the apartment numbers and frowned. "They have both been rented out again, but I don't know if the looters got there."

"It doesn't matter," Jack said. "We still need to search them."

"We're gonna have to go up another floor," Vernon said.

Jack nodded. "Yes, sir. We know."

Vernon moaned. "I'll take you up, but you're on your own after that. I had two residents on that floor who refused to evacuate, and I haven't heard from either of them since the fourth day of the hurricane."

Lloyd muttered beneath his breath.

"So are you saying they're dead?" Jack asked.

Vernon shrugged. "That would be my guess. This whole place stinks to high heaven, as my mama used to say. There could be others. Let me get the pass key," he said, and pushed past the jumble of furniture and disappeared down a hall, holding his candle to light the way.

When he came back, he was carrying his flashlight.

"I leave it beside my bed," he said, and walked out the door, wading through the agents to get to the stairwell they'd just left.

They followed him up to the sixth floor. Vernon led the way to Room 612 first, and unlocked it. "This here was Roy Baker's room."

Jack paused. "Lloyd, you take half the men and start searching. You know the drill. Try not to disturb the current resident's personal belongings. The rest of you come with me."

Lloyd pointed out the men he wanted, and they followed him inside Room 612.

"Follow me," Vernon said, and led the way farther down the hall and then just around the corner. "Right here is 620. It was Hershel Arnold's room." He unlocked it and then covered his face as the stench within slipped out into the hall. "I'm going back to my room. Y'all don't leave without me, okay?"

"We won't," Jack said. "By any chance, did the resident in this room happen to be one that refused to evacuate?"

"No. They left. I don't know what went bad in there…maybe sewage backed up…who knows? That bitch of a hurricane ruined everything."

Vernon had already turned the corner and was heading back to the exit when Jack and his men entered.

"Same story I gave the other team. The personal items in here don't belong to Hershel Arnold. Start looking for loose floorboards, in all the vents, inside closets with loose boards or access spaces in the ceilings…anywhere big enough to hide two million dollars."

The second team scattered through the three-room apartment. There couldn't be all that many places to search. Just a kitchen/living room, a bath and a bedroom.

"Good God Almighty, someone open the damn windows in here," Jack shouted.

Santos was having brunch at an IHOP and reading one of the local papers, when a brief news item on one of the inside pages caught his eye.

FBI catch the suspected killer of local woman, Louise Bell. Bell's body was found in a storage shed on her property after the FBI made their arrest of the same suspect in the act of breaking and entering at the residence of Sam Quaid, a well-known private investigator here in Dallas. Details of the suspect still pending, although sources are claiming it was a woman.

Santos gasped, and then started reading all over again while syrup dripped from the bite of waffle on his fork.

Real maple syrup on his pale yellow shirt.

Definitely not on the IHOP menu.

His appetite was gone by the time he'd finished reading the article. He waved at a waitress for his check, and when she brought it, he tossed some cash down on top of it, and headed out the door.

He'd rented a car when he landed in Dallas, as opposed to depending on rides from Uber, and the moment he was inside he cranked up the air-conditioning and drove away.

There were a few scenarios he had to consider. He could try to get the hell out of the States before Ledbetter had time to give him up, or he could try and make a run for it and leave Texas, but go where?

He'd known Ledbetter long enough to know she didn't have a drop of loyalty in her. Her loyalty was to the money, and her well-being. His first need was an immediate exodus out of Dallas. No need making it easy for the Feds to find him.

So where in hell could he hide until he figured out where to go? What was the last location in the entire United States that the cops would expect to find him?

And then it hit him. It was the afterthought of info that Miles Rafferty had included with the information Santos had paid for. He knew the perfect location where he could hide.

Hot damn, he was heading back to Houston after all.

It was just after 2:00 p.m. when Sam and Haley arrived at the Hillcrest Memorial Park cemetery off Boedecker and West Northwest Highway. There were distant clouds on the horizon, a promise of storms tonight, which matched a bit of what Haley was feeling.

She hadn't been back here since the day of Robbie's funeral, and was clutching the bouquet of flowers they'd bought like a shield. Part of her felt guilty for not having done this before, while the rational side of her knew that the people who made annual pilgrimages to places like this did it for themselves, because their loved ones were no longer here.

Sam glanced at Haley before he turned off the street. She was pale and shaking, but he had a knot in his belly, too, so he understood how she felt.

"It's pretty here," Haley said, and then glanced at Sam.

"Yes, it is. Are you okay?" he asked.

She nodded, and turned her head away so he

wouldn't see her tears, focusing on the acres of tombstones spreading out around them instead. As Sam turned right at the next corner, a cardinal flew across their line of vision.

"Look, honey, a red bird," Sam said.

Haley followed the bird's flight until it flew out of sight. "Remember how Robbie always put cardinals in all of his pictures, when he was little?"

Sam smiled. "He did, didn't he? I'd forgotten that." Then Sam pulled over a bit and parked. "We walk from here."

Haley got out without waiting for Sam, and then turned away from the sun. It was in her eyes.

Then Sam slid his hand beneath her elbow. "We go this way," he said, and steadied her as they walked across the grass to a white heart-shaped headstone with a white marble vase affixed to the base.

Sam took the old flowers from the vase, while Haley put in the ones she'd been carrying. Red carnations, white roses and Texas bluebells…red, white and blue, the colors of the Texas Rangers, Robbie's favorite baseball team.

It wasn't until she stood up and stepped back that she allowed herself to read his name.

Samuel Robert Quaid III
September 4, 2003–April 6, 2015

Haley took a slow, shaky breath, and then quietly reached for Sam's hand. They stood together in mutual grief and silence, each lost in thoughts of their own, forever bound by the loss of their child.

Then Sam pulled a quarter out of his pocket, flipped it over a couple of times, then held it up between his thumb and forefinger.

"You call it, son. Heads or tails?"

Haley's eyes widened. This was something new to her. What did this mean? How had she not known?

Sam tossed the coin up in the air, then watched it tumble to the grass.

"You chose heads, remember? You always chose heads," he said, and then laughed as he reached down and picked it up. "You win again! Man! You are the luckiest guy I know."

He dropped the quarter into the vase of flowers, and then rubbed the top of the stone, almost as if he was rubbing the top of a child's head.

"We miss you. Make sure Mama's angels stay close to her. She needs all the help from us she can get."

Haley leaned against Sam's arm. "I need to talk to Robbie."

Sam brushed a kiss across her forehead and then walked a short distance away.

Haley glanced down at the marker again, and then looked off across the graveyard, wondering if she willed it hard enough that he might suddenly appear?

"I didn't forget you, my son. When I lost you, I also lost myself. You are forever in my memories, and always in my heart. If you still play ball in heaven, hit a home run for me."

Then she turned around, saw Sam standing beneath a shade tree a short distance away. When she started toward him, he met her halfway and put his arms around her.

"Ready to go?" he asked.

She nodded, and as they began walking back to the car, she glanced up.

"What is the quarter toss about?"

"Oh, the last year he was with us, when he spent most of his time in and out of the hospital, he and I watched a lot of sports on TV. So you know how the captains of football teams meet in the middle of the field and choose who kicks and who receives by the toss of a coin? That's what we would do, too. It was just a little thing to make him feel part of the game, after he got too sick to play."

"That's awesome," Haley said. "I never knew that."

"You didn't like sports, remember?"

Haley nodded. "I remember. But I baked cookies on game days, and you two ate your share of those."

Sam put his arm around her. Haley couldn't describe the way she was feeling, but she felt lighter at heart than she had in a long time, and she knew why.

"We just shared our first good memory, didn't we, Sam?"

Sam nodded. "It should happen more often, I think."

They walked the rest of the way back to the car in a comfortable silence, and they drove home the same way.

* * *

Amy Ledbetter did not like her accommodations while waiting for arraignment, and was anxiously awaiting the arrival of her lawyer, Rance Wesley. Originally, she'd chosen him years ago because he was good-looking, but when he turned out to be gay, she kept him because he was also damn good at his job.

When Wesley finally arrived, a guard took her in handcuffs to a room where he was waiting, then handcuffed her to the table.

"Call when you've finished," the guard said.

Wesley nodded, waited for the door to shut and then sat down on the other side of the table, opened his briefcase and pulled out a folder.

"Well, this is a fine kettle of fish," he drawled.

"Just shut up," Amy said.

Rance raised an eyebrow. "Is there any part of the charges you intend to dispute?"

"No. But I am willing to barter myself to life without parole instead of a death sentence, in exchange for the name of the man who hired me, and what he hired me to do."

Rance frowned. "I don't know if that's enough info, Miss Ledbetter. You did kill an innocent woman in cold blood just so you'd have a comfortable place for your stakeout."

Amy shrugged. "You do what you have to do in life. Then if that's not enough, run this past the prosecutor. I can attest to the fact that the man who hired me is also the third man from that armored car heist. The Feds aren't the only people trying to find that missing money."

Rance Wesley rarely thought about his client's personal lives, but this one was an exception. She was as cold and heartless as anyone he'd ever known.

"I'll run this by the law and see where it falls. Your testimony would be in regard to a federal case. But your crime is going to wind up in a state court. You never make anything easy."

"Bullshit," Amy said. "I've been paying your retainer for four years without needing you to even break a sweat for me. I've never been in this situation before, and you know it. Go! Do what you do! Just get me off death row and into a decent prison."

Rance Wesley grinned, put his file folder back into his briefcase and then paused.

"Is there anything else you're not telling me?"

"Only that he ordered me to kill the Quaid woman when he was through talking to her."

Rance nodded. "I'll be in touch." Then he knocked on the door to be let out.

He was escorted out of the jailhouse, as Amy was escorted back to her cell.

Rance got to his car and turned on the air conditioner to let it cool while he made a quick call to the district attorney's office.

"Good afternoon, District Attorney's Office."

"Good afternoon to you, too, Helene. This is Rance Wesley. I need to speak to the man. Is he in?"

Helene giggled. "He's in, but I don't know if he's free to take a call. I can check."

"What I need is to talk to him in person. I'm at the jailhouse."

"Let me check his calendar," she said.

Rance was put on hold, which meant she'd gone to talk to Parker Austin himself. A couple of minutes later she was back.

"Thank you for holding. Mr. Austin says if you're heading this way, he'll make time."

"Awesome," Rance said. "I'm already leaving the parking lot. See you soon."

He pulled out onto the street, heading straight to the DA's office. He didn't know how this was all going to go down, but it was going to take Parker Austin and the FBI to figure out who benefited more from Amy Ledbetter's testimony, and where she was going to land in the prison system when it was all said and done.

The search team, headed by Special Agents Gordon and Townsend, came out of the Houston Arms Apartments hours later, choking and gagging and stripping out of their coveralls where they stood, then bagging them all up and throwing them in the back of the vans, leaving them standing in the parking lot in the gym shorts and T-shirts they'd had under them.

Vernon Winkler had a bag of his own clothing, none of which was clean, and was sent off to an evacuation center for food and clean clothing, while Gordon was making a call to the Houston PD to report the odor of dead bodies in the Houston Arms Apartments.

The search team had found everything from mold to fleas to rotting garbage teeming with maggots, but no money. The disappointment was weighing heavy on all of them. They'd been so hopeful—so sure.

"You want to call the Quaids, or do you want me to do it?" Lloyd asked.

Jack was still wiping himself off with disinfectant wipes, and reached for two more. "As soon as I get through here, I'll do it," he said.

"She's not going to be very happy. With the money still missing, the pressure stays on her," Lloyd added.

"I know," Jack said. "Give me a couple more minutes and I'll be ready to leave."

"Are we going back to headquarters in these shorts and tees?" Lloyd asked.

"No other options," Jack said.

Lloyd rolled his eyes. "We're never going to hear the end of this. And they'll have to disinfect the coveralls before they can be washed."

"If it was up to me, I'd just burn them," Jack muttered, and then tossed the last of the wipes he'd been using into another garbage bag, and then loaded it up, as well. "Okay, I'm ready to get away from this hellhole."

"Want me to drive?" Lloyd asked.

"Sure," Jack said, and tossed him the keys.

Minutes later, the FBI vans and the agents in them were gone.

* * *

After they came home from the cemetery, Haley traded her pants and a shirt for shorts and a tee and then fell asleep in one of the recliners.

Sam covered her up, and then went down the hall to his office to see what was popping on the open cases. While he was there, Deborah called from his office.

"Hello, Deb. What's up?" Sam said.

"One of the missing persons cases just solved itself."

"Oh yeah? Which one, and how?" Sam asked.

"The teenage girl from Fort Worth? Her mother just called to let us know she came home. Been gone six months, not a word, and then shows up ready to deliver a baby any minute."

"Oh wow…so now they know why she ran away. Three months pregnant and too scared to tell. At least she had the good sense to come home."

"That's what her mother said. They're so happy to have her back that they don't even care she's going to become a mother at sixteen."

"Better than becoming a statistic," Sam said. "Send them a paid-in-full notice."

"But they still owe you," Deborah said.

"They're going to need all they have to raise another child. It's all good."

Deborah sighed. "You're a good man, Sam Quaid. My best to Haley. Call if you need me."

Sam disconnected, then leaned back in the chair, imagining the joy of having a child you feared was dead walking through your front door. After losing his own son, missing children had become number one on his list of cases he would take.

He opened his email, found one with Haley's name in the heading and opened it. It was a letter of recommendation to her from Will Truman, the owner of Truman Realty. And he'd attached a personal note on a second page telling her that he'd already spoken to his brother, Larry, on her behalf, should she desire to go to work at the Truman Realty in Dallas.

He smiled, printed it all for her and slipped it in a file folder, then worked for another hour or so until he realized it was getting dark in the house. He went to the window to look out. It appeared those clouds they'd seen at the cemetery had worked themselves up into a thunderstorm.

He left the office and went to check on Haley. She was still sleeping, so he headed for the kitchen. It was going to be too rainy to grill this evening, so he started digging through the groceries they'd bought, trying to figure out what to cook, when his cell phone rang. Then Jack Gordon's name popped up in Caller ID, and he wondered what the hell else was going wrong.

"Hello?"

"Hey, Sam, it's me. We took a twelve-man search team into the apartments where Baker and Arnold were living when they were arrested, and found every stinking, crawling, noxious thing there was to find, except money."

"No way," Sam said. "Man, this is not what we were hoping for."

"I know. Not what we were hoping for, either."

"So what do you do now? Or is there even anything you *can* do at this point?"

"Just keep trying to build a case against Santos so we can get an arrest warrant. If Haley remembers anything else, however miniscule, give us a call."

"You can count on it," he said, and disconnected.

"Who was that?" Haley asked.

He turned. She was standing in the doorway with a worried look on her face.

"It was Jack Gordon. They searched the apartments. No money," Sam said, and then watched her expression go flat. But instead of bemoaning the situation she was still in, she saw the hamburger on the counter and pointed.

"Is that dinner?" she asked.

"It's going to be, once I figure out what to do with it."

"If you have what we need I'll make chili."

Sam wanted to hug her, and he took a cue from her not to talk about the call anymore.

"I have diced tomatoes, onions, peppers and the spices you'll need. What else?"

"Garlic and jalapeños?"

"Yes, yes, we bought some, remember?"

"Then we're good," Haley said, and went to the sink to wash her hands.

"Want some help?" Sam asked.

Haley paused, then looked around the kitchen.

"No, the cooking, measuring and chopping will be a welcome task. I haven't cooked a meal since the day before I fell."

"So, make friends with my kitchen. Let her know the woman of the house has arrived."

Haley smiled—the first one in hours.

"That's awesome, Sam! Thank you!"

Seventeen

As much as Sam wanted to be in the kitchen with Haley, he knew the smartest thing he could do was leave her on her own. She'd find what she needed, and if she wanted help, she'd ask for it. He wanted her to feel comfortable in his house, and she had always loved to cook. The best way for her to feel at home was to cook in that kitchen. So he grabbed a bottle of beer from the fridge, meandered back to the living room and turned on the TV.

He could hear Haley digging through his cookware, and then a couple of cabinet doors banging. Soon the scent of cooking meat and spices drifted into the room. He leaned back in the recliner and closed his eyes. It felt like before.

The love was still there.

The only thing missing was their son.

He sat in that way without moving, absorbing her presence.

God, how he loved her. She wasn't the same anymore, but neither was he. They had everything they needed to build a life on. All that was standing in their way was two million dollars of stolen money.

He heard a timer go off, and then another scent was added to the mix. He sniffed.

Oh man...corn bread! This meal was a flash from their past.

Then he heard her footsteps and opened his eyes, as if he'd been watching TV all along.

Haley leaned over the recliner and kissed his forehead.

"Food's ready."

"I'm ready for it," he said, then got up and followed her to the kitchen.

The table was set. A wheel of corn bread was on a platter, already cut in pie-shaped wedges. There was a little bowl of chopped onions, a larger bowl of grated cheese, and the butter, all within reach.

"What do you want to drink, Sam? There's sweet tea, or longnecks."

"I'll take another longneck," he said. "Goes good with chili."

"Agreed. I'll have one with you," Haley said, and got them out of the refrigerator, opened them and then handed them to him.

"Sit down and I'll bring the bowls," she said.

"I can—"

"Let me," Haley said.

He put the beers down at their places then sat,

watching the easy sway of her hips as she moved from counter to stove and back again, and the length of the dark ponytail hanging down her back as she went about filling the bowls.

She carried them, one at a time, to the table, and then slid into her chair.

"Bless this food, and the hands that made it," Sam said.

Haley looked up, then smiled. "Thank you."

"No, thank you. Eating this is going to be my pleasure."

Amy Ledbetter sat on her cot in the holding cell, staring at the tray of food they'd given her for dinner. It smelled a little like beans, but she didn't see any, and since she couldn't distinguish what kind of meat that was, and what the dark stuff was beneath it, she opted to skip the meal, put it against the bars of the cell and went back to the cot and stretched out with her back to the wall. No way was she turning her back on the three other women in the cell with her.

"Hey, Sleeping Beauty! You gonna eat that?"

Amy stared at the woman who called herself True. She looked like a hooker. Everything was too tight and revealing, considering the size of her boobs and ass.

"No," Amy said, and then watched True get up.

At the same time, another woman in the cell who went by the name Ariel, "like the Little Mermaid," got up, as well. "I want her bread. Your fat ass don't need it all."

True backhanded her across the mouth. Blood spurted. Ariel screamed. And the fight was on.

Amy didn't bother to move. If they fell on her, she'd whip both their asses. But she didn't have to bother. Two guards were already coming in, and two more were standing outside the cell with their weapons drawn.

One guard put True in a choke hold, twisted her arm behind her back and shoved her down onto her cot, while the second guard yanked Ariel up off the floor, and sat her down, as well.

Ariel was bleeding from both lips, and had the beginnings of a black eye. True had a scratch on her arm.

"Who started this?" the first guard asked.

The women pointed at each other.

Amy sat up and pointed.

"They're fighting over my tray of food…the one that's now upside down beneath that cot. I didn't want it. That one asked if she could have it, and I said, yes. That one jumped up and said she wanted the bread, then insulted the size of the other one's ass. All hell broke loose. Shit happens."

The women stared at Amy in disbelief.

"Are you crazy, bitch? No one squeals in here," True said.

Amy lifted her chin and stared straight into True's eyes.

"I'm not a bitch, and I'm not no one. I'm someone

you don't want to fuck with. Don't look at me again. Don't talk to me again."

One guard frowned at Amy. "You're not in charge here. Sit down and shut up. Anyone so much as raises their voice in here again and I'll handcuff all four of you to your cots, understand?"

Three of them nodded. Amy stared. And didn't blink.

The guards left.

Food was all over the cell floor, and so was a goodly amount of blood.

With no paper towels and no toilet paper, they were stuck with the mess and the smell.

Amy lay back down, but didn't take her eyes off either one of them.

"You acting all tough," True drawled. "What you get jailed for? Shoplifting?"

"Murder, and it's far from my first. Don't talk to me, I said. Next time you do, I'll shove your tongue down your throat," Amy said, and watched the blood fading from True's face.

True looked away.

Ariel was all busy trying to stop the blood flow with her shirttail.

The third woman crawled beneath her cot.

Amy sighed. If this was what prison was going to be like, she was going to lose her fucking mind.

Dude Santos managed to get all the way to The Rochester Apartments in downtown Houston, with only two detours. The floodwaters were receding quickly, now that the rains had passed, and he saw signs of power being restored in some areas.

He'd brought groceries, a rolling suitcase full of his clothes, a twelve-pack of bottled water he'd brought from Dallas, and was ready to move in.

There were around twenty cars parked within the lot, and he was guessing residents were beginning to return, if only to see the conditions of their belongings. The first thing he had to do was find out if he could get in without being challenged. It was an upscale area, and it was a good possibility there was security check-in somewhere in the lobby. So he adjusted his clothing and entered the lobby as if he'd lived there for years.

It was an obvious disaster—muddy and water-stained at least six feet up the walls—and smelled disgusting. Lobby furniture had floated up against pillars and walls, and were evidence of the chaos this once had been. There was a security station, but it was unmanned, and all the power was off.

Hot damn. That means building security is down.

He heard footsteps in a hallway somewhere near, and voices, but couldn't make out what they were saying. After a brief search, he located the stairwell, only to find the same level of mud and water stains there.

He took the stairs two at a time, exiting on the fourth floor and pausing a moment to orient himself with numbers. Apparently, apartment 404 was down the hall to his right.

The hallway was empty and as he proceeded he still didn't hear any signs of residents. Once he reached 404, he paused a moment to check the door locks. One lock was in the knob, the other above it was a dead bolt. Both opened with a key.

He pulled out his little wallet of lock picks, chose a couple and went to work.

Dude had been picking locks and stealing for years, long before he moved into the big time, so he did not doubt his ability to get in, and he was right. It didn't take him long to pick the first lock, and he was hoping the homeowner had not locked the dead bolt, too. He turned the doorknob, but the door didn't give.

"Shit."

One more lock to pick, after all. By now, he was wet with sweat. It was coming out of his hairline, burning his eyes and blurring his vision. His hands were so slick with sweat that he kept dropping the picks, but he persevered, and finally, he heard the last tumbler click.

"About damn time," he muttered, picked up his stuff, opened the door and walked in, closing the door behind him. The lights didn't work, but the windows did. He began opening them up as fast as he could. It was hot outside, but it was hotter in here. At least he'd get a better mix of air.

Once that was done, he headed back downstairs on the run. It would probably take him at least three trips, maybe four, to bring up his things, but once he was inside and locked into that apartment, he was good as gold.

After driving the car into the parking garage all the way up to the fourth floor, he began carrying everything inside. The sun was less than an hour from sundown when Dude headed down the hall again with the last load. He locked the car, hoping that was enough to deter thieves, but if not, it was a rental, and he could always steal another for himself.

Once he was inside, he turned both locks. It was getting darker, which meant he needed to find the flashlight he'd purchased, and began digging through the sacks of groceries until he found it and the batteries.

"And then there was light," Dude said, and began to sort through his things.

He'd made certain that none of the food he bought had to be refrigerated, so he was good there. He tried the water faucets and the water came out with good pressure, and smelled clean. He dared to take a little sip, and it tasted as clean as it always had, so if the plumbing was draining, he could shower. That would be a huge plus.

He grabbed the flashlight and headed down the hallway, looking in on one bedroom that looked unused.

"Guest room," he said.

The next room on the other side was smaller, and was being used as an office, but the one across the hall proved to be the master.

He eyed the king-size bed approvingly, and then walked into the master bath and smiled. Big glassed-in shower, even larger jetted soaker tub. He'd have to forego the jets and warm water, but it was already hot enough in here. Hot water was not on his wish list.

Satisfied that he was going to be quite comfortable in his hiding place, he went back to get his suitcase. Tomorrow he'd have daylight again, and maybe he'd get lucky and some power would be restored. For now, he was sitting pretty.

He went into the walk-in closet to look for a few empty hangars, and then got sidetracked, going through the clothes hanging there.

He recognized a couple of high-dollar designer dresses, and eyed the array of shoes on the racks.

"Nice place, nice clothing, Haley Quaid. Take your time coming back. I'll be here waiting when you finally show up."

Sam was on the phone regarding some of his work, and Haley didn't want to watch TV. She wandered back through the house, then saw the pool beyond the sliders and went outside.

With the sun going down, the backyard was in shade. The water looked so inviting, and she was wishing for a swimsuit. But she could still dangle her legs in the water, so she kicked off her flip-flops and sat down at the edge of the pool.

The water was warm and felt like silk against her skin. This night, the neighbors were quiet. *They must be inside*. The privacy fence was eight feet tall. She looked up. The first stars were visible, as was the half-moon above.

Traffic, sirens and screeching tires were part of the background of Dallas living. There was no privacy fence that could keep all that out. But it made her safe from prying eyes.

She got back out of the pool, stripped down to her underwear, and dived into the deep end, cutting through the water with hardly a splash. She bobbed up like a cork, and swam to the other end of the pool, then back again and had to stop. She hadn't been swimming in ages and it showed.

She was semifloating on her back and looking up at the night sky when she heard the sliding door open, then shut.

Then she heard Sam laugh.

He must have found her little pile of clothes.

All of a sudden, the lights beneath the water were on, and Sam was walking toward her. Somewhere between his laugh and the pool lights, he'd shed every stitch of clothing he was wearing.

Naked beneath the moonlight, he towered over her.

"Is there room for me?" he asked.

"Always," Haley said, and then watched the play of muscles in his arms and belly as he dived into the water. "Beautiful man," she whispered, and then he surfaced, and swam over to where she was floating.

"What are you thinking about?" Sam asked.

"Oh… I guess how wrapped up people can get about money," she said.

"Are you referring to Santos?"

"Him, and I guess, in a way, all of us. When I didn't have anything to focus on in Houston except my job, making the big sales became the gold ring I kept striving to achieve. And I did it, only to find that no amount of money could replace what I'd lost."

Then she bobbed up from a floating position and wrapped her arms around Sam's neck.

He pulled her close and brushed his mouth across her lips.

"But I'm here now. You still have me."

Haley leaned back enough that she could see his face.

"And you are enough," she whispered. "Make love to me, Sam. I have an overwhelming need to feel alive."

The fear from nearly dying was still in her voice, and Sam would do anything to take that away, so he leaned back into the water, taking her with him, becoming the raft that moved them into the shallow end of the pool.

Haley came out of her underwear within seconds and tossed it out onto the concrete. Sam's hands were beneath the water, lifting her up and then easing her down onto his erection. Haley wrapped her legs around his waist and buried her face against his neck as he filled her.

Sam closed his eyes as he went deep, accepting

everything she gave him as a blessing. She was the only woman he'd ever loved—would ever love—and she was right where she belonged. In his arms.

He turned, putting himself between her and the back of the pool and started to move in a repetitive, rolling thrust. The pool lights became their spotlight, distorting movement and bodies as the act of love took on a life of its own.

Waves rocked them. The night air slipped around them, between them. The sound of disappearing sirens mimicked the scream inside Haley's head.

She was coming, falling, burning, then shattering… and shattered.

Sam was on his own quest when he thought he heard her groan. Her breath was hot against his neck when she suddenly tensed in his embrace. He thrust once, twice, then every muscle inside her contracted around him like a vise, and it was all over. The climax rocked him to the core. He was still spilling his seed inside her, and trying not to stumble as he locked his arms around her and carried her up the three short steps and out of the pool.

Sam sat down on the first thing he came to, which was the bench next to the picnic table, and then held her without speaking until the air had dried their bodies. It was with great reluctance that he pulled out of her, and was already getting hard again when they went inside and locked the door.

The lights went out from room to room as they

walked their way down the hall. Sam set the security alarm and followed Haley into the bedroom.

She paused in the doorway to the bathroom, and then turned to face him. "I love you, Sammy. Every time you touch me, I am healed a little bit more. God willing, maybe one day I will give you another baby."

And then she walked into the bathroom and closed the door.

"I love you, too, Haley Jo. From your lips to God's ear."

Mae Arnold was moving, and eating and sleeping, and now and then still knocked off her feet by the shock of what had happened to her life in such a short time. After doing morning chores and making herself some cinnamon toast with her coffee, she had driven into town this morning to talk to a Realtor. There was only one person with a Realtor's license, and he also owned the only bar in town. He sold drinks at the bar, and used the little office in back for his real estate business. Out of consideration for the people who did not approve of drinking, he'd put a door at the back of the building that led straight into the office, and that's where Mae was now—standing on the stoop, staring at the hand-painted sign hung by the door.

Emmit Watkins—Licensed Realtor.

Emmit knew she was coming, so she promptly knocked.

Emmit opened the door, and then stepped aside for her to enter.

"Come in, Mae! My sympathies on your recent losses. Take a seat right here where it's cool."

She eyed the window unit air conditioner above his head, and then scooted her chair a bit to the right to get the full blast of refrigerated air.

"So. How can I help you?" Emmit asked.

Mae gripped the arms of the chair, wondering if God was going to strike her dead for this decision.

"I want to put my farm up for sale. Livestock and all."

Emmit blinked. "But Arnolds have always lived on that property. For nearly two hundred years!"

"I'm not an Arnold," Mae snapped. "I just married one and gave birth to one…fool that I was for both choices."

Emmit blinked again, and then shifted into his business mode. "So, how many acres do you have with that property?"

"There's a hundred and fifty acres, two ponds, four outbuildings including a barn, and a corral. One dry milk cow, one fattening hog and a chicken house full of chickens."

Emmit was writing it all down as fast as she was talking. "And the house, how many square feet?" he asked.

"It's a single-story house with porches on front and back. There's about fifteen hundred square feet, one bath and three bedrooms with a utility room added later that's attached to the kitchen. Nice-size living room, separate dining room, eat-in kitchen and all furnishings stay with the house."

Emmit's eyes widened.

"But, Mae, where will you go, and what will you do for furnishings when you get there?"

"I know where I'm going. I'll deal with the rest when I get there."

"Do you have an asking price?" he asked.

"It's all old. I don't know what anything sells for," she said.

Emmit saw the pain beneath her bravado. He'd heard the stories about Pete Arnold. Hell, most every man in town knew the old fart was a womanizer, but they also thought Mae knew it, too. Now it was obvious that she had not. And he also knew their son, Hershel, was dead. He guessed he understood why she wanted to leave. There wasn't anything good left for her here.

"All right, then," Emmit said. "I'll come out and take some pictures, and we'll discuss a price then."

"Much appreciated, Emmit. Give Bessie my regards," Mae said, and stood. Her business here was done.

"Yes, ma'am, I sure will. Thank you for the business, and if the weather stays nice and sunny like today, would it be okay if I came out tomorrow and took the pictures?"

"In the morning?" she asked.

"Yes, ma'am. In the morning," he said, as he opened the door for her.

"I'll be waiting," Mae said, and made a hasty exit. She had one more stop to make before she left town— back to the funeral home, but not to see Pete, who was still on display in the viewing room. He was on his own now. He and his women. She was going back to make arrangements for Hershel, too.

When she pulled up at the one stoplight in town, the pickup backfired. She rolled her eyes. Great. Now everybody was staring.

When the light turned green, she drove on to the funeral home and parked under the only shade tree. The sun was hot on her head as she walked across the parking lot, and when she opened the door, a chime sounded somewhere in back to let them know someone had entered. Moments later, George came through the double doors.

"Mrs. Arnold. I didn't expect— Um... I mean, how can I help you?" he said.

"They're shipping my son's body here. He's already on the way, but I don't have any kind of an arrival date for you."

George nodded. "Then we'll let you know when he arrives."

Mae shook her head. "No. I've decided I don't want to see him dead, since he didn't care enough to come see me when he was alive."

George didn't bother to hide his shock. Mae Arnold was turning into quite a surprise. "I see, then how do you—"

"I want his body cremated. He's not worth the time

it would take to dig a hole. After you bury Pete, just sprinkle Hershel's ashes on his grave. They're two of a kind. They deserve each other."

George just kept nodding. There was no need to comment on anything she was saying.

"Do I need to sign something?" she asked.

George nodded. "Uh…if you'll follow me to the office—"

Mae stood there, waiting. "George!"

"Yes, ma'am," he said.

"I can't rightly follow you to your office unless you lead the way."

"Oh my word, of course, I'm sorry. It's just been a shocking…um, I mean a very busy day."

Eighteen

Amy Lynn Ledbetter choked down her breakfast of jailhouse oatmeal, ignoring the nervous looks from the other three women in the holding cell, and then was given a clean prison-orange jumpsuit to wear to her arraignment. She'd stripped without care for who was looking to put it on. It went well with the felt slippers they gave her for shoes.

As she was driven to the courthouse from the jail, she thought about the freedom she had taken for granted. No more impulse shopping. No more going to a movie, or swimming at the beach. No more summer rain on her face. Would she ever stand in snow again?

Every thought she should have had when she made her first trip to juvie was now going through her mind. She thought back to all the people who tried to warn her where she was heading. The judge who lectured her sternly when she was on the verge of aging out of the juvenile court system, warning her if she got caught again, it would be doing hard time in prison.

Instead of changing her ways then, she just learned how to be more careful, and how to be a better thief, and how to clean up after a kill without leaving a trace of herself behind.

She leaned back against the bench seat in the prison van and closed her eyes. No regrets. No feeling sorry for herself. It was an inevitable conclusion. She'd laid the trail for herself all the way to this destination.

Once they reached the courthouse, she was put in a holding area with a guard inside and two guards outside her door. No one talked to her. No one looked at her. Before, she had worked hard to be invisible. Now it was because she was too evil—too disgusting to acknowledge.

When it came time for her to go before the judge, she was taken out of the holding room and paraded through the halls of the courthouse under guard, while reporters shouted at her, asking questions she had no intention of answering, and thrusting cameras in her face. She hadn't really thought about this aspect of getting caught, but it appeared word was out that she'd killed that old woman. Whatever. She'd killed young ones, too.

One cameraman got too close to suit her, so she spit on the lens. The reporter standing beside him gasped, suddenly indignant without caring that they'd entered personal space. But it went by the wayside when the guard yanked Amy forward into the courtroom.

The first person she saw was Rance Wesley, her lawyer. His face was expressionless, so she tried to read his body language, but to no avail. Once she was seated at the defense table, she began grilling him.

"What do you know? What am I supposed to do?"

"This is your arraignment, not a trial. You'll stand when I say so, and admit your guilt when you are asked how you plead."

"But what if—"

Rance glared. "You said you didn't want to go to trial."

"And I don't. Did you get me a deal?"

"Maybe."

Before she could ask anything more, a man with a deep, booming "James Earl Jones voice" shouted "All rise," and then Amy zoned out. She was living out a scene in fucking *Criminal Minds*, only she couldn't hit Pause and go pee, or get herself a snack. This was the real deal, and life as she'd known it was officially over.

Two days later she was pulled out of the cell again, this time for a consultation with her lawyer. Like before, she was handcuffed to the table, and as soon as the guard stepped out of the room, she leaned forward.

"Did I get the deal?"

Rance nodded. "You will give your statement to the Dallas District Attorney Parker Austin, and to an official from the FBI this afternoon at 2:00 p.m. Not sure who the Feds are sending. Austin worked all that out. You do not have a choice of prisons."

"This isn't what I asked for," she snapped.

He stared at her a moment, watching the crazy way the pupils of her eyes kept widening and retracting, like a tire that couldn't decide to blow out, or just go flat, then he held out both hands.

"Look at me, Ledbetter. Not the walls. Not the bars on the windows. Look at me."

Amy focused in on the calm demeanor of his voice and leaned back.

"Thank you," Rance said. "So…in this hand, you have the 'Texas prison sitting on death row' choice. And then in this hand you have the 'Texas prison and life without parole' choice. You choose."

It was a bit ironic that after all the people Ledbetter had killed, she was afraid to die.

"Fuck," she muttered, and pointed to the life without parole.

"Fine. I advise you not to be a smart-ass on film. I advise you to say what you have to say without elaborating. I advise you not to insinuate in any way that you have ever killed anyone else."

Amy frowned. "Well, of course I won't. What do you think I am?" she muttered.

"I think you're a smart-ass. I think you are proud of your occupation. If you don't like what I said, next time don't ask me a question you don't want answered. I'll see you at two."

Amy shrugged. "Yeah. Okay. Whatever."

He went to the door and knocked. One guard escorted him out of the jail while another guard took Amy back to lockup, and then had to wake her up to bring her back.

Now here she was, sitting in a lawyer's office, handcuffed and shackled, giving her testimony in front of a video camera, with District Attorney Parker Austin, and Deputy Director Bob Richmond of the Texas branch of the FBI as witnesses. When it was over, the Dallas DA got Ledbetter in a state prison, with a life without parole sentence, and Deputy Director Richmond got Santos on Federal charges for robbery and murder.

The power came back on at The Rochester on the morning of the third day of Santos's arrival. It was one thing for the power to be on, but it was great news that the central air-conditioning for the building still worked. Obviously it was not housed in the basement or the first floor, because both had flooded. He was so elated that he let out a whoop, and then began closing windows.

Now that the refrigerator was working, Dude debated with himself about cleaning it out so he could use it, or just doing without. But ice and creature comforts won out, and after looking around for a box of garbage bags and finding them on a back shelf in the small pantry, he tied a tea towel around his face to mask the smell, opened the refrigerator door and began dumping everything inside into the bags.

He had two filled, and was working on a third before he finally finished. And then he remembered the freezer, and pulled everything out of there, too, including a box of once-frozen shrimp and a container of melted ice cream. As he was emptying the water from the ice basket that had once been full of cubes, he heard the ice machine in the freezer beginning to fill. One more plus for which to be grateful.

What caused him some concern was that residents were returning, but he need not have worried. Yes, people were returning to their apartments, and yes, he was a stranger to them, but they thought nothing of it. The hurricane had displaced thousands. Maybe the woman who'd live there before wasn't coming back. Maybe she died. Maybe this guy's place was uninhabitable, and this was his new home. They had their own set of problems, and didn't care to inquire about his.

It took Dude a couple of trips down the hall to the garbage cans before he got everything hauled out. Then he thoroughly cleaned the interior of the refrigerator with soap and water. And to celebrate the return of electricity, he also tossed all of his sweat-stained clothing into the washer.

He was a killer-in-waiting, playing house in his next victim's home.

Now that that was all done, he turned on the TV

to catch up on the news, but channel surfed without finding anything of interest. It was too late for the noon news, and too early for evening news, so he turned the sound down a bit and stretched out on the sofa.

The room was cooling off nicely, and between cleaning the refrigerator and the load of laundry washing, the whole place smelled fresh and clean.

He fell asleep thinking about the beautiful blue of the water in Cozumel, and dreamed of Marigrace riding his hard-on like a jockey at the Kentucky Derby.

Sam was outside mowing the front yard when he saw a neighbor from up the street out walking her dog. She waved, and he waved back, but then she stopped to talk, so he killed the engine, then pulled a handkerchief out of his pocket to wipe the sweat from his face.

"Good morning, Helen. How's Petey?"

The little pug-nosed Frenchy heard his name and yapped. Helen Worth just smiled. "Petey and I are fine. It sure is a hot one today, isn't it?"

"Yes, ma'am, it is."

"I won't waste your time because I see you're busy, but I wondered if you'd heard about the details of the service for Louise?"

Sam felt a twinge of sadness. "No, I had not."

Helen's eyes welled with tears. "Some family flew in from Tennessee. They're taking her body back to Memphis for burial. It's where she's from."

"I didn't know that," Sam said.

"I did, but then she and I have been neighbors on this street for over twenty-two years. It sure was a shocking thing that happened to her."

"Yes, ma'am, it was," Sam said.

Petey yapped again.

Helen sighed. "Well, Petey wants his walk over with and so do I. I saw you on TV, you know." Then she grinned. "You were quite the hero. Is your girl, okay?"

"Yes, ma'am, my girl is more than okay. She's just about healed. Only a few fading bruises left."

Petey yapped again.

"Oh hush, Petey," Helen said, and picked him up in her arms. "Give her my regards. Maybe I'll meet her one of these days."

"Maybe so," Sam said, and then waved as she walked away, still carrying her dog.

Sam stuck the handkerchief back in his pocket and started the mower back up. Only a few more rounds to go, and he'd be through.

Haley heard the mower go off and went to look out the window. That's when she saw the woman and her dog stop to talk to Sam. She felt like she was spying, so she went back to folding laundry. She kept having to wash the same few outfits over and over and was wishing she had her own clothes again.

Then she wondered if the power had come back

on at The Rochester, and what shape the bottom floor was in.

She was debating with the notion of just hiring a moving company to go in and pack up her stuff and bring it here, but there were some things she wanted to bring, and more that she didn't. The only way to make sure she got what she wanted, was to go do it herself, but Lord, how she hated the act of moving.

She finished folding laundry, then went to hang up the blouses in the closet. Sam came in while she was putting laundry away. She could hear him calling her name, and stepped out of the closet.

"In the bedroom!" she shouted. She was putting clean underwear in the dresser drawer when he came loping into the room.

"Hey…let's go eat lunch somewhere today, okay?"

She smiled. "I'd love to."

"I'll have to shower, so you choose a place, okay?"

"Good thing I just did laundry. My wardrobe is limited. I've been thinking about going back to Houston to pack up. I have a lease, but there's always a waiting list, so I know they'll let me out of it."

"No problem, baby. We'll talk about it more over lunch."

"Okay," she said, then stopped to watch him strip on the way to shower. He had a body worth appreciating.

While Sam was in the shower, she called the manager's office at The Rochester.

"Rochester Apartments, Frances speaking."

"Frances, this is Haley Quaid. I'm a resident on the fourth floor, but am in Dallas at the present, and was wondering what the conditions are there now."

"Of course the basement and first floor received the flood damage. We've been removing the debris from the lobby, and now that the power is on, we can also begin cleanup."

"Oh, the power is on?"

"As of today," Frances said.

"I'm in Dallas now, and intend to move back here as soon as I can pack up. My lease isn't up yet, but I know you have a waiting list for tenants, and wonder if it would be possible to get an early release?"

"What size apartment do you have?" Frances asked.

"It's a two-bedroom, two-bath. Right at a thousand square feet."

"We have several names on the list waiting for that size to open up. I'm sure we can do that with no problem whatsoever."

"Wonderful," Haley said. "Rent is still paid until the end of the month, and I will certainly have it cleaned before I leave. We'll be heading back that way soon. I'll see you then."

"Of course. See you soon," Frances said, and hung up.

Haley sat for a few moments, thinking about how life was taking her back to happiness without her planning any of it. It had been a miserable trip to get here, but she'd do it all over again, to be able to spend the rest of her life with Sam.

Happy that much of the unknown had been settled, she hurried to change her clothes, and when Sam came out of the bathroom, she went in to fix her hair. She was wiping the steam from the mirror, and had cleaned a space just big enough to see her face when she stopped, then leaned forward, turned her head from side to side, and fingered the new scar on her cheek and the nearly faded bruises.

"Hey, don't worry about any of that. You look beautiful," Sam said, as he came in to hang up his towel.

Haley eyed the faded Wrangler jeans and the blue-and-white-striped cotton shirt he was wearing.

"So do you," she said, laughing at the expression on his face as she finished wiping off the steam.

Sam blew her a kiss, then began finger-combing his hair until the black spikes suited him, while Haley began putting on her makeup.

Before, she'd had too many wounds to hide, but now that she was nearly healed, she reached for concealer, dabbed a tiny bit beneath both eyes and on the scar, then worked it in. She opted out of face powder, because she'd only sweat it off before they ever reached the restaurant. Satisfied that it had taken the shock value out of her face, she finished up with a little mascara and lipstick and called it done.

"I'm ready when you are," Haley said.

"I'm always ready," Sam said, and then grinned.

Haley was still laughing when they got into the Jeep and drove away.

"So, where are we going?" Sam asked, as he wove his way out of their neighborhood.

"Wherever they serve the best fried catfish in Dallas," Haley said.

"Okay, then, we're going to Whiskers Fish and Burgers. It's a distance away in the 1700 block of Singleton Boulevard, but it's worth the drive. What it lacks in ambiance, it makes up for in food and service."

"Sounds like my kind of place," Haley said.

"So, while we're driving, let's talk about your apartment," Sam said.

"I called while you were in the shower to find out what the conditions were. The good news is most of the damage is confined to the basement and first floor, and that the power was restored there today. That will make everything much simpler for me."

"What about your lease?" he asked.

"They have a list of names waiting for an apartment the size of mine, so I'm good to go on the release."

"One step closer," Sam said, and gave her fingers a quick squeeze.

Haley nodded. One step closer, indeed.

By the time they reached the Whiskers Fish and Burgers Shack, Haley was starving. Then, when they parked and got out, the scent of frying fish overrode any opinion Haley might have had of the outside decor.

The parking lot was already filling up, so they

wasted no time getting out. The iron fencing all around the front of the little place looked like the walls of a prison. The bars were the same height as the roof.

"I assume this is to keep thieves out, not pen people in," Haley said.

Sam nodded. "I found this place a couple of years back when I was on a stakeout. The fish is so good in here that you wouldn't mind being penned up inside. I eat here at least two or three times a month."

"Awesome," Haley said, as they walked inside. Then somebody called out from across the room.

"Sam! You're the man! I saw you on TV, swinging from some rope. You trying out for *Tarzan* next?"

Sam was grinning. "I told you I eat here a lot." Then he put his arm around Haley's shoulders. "Guys, this is Haley. Be nice."

There was a brief moment of silence, which Haley read as shock, and then it erupted in noise.

"You the lady who was trapped with those thugs? The one Life Flight rescued?"

"Yes, she is," Sam said.

They all gave her a thumbs-up.

Haley smiled.

A waitress swung by them with a tray full of food.

"Good to see you down on firm ground. Nice to meet you, Haley. Y'all take that table over by the window. Someone will be with you shortly."

And just like that, she became one of the crowd.

And when the food came, it was the best fried cat-fish she'd ever eaten.

"Aren't you going to eat your fries?" Sam asked.

Haley groaned. "I ate some. And some of the pick-les, and all of the tartar sauce, and you already ate my bread. I'm stuffed. Help yourself to whatever is still here."

And Sam did. She was still laughing at something he said when someone tapped her on the shoulder, then moved into her line of vision. There was a mo-ment of complete shock as her stomach rolled, and then she got herself together.

"It is you!" the woman crowed. "I told Charlie it was, but he didn't believe me. We heard all about you on the news! It's good to see you again. We haven't seen you since—"

Haley watched her face flushing, and felt obliged to rescue her.

"Since Robbie's funeral, I think. Isn't that right, Sam?"

Sam nodded. "Sounds about right. Good to see you, Mavis. How's your son, Andy? He and Robbie played baseball together, right?"

Mavis nodded. "So, you live in Houston now," she said.

"Yes, but not for long. I'm moving back with Sam," Haley said.

Mavis exhaled slowly, and smiled. "That's great news! I know y'all will be happy, just like you were be—" She stopped talking and then rolled her eyes.

"I never know when to shut my mouth. It's good to see the both of you."

She was gone as abruptly as she had arrived.

Sam was watching Haley's face for signs of distress, but didn't see it.

Haley caught the intent look he was giving her and lowered her voice.

"For the love of God, Sam. I am not going to fly apart. This is going to be awkward for a while for the people who knew us, but it doesn't mean it's awkward for us, right?"

Relieved, Sam shrugged. "Sorry if I was staring, but I was so intrigued by the way that green and purple under your eye is blending now that it's fading away, that I got caught in the beauty."

Haley burst out laughing.

Sam grinned.

Their waitress appeared. "Y'all want anything else?"

"Just the ticket, please," Sam said.

She pulled it from the pocket of her apron and slapped it down on the table.

"It's been a pleasure serving you. Y'all come back."

"Oh, you know we will," Sam said. He fished some bills out of his wallet, leaving a hefty tip to boot, and then escorted Haley out.

The heat hit them both in the face. Beads of sweat broke out on Haley's upper lip as Sam used the remote to unlock the doors.

"I'd run to get out of the sun, but I'm too full to move that fast," Haley said.

"I'm glad you liked this place," Sam said.

Haley nodded. "It's a keeper, for sure."

A few minutes later they were back in traffic with the cold air on blast and the vents aimed at their faces. It felt so comfortable, so natural to be doing this together again, that Sam forgot about polite conversation, and Haley fell asleep on the way home.

Sam glanced at her once and smiled. This was just like before, when their world was whole and their lives were happy. He sighed, then signaled a lane change as they were coming up on the exit to go home. They were already in happy mode. If they could just get the two-million-dollar monkey off their backs, they'd be in work mode, building that new world.

Mae had mentally separated herself from this farm, but as she went through the farmhouse that night, locking up and turning out lights, the emotion of what was happening sent her to her knees in the middle of the kitchen floor.

She threw back her head and screamed out in anger, then broke down in sobs—each one ripping up her throat and out her mouth to the point that she couldn't catch her breath.

"I didn't kill anyone! I didn't cheat on my husband! I didn't steal money! I didn't do harm to any living thing, and yet you have gutted me, Lord! I stayed faithful to Your word and this is my reward? Why didn't I die instead? Why didn't You take me, instead of leaving me to bear this shame and heartache alone?"

Without waiting for an answer, Mae went from her knees to the floor, then curled herself up as tiny as she could be and cried herself to sleep.

She woke up once to the sound of coyotes yipping, and for a moment was trying to figure out why she was on the floor. Then she remembered she'd had herself a bit of a fit. Morning was too far away to stay where she was, so she got up and finally made her way to bed.

The next time she woke up, the sun was shining in her eyes, and she remembered Emmit Watkins.

"Oh Lordy, Emmit will be here and catch me in my gowntail. I better get a move on."

She washed her face without looking at herself, and then combed her hair and ran to get dressed. She was drinking her second cup of coffee and finishing up her bowl of cereal when the phone rang.

Mae hurried to answer.

"Hello."

"Mae, this is Emmit. I'm about to head your way, okay?"

"Yes, it's okay. Come right ahead."

After that, she hurried to clean up the kitchen, and then went through the rooms, making sure everything looked neat and tidy, the same way she'd gone about preparing the clothes to bury her men in. Even though her dreams had been shattered, she didn't know any other way to be.

Nineteen

As of 10:00 a.m. that morning, the Federal Bureau of Investigation had an arrest warrant for one Alejandro Santos, aka Dude Santos, with the last known address of the town house he'd just rented in Dallas.

After a futile attempt to serve the warrant, they now knew he was in the wind. All of his personal belongings were gone, as was the rental car he was driving.

They put out a BOLO for the make and model of the rental car, and issued notices to all law enforcement agencies that Alejandro, aka Dude, Santos was wanted on federal charges of robbery and murder. They'd finally found their third man.

And someone tipped off the media that the third man in the First State Bank robbery in Houston had been identified. The news item initiated all kinds of wild suppositions that Santos had been the one with the money all along.

Before the FBI knew it was happening, Santos had

become a bigger target to criminals like him, thinking they might find him first and get all of the money.

The irony of this was that the FBI knew he didn't have it, or any knowledge of where it was because of what Haley Quaid overheard. They also knew, thanks to Amy Ledbetter's testimony, that he'd gone so far as hiring her to get to Haley Quaid for information, too.

After all this time, and all the work they'd put into this case, there was a real good chance this could become a cluster fuck.

Dude was in the kitchen making coffee to have with his lunch. He'd turned on the small television earlier, and was listening as he worked when he heard one of the newscasters say his name.

He turned around just as one of his old mug shots flashed on the screen, and then he ran to turn up the volume, then listened to the story in total shock. They knew he was the missing man from the robbery! Ledbetter gave him up. It was the only way they could have known. But it was the last part of the story that freaked him most. It appeared the media was throwing out all kinds of suppositions about the possibility that he might be the one who had the missing money, which was why it couldn't be found.

He went from shock to true fear as reality set in. Not only was there a federal warrant out for his arrest, but there would be dozens of scumbags already playing their own game of bounty hunter to find him and the money he didn't have.

He turned around and looked back into the kitchen at the food on his plate and the coffee that had finished brewing, thinking how quickly the hiding place he was in had turned into a prison. He needed to be somewhere else real bad.

He'd grown enough of a beard while he was here that he was hoping anyone who'd seen him here would not connect him to that picture. The mug shot was an old one and in it, he was clean-shaven. He was also forty pounds heavier now than he was when that mug shot was taken.

If he left here right now in broad daylight, he wouldn't get out of Houston. Either the cops would spot his rental, or one of the hunters would spot his face. He had a slim chance…and it was a very slim one, but he was going to take it.

He'd leave here after dark, steal a car from the parking garage and take off for the border. If he got that far, he would still be in danger of arrest. At that point, he had one option left, and he wondered if he would be the only Latino ever to try and sneak out of the US to get back into Mexico. But he already knew that river ran the same direction, whether you were coming or going.

He ran back to the bedroom and began going through his things, figuring out what he needed most. He was going to have to leave all his nice clothing behind, packing only what he could carry in his smallest bag.

* * *

Sam and Haley were on their way to Houston in one of the smaller truck rentals from U-Haul, and had been on the road since just after 9:00 a.m. It was just before noon when Sam's phone rang. He answered the call on Bluetooth and kept driving.

"Hello, this is Sam."

"Sam, it's Jack Gordon. I swung by your house this morning, but you were gone."

"Haley and I are in a U-Haul on our way to Houston to get her things from her apartment. What's going on?"

"I just wanted you to know that this media coverage of Santos did not come from us."

"I wondered," Sam said.

"Yes, and not only does this give Santos a warning that he's been identified, but the media spin of him in possession of the missing money has also given every desperate man in Texas the urge to go looking for him, too."

"Ah…that hadn't occurred to me yet, but thanks for the heads-up."

"Just pay attention to your surroundings. We have no idea where Santos is, but if he is really that desperate to get to Haley, he could be anywhere. He could have had eyes on you ever since Ledbetter's arrest, just waiting for his own chance to get her."

"What was he driving?" Sam asked, glancing up into the rearview mirror.

"A 2015 model white Ford Focus rental, but since

the BOLO is out for that, he may have already ditched it and be driving something else."

"Well hell," Sam said. "Thanks for the update. We're headed back to Dallas as soon as we have what we need. Probably get home sometime before daybreak." Then he disconnected and glanced at Haley.

"He talks loud. I heard all that," Haley said. "But with all that going on, I don't think I'm his target anymore. He has too much pressure from cops to worry about what I might or might not know. And I have you, so I'm not freaked out. At all."

Sam nodded. "Agreed."

Satisfied that they were no longer a target, they kept driving and drove through the city limits of Houston just before 1:00 p.m. It took almost another hour to get to The Rochester.

Haley pointed at the parking garage. "Do you think there's enough clearance for us to drive in?" she asked.

Sam glanced at the clearance height painted on the entrance.

"Yes, easily," he said.

"Then take it inside and go up to the fourth floor. It will make loading stuff up so much easier if we don't have to do any stairs. Park as close to the entrance door as possible. It will be right beside the elevators."

"Okay," Sam said, and drove through the entrance and drove up the landings one by one until he reached the fourth floor. He saw the elevators within moments.

"Oh, this is great," Haley said. "Usually this place is packed. A few residents have obviously returned, but not nearly all of them. We can park within twenty feet of the door. This is awesome!"

Sam killed the engine, and then looked at Haley and grinned. "We're here, baby. There are quite a few boxes in the back, and the dolly to move them. We have ten garment boxes. If that's not enough, we can fold up the rest and box them rather than hang them."

Haley shivered with excitement, and began digging through her purse for the keys.

"Okay, I'm ready to go."

They both got out, and then Sam opened the back doors of the truck, jumped up to get the dolly out first. Then he stacked a load of the flats in an upright position on the dolly, and strapped them in, then locked the U-Haul before heading into the building.

Haley was carrying the sack with several rolls of packing tape and a tape dispenser. She could fold boxes and seal the bottoms in no time at all, and if they needed more boxes than what they were bringing in, Sam could go back for the rest.

"What's the room number?" Sam asked.

Haley pointed. "404. Just a couple more down and on the left."

"Here we are," Sam said.

"I dread cleaning out the refrigerator most of all," she said, as she put the key in the first lock and turned it, then moved up to the dead bolt and unlocked it last.

She tried to turn the knob, but it didn't give. Frowning, she used her key again. It turned freely the second time and she swung the door inward, grateful to be met by cool air.

"That's weird. Like it was unlocked and then I locked it when I tried to get in," Haley said, as she closed the door behind Sam.

He frowned. "What do you mean?"

"Oh… I always lock both locks. Always. I guess I was in such a hurry to get out that morning that I forgot. At least it's cool in here now. And… I see I also left lights on, which I did do from time to time. You can unload those boxes in that open space between the kitchen and the living room. I'll be right back."

"Where are you going?" Sam asked.

"Down the hall to my bedroom. I want to change into a comfortable pair of shoes."

Sam rolled the dolly over to the open area, released the straps and then began taking the flats off and stacking them on the floor. He had everything unloaded and Haley still hadn't returned.

Curious, he opened the refrigerator to see what shape it was in, and then stood there staring, trying to wrap his head around what he was seeing.

"Hey, Haley…you need to see this," he yelled.

She didn't answer.

He frowned again.

"Haley! Are you okay?"

She still hadn't answered.

And then everything suddenly clicked into place. The lock that wasn't locked. The lights left on. A refrigerator practically empty and cleaned.

He turned and looked straight down the hall, then pulled up his pant leg, slid the handgun from the holster on the side of the boot and took it off safety. He walked down the hall and pushed the door inward.

His mind went through a thousand different scenarios in less than ten seconds, but it all boiled down to Haley on her knees, in front of a man holding a gun to her head.

"One wrong move and she is dead," Santos said.

Sam didn't like her odds.

"Aw, *hell* no," he said, and swung the handgun up so fast Santos never saw it coming.

But Haley did. She flung herself sideways just as Sam's bullet hit him right between the eyes.

Santos's gun went off, but Haley was six feet away, watching him fall.

Sam ran toward Haley and helped her up, then wrapped his arms around her.

"Oh my God, oh my God, baby, are you okay?"

"Yes. He took me by surprise. I opened the closet and he was right in my face. He put a finger to his lips as he came out, shoved me to my knees and grabbed a handful of my hair. And then we waited."

They could hear footsteps of people running in the hallway, and then someone knocking on the door.

"We better answer that," Sam said.

Haley moved ahead of him to open the door and found Frances, the manager, and the security guard from downstairs.

"We're okay. This is Sam, my ex, soon to be husband again. We just got in from Dallas to pack up my things, and found an intruder in my place. He surprised me…held a gun to my head, threatening Sam not to move."

"So I shot him, instead," Sam said, then presented his PI badge and his license to carry before the security guard could freak out. Then he flipped the safety and laid the gun on the little table by the door.

"Has anybody called the police?" Haley asked.

"I will," Frances said.

Haley turned around, reached for Sam, and once again, fainted in his arms.

The Houston police were all over the apartment, looking for evidence that would corroborate the stories the Quaids gave them. First, taking into consideration the still-warm engine on the U-Haul, indicating they hadn't been there long enough for it to cool. The dead man's clothing hanging in Haley's closet. His toiletry bag in the master bathroom with his things spread out all over. And the clean and empty refrigerator that Haley had been dreading to tackle. Everything pointed to the obvious.

He'd been there for days and they walked in to a surprise.

When the crime scene crew arrived and began finding his fingerprints all over everything, from the coffee maker to the handles on cabinets, and the body hair recovered from her shower that was so obviously not hers, it only added to what they already knew.

A detective from homicide had been on scene for only a few minutes when he walked back into the living room where Sam and Haley were sitting.

"Has anyone found a wallet? There's no ID on him and his pockets are empty," the detective said.

"It's Alejandro Santos," Sam said.

The detective frowned. "Who?"

Three different officers looked up, all talking at once. "The third man? The missing man from the bank heist? The one the Feds are looking for?"

Sam nodded.

The detective frowned at him. "And how do you know all this?"

"Santos has been after Haley ever since his two partners took Haley hostage during the hurricane."

A cop standing by the door suddenly pointed at Sam. "I know who you are! I've been trying to place you ever since we walked in. You're the thumbs-up guy from that first air rescue. And this Haley is Haley Quaid! The woman who was kidnapped by the escaped prisoners the US Marshals were after. Life Flight airlifted a Haley Quaid from that house in Thornwood. That's you!"

Everyone turned and looked at Haley again. Now the fading bruises and the scar on her cheek were making sense.

"Yes, that was me. I heard a lot while I was trapped with them. They were talking about betraying someone named Dude Santos. I didn't know who that was at the time, but when I told the Marshals and the FBI about it, they figured it out."

Then Sam began to explain how Santos went after Haley, believing she could help him find where his buddies hid the money they'd stolen, and killed Sam's neighbor in the process.

By the time he laid the whole story out, the FBI had arrived on the scene. Jack Gordon flashed his badge as he entered, took one look at Sam and Haley and then shook his head.

"Really glad to see you two looking so healthy." Then he introduced himself to the detectives before he sat down with Sam and Haley. "I'll bet you're about sick and tired of all this."

"I'm hoping there's no more men after my girl, that's for damn sure," he said.

"Be right back," Jack said, then got up asking where the body was, and disappeared within the melee of cops. He was back within a couple of minutes. "Just wanted to confirm the identity for myself, and I'm going to say, I didn't give the bastard enough credit. After we arrested Ledbetter, I guess he decided to find Haley by himself. And what better way to do it than to hide out in her apartment and wait for her to return?"

"When is all this going to be over in here?" Haley asked.

Jack shrugged "Hard to say. Our crew will be in shortly. I'm sorry this is going to delay your packing a few hours."

Haley slumped wearily against Sam. "At least Santos isn't looking for me anymore." Then she gave Jack a hard look. "I expect someone to give a very public statement to the media, letting them know I knew nothing about the money, and that it was Ledbetter who gave him up as the third man. Not me."

Jack nodded. "We can do that much for you, ma'am. After all, you were the first one who brought them down. If only your shots would have been as clean as Sam's it might have saved you a world of hurt."

Haley shook her head. "You men all think the same. Women are good, but men are better."

Jack grinned. "My wife would certainly take me to task for that."

"I thought I did a pretty good job," Haley said. "I hit both of them with my first two shots, at night, in a hall with no lights."

Jack grinned. "That you did."

"Extremely lucky shots," the detective said, eyeing Haley with new understanding.

"No, sir," Haley said. "I heard them, saw movement in the shadows and shot toward the sound."

"Just like I taught her," Sam added. "And for the record, I have never been able to beat her at the gun range."

Numb to all of the shock and noise, Haley fell asleep on her sofa with her head in Sam's lap. He sat motionless, his hand on her shoulder and his thoughts on rewind, unable to quit thinking about how close they'd both come to dying today. All because three men decided to rob an armored car. Here they were months later, and the devastation they had caused during the aftermath was still being counted.

Frances came back twice to check on Haley and Sam. Once to bring one of her own blankets to cover Haley as she slept, and the second time she brought food and cold drinks in a covered basket, and set it in on the coffee table in front of them.

Each time, Sam thanked her, and each time, she would smile and nod, leaving with tears in her eyes.

The last time she came, it was with a whispered warning.

"I hate to be the bearer of more complications, but be aware that the media have caught wind of all this. The police won't let them bother you right now, but after they're gone might be a different story. Security won't let them in the lobby, but there are always ways for people like that to get where they want to be."

"Thank you for your kindness," Sam said. "These past few years have been hard for Haley, and for me. She's been through a lot since the hurricane, and this incident today was, I think, the last of her endurance."

Frances looked down at Haley. "I am horrified for her beyond words. That's all I can say. We'll do anything to help her exit from The Rochester as easy as possible, and we're very apologetic that someone like this Santos man slipped under our notice."

Sam shook his head. "He just took advantage of

a dire situation and got away with it. As for helping her transition out of here…any amount of help you can muster to carry boxes as we can get them packed would be awesome. Our U-Haul is just down the hall and through the exit door to the parking garage."

"Yes, of course, and happy to do it, and we'll see to the cleaning after she's gone, so no worries on that end, either," Frances said. "I'll leave you two on your own for now, but if you want another place to sleep tonight, I'm sure we can—"

"We slept in an attic for days in sweltering heat with a hurricane on top of us, and two dead men down the hall from us. We'll be fine, here," Sam said.

"Oh my, oh bless you both," she whispered, and then slipped away.

Two more hours passed before the medical examiner arrived, and a short while later they hauled Santos out in a body bag, on a gurney with a wobbly wheel. It was an undignified exit, much like a dragging muffler. He would not have been pleased.

The Houston police were still on guard when the crime scene crews left, and then the Feds left with their people. The Houston police were the last to leave, and one of them approached Sam to escort Haley and him out.

"Sir, this is an official crime scene. We're going to tape it off and—"

And then Haley woke up. "What's going on?" she asked. "Where did everyone go?"

"I've got this, baby," Sam said, eyeing the cops. "Gentlemen, we appreciate everything you've done to help us, but your job is over here, and ours is just beginning. There are no questions left to answer. We'll be out of here by noon tomorrow. Okay?"

The cop frowned. "There's blood all over the floor in the bedroom."

Sam resisted the urge to roll his eyes. "I know. I'm the one who put a bullet in the man's head. It will be easier to ignore blood than a man holding a gun to her head. Besides, we won't be sleeping in there, so there's that."

The two officers looked at each other and shrugged, then pulled the door shut behind them.

Sam turned both locks just as Haley walked past him and down the hall to the doorway of her bedroom. He hurried down to join her, afraid of what her reaction might be. She kept passing out at times of stress, which he was still attributing to her concussion, and didn't want a repeat without anyone there to catch her.

"Honey?"

"Just look at this mess. And I told Frances it would be clean before I left."

Sam took her by the shoulders and turned her around, trying not to laugh.

"Damn, woman. Here I am worrying about your emotional status, and you're concerned with soap and water, so I can help you with that. Frances came by while you were sleeping. She's going to get us help in moving, then do all the cleanup after we're gone.

I think she's scared The Rochester might be sued for letting Santos hide in here under their noses."

Haley sighed. "That's the best thing I've heard since the thump Santos made when he hit the floor."

Sam shook his head and grinned. "Why don't we wash up in the guest bathroom. Frances brought food. We need to at least eat some of it or we might hurt her feelings. Oh…she also said the media got wind of what happened here, so we're not answering the door."

"Oh. My. Lord. There has to be an end to all this."

"And there will be," Sam said. "But not tonight. Tonight we eat, and then we'll sleep in the spare bedroom, and in the morning we pack and go home."

"Home. That sounds wonderful," Haley said.

As it turned out, they never made it to the extra bedroom. Haley fell back asleep on the sofa, so Sam covered her up, got a quilt from the extra bedroom, pulled the recliner up as close to the sofa as he could get it, pulled off his shoes, covered up with the quilt and closed his eyes. The last thing he flashed on was Haley on her knees in front of Santos, and then sleep pulled him under.

The next morning began with Frances knocking on their door at 8:00 a.m. with hot coffee and fresh doughnuts.

Sam peered through the peephole, then let her in.

"I smell fresh coffee," Haley said, as she came out of the guest bathroom, drying her hands.

Frances carried the tray to the kitchen counter, then gave Haley a quick hug.

"I told Sam yesterday while you were sleeping that we would see to the cleaning. I have six employees lined up to help you pack, then transport your things to your U-Haul. They will be here in about thirty minutes. Is there anything else we can do for you?"

"Yes," Haley said. "I will be leaving the furniture behind. So many people have lost everything during Hurricane Gladys, and I intended to donate it somewhere. If you would see to that happening, I would be grateful."

"Yes, we will be honored to help facilitate that for you, and I'll be sure and give them your name."

"Thank you," Haley said. "Now I think I better go grab a doughnut before Sam eats them all."

Frances waved as she went out the door, and was true to her word. Thirty minutes later, Haley's apartment was full of people again, but this time they were helping her and Sam pack.

It was ten minutes to twelve when Haley handed Frances the keys to her apartment, signed the release to her lease agreement, then walked out the lobby door of The Rochester.

Sam was parked at the front entrance, waiting for her to come out. As soon as she was back in the U-Haul, she buckled up.

"I'm done, Sammy. Take me home."

Twenty

George, the funeral director, was still troubled by yesterday's events.

Pete Arnold had been buried yesterday afternoon with no ceremony whatsoever. There was a gaggle of some people he grew up with, the four pissed-off women he'd been fucking, and Preacher Riley, who'd come at the request of the director of the funeral home.

It hadn't gone well, George thought, as he was finishing up the paperwork to close out the order, but it could have been worse. It was the first time he'd ever had a widow boycott her own husband's burial.

And today was going to be another first. George had in his possession Hershel Arnold's cremains, and as soon as his assistant arrived to take over, he was going to the cemetery, at Mae Arnold's request, and scatter them on Pete Arnold's grave.

His assistant, Delroy, finally arrived a few minutes later, flustered and angry.

"What's wrong?" George asked.

"Ohh, as luck would have it, the toilet overflowed at home. Only when it happened, it didn't smell like someone had dumped a big load. All I could smell was something burning. But since nothing was on fire and the water was all over the floor and running out into the hall, I snaked it out myself. In the process, I rescued from the depths of sewer hell, one slightly charred, heavy-duty-for-extra-flow-days sanitary pad belonging to my wife, a Cyborg action figure belonging to my eight-year-old son, Junior, a handful of broom straws that had been cut from the backside of the broom I use to sweep out the garage and a book of safety matches, all but two of which had been struck."

George was smiling, something he rarely enjoyed at his job.

"So what was going on?" he asked.

Delroy rolled his eyes. "It's all his mother's fault for what she lets Junior watch on the TV. Anyway, he saw some movie with a bunch of Vikings in it, and fixated on the way they dealt with their dead."

"I'm not following you," George said.

"Oh, well hell, let me enlighten you! When someone of importance died back in those times, they put the body on a pile of firewood, that is either in one of their long boats, or on a raft, set the wood on fire, and floated the body out to sea, all aflame and dramatic like that. And that's why the sanitary pad and broom straws were singed, and why the arm on the cyborg action figure was partly melted. The significance of the matchbook, I am sure you understand."

George was laughing so hard now, he could hardly catch his breath.

"So... Junior set it ablaze and then flushed it?" George asked.

Delroy sighed. "There wasn't much sea in the toilet, so he sent it down into a whirlpool, because... Vikings. Anyway, I'm sorry I'm late. Feel free to leave anytime you're ready."

George felt all the heaviness of the past two days leaving him as he carried Hershel to the car. He was certain that in their younger years, Pete must have been a good and patient father, like Delroy, and Hershel would have been just a happy little kid, like Junior.

He drove down Main and out to the west side of town to the Carytown Cemetery, proceeded down to the freshest grave in the lot and parked.

The flowers from the service were still scattered about on the raw pile of dirt over Pete Arnold's grave. They were wilting, and the ribbons were coming untied, but George was certain those details would escape Pete's notice.

He walked up to the side of the grave, took the lid off the urn and then hesitated.

"Uh...Pete, thought I should give you a heads-up that Hershel is on his way to visit. I know it's been a while, but I'm certain you two must have a lot of catching up to do. Here he comes now, knocking at your door."

And with that, he tilted the urn and began scattering the ashes like his mama used to scatter the scratch for the hens in the chicken house, flinging it about and letting the breeze carry it at will.

For a few moments, the air was awash in a gray, powdery ash, whirling about like snowflakes too light to fall. Then the ash began to settle, onto the flowers, and on the ribbons and into the raw, upturned earth.

"Ashes to ashes. Dust to dust," George said. "You two caused way too much turmoil when you were here. It's time for the both of you to rest in peace."

The for-sale sign at the Arnold property had garnered more interest than Mae had expected, and at the present time there were three prospective buyers in a bidding war. They had until the end of the day to present their final offers to Emmit Watkins at the realty office. The highest bid at that time would be the one accepted.

Mae was pleased. The quicker she sold it, the sooner she would be gone. She'd been working all morning, going through things in the kitchen that she wanted to move with her. Her favorite cook pans and skillets, of course.

No Southern woman spent fifty-some years getting the seasoning just right on her cast iron skillets, only to turn around and leave them behind.

She had everything out on the kitchen table that she intended to take, and her mama's set of dishes on the kitchen counter. She would, of course, take her cookbooks, although most of them were just notes jotted in various spiral notebooks. The rest of how to do it was in her head.

She was tired and had the beginnings of a headache, so she started to take a break and grab a bite to eat before she pulled out all of the men's clothing for donation. There was a clothes closet charity in the basement of the Southern Baptist church and she'd donated Pete's and Hershel's clothing. The ladies from the church were coming out tomorrow with the church van to pick it all up.

Before she sat down to eat, she needed to find her To-Do list. She'd laid it down somewhere in this house. She searched the kitchen, the dining room and then into the living room without finding it. So she started down the hall. The first room to the right off the hall used to be Hershel's old room.

She walked inside with purpose, and then saw the notebook and her pen at the foot of Hershel's bed.

"There you are," she said, and went to get it. She picked them up and turned to leave, and as she did, she dropped the pen. Before she could catch it, it had rolled into the gap below the closet door.

"Oh, good grief," Mae said, and opened the door.

She bent down to pick up the pen, and as she did, saw the corner of a large cardboard box pushed to the back of the closet, and fell to her knees in shock.

With all the shock of Pete dying only moments after they'd brought this to the house, then the revelation of his lifestyle and the betrayal of their marriage vows, it had completely left her mind.

She was trembling, sweating and wondering if she was going to have a heart attack and die, too. All this time the evil that came with this money had been on the property, and then in their house. She crawled across the floor to the bed, pulled herself up and then ran for the phone.

Her legs were shaking as she dug through the stack of papers on the sideboard until she found the numbers she was looking for, written on the back of an empty envelope. She carried it to the phone, then pulled up a chair, because she needed to sit down to make this call.

She punched in the number, listened to it ringing, and just when she thought it was going to go to voicemail, she got an answer.

"Hello. Special Agent Gordon speaking."

"Mr. Gordon, this is Mae Arnold. Hershel Arnold's mother."

"Oh yes, Mrs. Arnold. How can I help you?"

Mae shivered suddenly, like she had the day she knew Hershel was dead, and then realized he must be with her now. Helping her get this back where it belonged.

"Well, sir, I am the one helping you. How fast can you get some of your people to my home in Kentucky?"

Jack Gordon frowned. "There are Federal agents in every state, ma'am, but why do you need the FBI?"

"I found the money. The money Hershel stole. It's a story in itself how it got here, but I want it gone."

Jack stood up. He didn't even know he was on his feet until his partner looked up from his computer and gave him a "what the hell" look.

"Are you talking about the two million dollars from the armored car robbery?"

"Well, I sure didn't count it. But it's a really big box, and it's full to the top."

"Holy… Uh…okay, do you live in a city?"

"No, sir. I live twenty minutes outside of a little town in Southern Kentucky called Carytown."

Jack frowned. He knew from experience that finding locations in the mountains of rural Kentucky was often unsuccessful.

"I'm going to need some information from you, in order to be able to find your location."

Mae proceeded to give them to him as he asked.

"Got it," Jack said. "I will have agents at your house within the next two hours, maybe sooner. Just don't go anywhere. Are you there alone?"

"Yes. There's no one left but me."

"Thank you, Mrs. Arnold. Thank you for calling."

Mae heard the disconnect, then hung up the receiver and wiped her hands on the skirt of her dress as her stomach growled.

"I'll be making that sandwich now."

Mae was sitting on the front porch in her rocker, listening to the bird calls from the trees, watching a rabbit eating at the edge of the yard as it hopped from place to place where the clover grew thickest, and realizing this was what she was going to miss most. The silence of humanity, and the presence of God's little creatures.

She'd been hearing the sound of multiple vehicles

for a while now as she rocked. Sound carried here in the hills, and some of the hills between here and town were steep to drive on, putting a strain on the engines. That's what she was hearing, and they were getting closer. She hoped it was the Feds. It would be a burden lifted when the box was gone.

When she heard them slowing down, and then the distant sound of cars driving on gravel as they came up toward her house, she smoothed down her hair, straightened her clothing and folded her hands in her lap just as they drove into sight.

They'd come in two vehicles. A black van, and a black SUV.

They parked, and then one man got out and called to her from the other side of the gate.

"Is this the Arnold property?"

Mae stood. "Yes, it is. I'm Mae. I'm the one who called."

It took a day after Sam and Haley got back to Dallas before they got everything she'd moved put in its place. With most of it being clothes, and with the huge walk-in closets in all three of the extra bedrooms in his house, the matter of storage was easily solved.

The only thing Haley had taken from their home before was their wedding china and her cast-iron cookware. In the South, cast iron was as valuable to a woman as her grandmother's pearls. And the fact that she'd brought them back where they'd first belonged was symbolic of where her life had taken her.

The other things of matter were her pictures and

her keepsakes, and they went right back into the decor of this house as if they'd always been there.

Sam was hanging the last picture when Haley stepped back a distance to get a better perspective.

"It looks great," she said. "What do you think, honey?"

"I think it's right where it belongs...like you."

Haley smiled, eyeing the way his muscles moved beneath that white T-shirt, and how blue his eyes looked in the sunlight.

Sam watched the expressions on her face coming and going, and when he saw her eyes widen, and her gaze track from one side of his chest to the other, he grinned.

"I know that look," he said.

Haley blushed. "What look?"

"The one where you want to take another look at my scar."

Haley laughed, and she was still laughing when Sam picked her up and carried her down the hall to their bedroom.

"It's a good thing that was the last picture," Sam said, as he began pulling off his shirt.

"Why?" Haley asked, as she came out of her clothes.

"Because this is going to take a while," he said, then pulled her into his arms and fell backward, with her still laughing in his ear, onto their bed.

It was nearing 3:00 p.m.

Sam was outside cleaning the pool, and Haley was in the house changing into her swimsuit to help, when all of a sudden she came running out onto the patio, as close to naked as she could be. She was wearing the bottom to a teeny blue bikini, but was carrying the bra.

"Sam! Sam! They found the money! It's over. It's all over. No matter what crazy story the media cooks up next, the price on my head is gone."

Sam whooped, dropped the dipper he was using to fish the June bugs out of the pool and ran to her.

She was both laughing and crying when he reached her. She threw her arms around his neck and then hugged him so tightly that Sam knew her emotions had taken hold.

"You're right, baby. That's the end of our past, and today is the beginning of our future. What do you want to do first to commemorate this day?"

Haley leaned back in his arms. There were tears in her eyes, but she was smiling.

"I want to make a baby with you. Can we do that, Sam? Can I do that with you?"

At that moment, Sam's heart came close to pain, but in the very best way. He saw himself in the reflection of her eyes as he ran a finger down the side of her cheek all the way to the valley between her breasts. And then he smiled.

"We did it before with stunning results. I think we should do it again."

Epilogue

One year later

Mae Arnold was at her favorite watering hole, watching a pelican come in for a landing on one of the pier posts. She liked to come down to the pier every evening around sundown to watch the sun setting off the Miami shore. Sometimes she had a margarita to toast the end of another fine day, and today was no exception. When the waiter brought out her order and winked, Mae grinned. He was funny and young, but he went out of his way to make her smile, which was more than worth the walk down here.

People were coming out of the restaurants now, and walking the length of the boardwalk toward the pier. Mae picked up her margarita and joined the crowd, smiling, talking a little to pass the time as they lined up along the railings, waiting.

As always, the talking stopped when the sun first kissed the water's edge. Their reverence for the dying day was palpable as they watched the sky's colors beginning to change. Minute by minute, the sun sank lower, and just as it was slipping out of sight in a glorious explosion of pinks and purples, they raised their glasses in a salute and said goodbye.

And in another part of the country, the arrival of a new life was happening in a birthing room in Dallas Memorial.

After ten long hours of labor, Haley Quaid was just about to give birth—again.

"She's crowning!" the doctor said.

Haley's face was beaded with sweat. She was so tired and drained from the long hours of painful labor.

"Oh God," she said, as the spasms expanded again, moving from the lowest part of her spine, then in a restrictive and ever-tightening band around her belly, and down.

Sam was standing beside Haley, helping her count, coaching her breathing and not once since they'd entered the last phase had he let go of her hand.

"You can do this, sweetheart… You are so strong, and so beautiful. Hang on to me. You know I won't let you go."

Haley heard his voice, but not the words. There was a roaring in her ears, and a rush of pressure that she remembered from before. It was happening! She bore down with every last ounce of strength she had left and rode the pain. The euphoria of that last push was all she had, and it was just enough.

"You did it!" Sam cried, raised her hand to his lips and kissed every white knuckle of her grip.

"It's a girl. Your little Sammie is here," the doctor said, and laid the baby onto Haley's chest before the cord was cut. The baby was crying, and Sam was laughing. Haley looked down, saw black hair and tiny hands curled into fists, and cupped her hand against the back of the baby's head.

"Don't cry, sweetie," Haley said. "You're going to love it here."

And in that moment when the baby heard her mother's voice, the fussing stopped. Her ear was near the sound of her mother's heartbeat. She knew the rhythm, and she knew the voice.

This must be home.

Sam leaned down to where the baby was lying and whispered in her ear.

"Welcome to the world, baby girl."

* * * * *